CURTAIN CALL TO MURDER

Julian Clary claims to have been born sometime between 1976 and 1992 and was educated at St Nancy's School for the Probably Theatrical.

His first novel, *Trouble at the Tradesman's Entrance*, won the Checkatrade prize for new fiction. His second novel, *A Night at the Lubricant*, shot to the top of Amazon's *Saucy But Not So Gay That It Will Frighten Off Little Old Ladies* section. *Dogging Down the Docks* was awarded best new fiction from Crufts.

Clary lives a reclusive life in Chatham, Kent, and is rarely seen in public.

He recently married Timothée Chalamet.

Also by Julian Clary

I Was Visibly Touched
The Bakewell Tart and the Nights I Spent with Him
A Warm Hand on My Opening
Queer Gynt
Moussaka of the Innocents
Another Fine Meze
Tess of the Dormobiles
Carry On Up the Towpath
Lord of the Rings: Not the Story You Were Expecting
I'll Be Up in a Minute
Enemadale

CURTAIN CALL TO MURDER

JULIAN
CLARY

ORION

First published in Great Britain in 2024 by Orion Fiction,
an imprint of The Orion Publishing Group Ltd.
Carmelite House, 50 Victoria Embankment
London EC4Y 0DZ

An Hachette UK Company

3 5 7 9 10 8 6 4 2

Copyright © Julian Clary 2024

A CIP catalogue record for this book is
available from the British Library.

ISBN (Hardback) 9781 3987 1730 5
ISBN (Export Trade Paperback) 9781 3987 1731 2
ISBN (Ebook) 9781 3987 1733 6
ISBN (Audio) 9781 3987 1734 3

Typeset by Input Data Services Ltd, Bridgwater, Somerset

Printed in Great Britain by Clays Ltd, Elcograf, S.p.A.

MIX
Paper | Supporting
responsible forestry
FSC
www.fsc.org   FSC® C104740

For Helen Reeve and Jenni Carvell – both dedicated dressers with a gift for pulling down my trousers with a deftness and determination that would not be out of place in a Barcelona dark room.

In the face of circumstantial and self-inflicted obstacles they have, on multiple occasions, ensured my presence on stage when, to be honest, I didn't know where or who I was.

Dressers are the unsung, underpaid, overlooked heroes of showbusiness and this book is for all of them.

And with affectionate thanks to David McGillivray who writes the filth for my live shows, some of which may have inexplicably found its way into these pages. God bless. I hope your trouble clears up soon.

'If a leopard licks your nose,
it is your flesh it is hoping to eat!'

African proverb

Prologue

Dear Reader,

You know me, I suspect. I am a camp comic and renowned homosexual. Let's get that out of the way straight away. I am apparently the master of the rolls, the mistress of the brioche, the meat and two veg of innuendo.

So what am I doing here in the gingham-curtained world of cosy crime? Please don't think that I'm just an opportunistic slapper whose literary agent told him this was where the money is and to jump on the bandwagon asap. I can assure you it was not for the financial rewards. I was set up for life in the early 1990s when I did an advert for Toilet Duck. And I was, lest we forget, the voice of Scottish Laminate Flooring for nigh on fifteen years. Had I not squandered the cash on illegal stimulants and instead settled down sensibly to a quiet life somewhere dreary on the south coast, I might never have troubled the general public again.

But alas. We can all be wise after the event. Anyway this 'genre' has all become too cosy for its own good, if you ask me. It needs shaking up a bit. The reader has too often been visualised as a spinster-ish Tory dressed in pastel shades whose idea of a wild night is a bitter lemon with not too much ice. This is nonsense. Mature people were young once. What they don't know about recreational sex you could write on the back of an incontinence pad. I did a gig on a cruise ship recently and they loved the filth. I got a Mexican wave of Zimmer frames after my encore which was a song called *Sometimes Life's a Cunt* (written for me by that well-known family entertainer Gary Wilmot).

No. Circumstances have driven me here. I was as horrified as everyone else about the murder at the world's most famous theatre. More so, as I know every inch of the Palladium stage intimately from my tenure there in panto each year. I have stood on the very spot where it happened, delivering my usual nonsense and little suspecting that a person I knew well would one day die a horrible and premature death right there. Awful, isn't it?

I feel it's my duty to write this book for you to read. And along the way you can learn what showbusiness is really like. It's not all air kisses and fingering the ensemble, let me tell you. Get your smelling salts ready, dears.

Let's start with the scene of the crime: the London Palladium. The Palladium is an extraordinary place. It has a magic about it that I've never experienced anywhere else, unless you count the time, I was stuck in a lift with the Lowestoft rugby team.

As you walk from the darkness of the wings into the light on stage something happens, as if you are entering another sphere. A bit like taking your first bite of a Walnut Whip. I speculate that it may have something to do with those who have trod these boards before you: amazing performers from every age, including Louis Armstrong, Bob Hope, Arthur Askey, Liberace, Gracie Fields, Shirley Bassey, Nat King Cole, Judy Garland, Max Miller, Bruce Forsyth, Clare Balding and many, many other legends. (Brucie's ashes are interred in the wall under the stage.)

It is as if the energy and goodwill of all these people infuses

2

you, enters you via the portal of some psychic anal fissure that opens up during the heightened state of nervous excitement you feel as you wait there for your cue.

Which makes what happened on that dreadful night all the more surprising. Something so dark and evil it had no place there, or anywhere. Like finding Jacob Rees-Mogg in a gay sauna.

Showbusiness is a relatively small world. As I have told you, I know the Palladium inside out, onstage and off. But, as far as this story goes, I also, as it happens, know most of the people involved. It's uncanny. Weird. Having worked with some of them over the years, I followed the story avidly as it unfolded, and I now feel uniquely qualified to write it all down.

This is a story of tragedy and revenge, and I have, in my tireless research, uncovered many layers, both surprising and horrifying, to finally reveal the truth of what happened to cause this Curtain Call to Murder. Fasten your seat belts . . .

As the chihuahua said to the great dane, it's a lot to take in.

Disclaimer

I know there is a suspicion with 'celebrity authors' that we don't really do the hard graft of writing the books that bear our names. I also know that this is true in some cases. They know who they are. Not only is it obvious when you read them, but they've also told me themselves. I think it's a grubby deception to play on the general public and I want no part of it. I don't know how they sleep at night.

So just for the record: I WROTE THIS MYSELF! I toiled away at the kitchen table in my luxury home, in theatrical digs around the country while on tour with *Jesus Christ Superstar*, in my dressing room at the Palladium during *Peter Pan* and on

the terrace of my holiday bungalow on the island of Huvafen
Fushi in the Maldives. It's all me, all mine.

I thank you.

JC

Dramatis personae

Jayne Oxley – dresser
Cheerful and content with her own private thoughts. Prefers not to be noticed. And dresses accordingly. Happy to go where life leads her.

Peter Milano – actor
Blessed with charm and cheekbones, but now well past his sell-by date. Could be a silver fox but instead presents more as a grey stoat.

Miriam Haughton – actor
Experienced and professional, she floats through life with just the occasional sigh of discontent. Success has eluded her as she always knew it would. Takes comfort in dairy food, which no doubt accounts for her creamy complexion.

Simon Gaunt – actor/comedian
One of the new wave of 'geezer comics' that are all the rage. Rough around the edges. No stranger to carbs.

Hermia Saunders – actor
Inconsistently brilliant on stage and rather too fond of intense eye contact and American seriousness off stage. Has had a lot of therapy but sadly still not enough. Lovely cheekbones, possibly from a catalogue.

Ken Thomas – journalist
Prolific, usually bitchy reviewer and gossip columnist. Ruddy complexion a testament to the fact that he drinks too much and sleeps too little as he's busy lying awake thinking vitriolic thoughts.

Trevor Millicent – playwright/director
Writer of profound dramas that reflect the dilemmas of the human condition, he likes to think. A little stooped by the burden of his own superior intelligence, you wouldn't want to be sat next to him on a long train journey.

Alice Haughton – mother of Miriam, retired actor
A former beauty and now long-term resident in a luxury dementia care home. Occasionally incontinent.

Harry 'Spud' Grimshaw – theatre technician
A moody, uncommunicative punk who wears tight black jeans that have never been washed.

Robin Kowalski – Jayne's Tinder date
Compact, terrier-like. Looks over your shoulder as he's talking to you in case someone more interesting is on offer.

Taffy Evans – head of wardrobe
World-weary but honest. Baggy jumpers and wild, grey

candy-floss hair. She is straight-talking and loyal but not someone you'd want to cross.

Gordon Griffiths – ex-dresser
Young and self-absorbed. Searching in vain for love, happiness and a personality that might suit him.

Katheryn Milano (married to Peter Milano)
Horsey, well-heeled country type. Sells overpriced, high-end properties to mousy men with more cash than sense.

Laura Porter (married to Simon Gaunt)
Former model, now an avid shopper. Avoids food.

Julian Clary – narrator
Comedian, actor, writer, musical theatre star, ballroom dancer, dog lover, *Celebrity Big Brother* winner, left-wing luvvie and panto legend. Possibly spreads himself a bit thin in some areas.

Act One
Chapter 1

Headlines
Horror at the Palladium!
Audiences witness onstage tragedy
How could it happen?

Breaking News, BBC News website, 11 p.m, Tuesday, 29 August 2017
The theatre world was in shock following a horrific death during a performance of a new play at the London Palladium this evening.

Audience members screamed in horror during a celebrity-filled press night performance of Leopard Spots *at the Argyll Street theatre. Distressed members of the public streamed out of the theatre and were seen weeping and trying to comfort one another on the pavement. Several people collapsed and had to be tended to by the St John Ambulance staff present.*

'There was a lot of blood,' claimed one witness. 'I don't know if I'll ever be able to go to the theatre again after this.'

Julian on the murder
And it wasn't fake blood, unfortunately. Awful to see such a thing. Traumatising, especially in such a setting. You might witness a road traffic accident if you're unlucky. But you're

unlikely to be staring intently at the very point of impact as you are in a theatre. Imagine. An audience is engaged, concentrating and then *that* happens. Seared into the memory, I'm afraid. I've told you when, so now begins the telling of this tale: the why and the who. And, to do that, we must travel back in time to the Edinburgh Festival 2016.

12 months earlier

The Scotsman, 12 August 2016
By Stephanie McDonald.
Headline: *Leopard Spots* [*****], Edinburgh Festival Traverse Theatre.

This refreshing and original play is just the breath of fresh air this festival needs and gave hope to this reviewer that innovative and creative work is still alive and well. (I was beginning to lose faith after watching an experimental LGBT dance company piece yesterday that involved two lesbians wrestling in a bath full of gravy.)

Written and directed by Trevor Millicent, Leopard Spots *stars the comedian Simon Gaunt in his first major acting role and he certainly makes the most of every scene, sparring with the other 'name' – a rather gnarled but still enigmatic Peter Milano.*

The story revolves around a married couple, George and Geraldine (Milano and the ever-fragrant Miriam Haughton) having a make-or-break holiday to revive their fractured marriage in a rundown holiday hotel in an unnamed tropical location. The only other guest is a mysterious American heiress, Miss Simpson (a languid Hermia Saunders), who may or may not be suicidal or terminally ill – or neither.

Gaunt plays the hotel manager, but as his staff have all gone AWOL, he has to multitask as a cook, a waiter and even a masseur

10

– with hilarious results. It is a masterclass of comic brilliance. Think Basil Fawlty on steroids. George and Geraldine's marital spats fizz with authentic venom or reignited lust, depending on how many glasses of champagne they've consumed.

When a leopard is seen roaming the grounds and the mystery of what became of the missing staff dawns on those who remain, all four end up locked in the hotel's booze-filled storeroom and the stage is set for the messy, terrifying climax – which I won't spoil.

But I can inform the reader that their hearts will race, their sides will ache and their spirits will soar with delight. An astonishing and accomplished piece of work that thoroughly deserved the standing ovation it received. A proper well-written, well-acted play – quite a rarity here this year. And not a drop of gravy in sight.

The Sunday Times, Sunday, 14 August 2016
By Michael Billingshurst.
Headline: *Leopard Spots* [*****], Edinburgh Festival Traverse Theatre.

A new play by Trevor Millicent, at least for the last few decades, has usually been a date with Dame Disappointment. He has persistently failed to enthral since his remarkable debut Who Are You and What Do You Want? *set pulses racing in the 1990s. Leopard Spots is therefore a surprising delight. My cynical expectations dissolve within moments of the curtain rising. What a surprise! There's life in the old dog yet.*

The play sparkles with witty dialogue throughout and benefits from a plot that has you leaning forward in your seat with anticipation. All this is delivered with panache and pathos by a stellar cast led by the cheerful Simon Gaunt, and the presence of that lecherous old lush Peter Milano provides him with a perfect foil. Miriam Haughton and Hermia Saunders add to the fun.

11

The laughs come thick and fast until the final minutes when they are replaced by genuine fear. To carry off such a segue is a remarkable feat of both writing and performance. Comedy and terror? Who knew they would mix together so well, much like one of the many generous cocktails the characters in this sharp and clever play neck during the course of their endeavours.

At last, Millicent has found his form again. Smelling salts recommended and not, on this occasion, to keep you awake.

Trevor Millicent: notes for archive
The fact that Simon Gaunt and Peter Milano loathed each other rather added to the frisson of their on-stage relationship, I feel. I couldn't have planned it better. It is even possible that I did everything in my power during the rehearsal period to ignite this friction. This is sometimes a director's solemn duty. The play's the thing. Collateral damage is not my concern.

***Daily Express**, Tuesday, 16 August 2016*
By Ken Thomas.
Headline: *Leopard Spots* [*], Edinburgh Festival Traverse Theatre.

Hopes were high as I took my seat at the Traverse. The smell of sweaty punters and chips wasn't going to spoil my enjoyment of a show that was the talk of the festival. But how wrong I was. I staggered out two hours later in a cold sweat of bewilderment, feeling so empty that I needed some fast food myself.

It starts on a bucolic veranda with cocktails and Coward-esque banter, but there's worse to follow. There's a man-eating leopard on the loose in this jungle jape, you see, and a gaggle of hapless guests and the hotel manager decide it's best to lock themselves in the pantry for safety. This stifling, windowless room is a metaphor, wouldn't you know it, for the fractured marriage of the ill-suited George and Geraldine. Why not get a divorce and shoot the big cat?

There's also a Yankee Camilla Parker-Bowles rich-bitch-type wandering around and him-off-the-telly Simon Gaunt doing a turgid turn as a waiter. Neither silver-tongued nor silver service, unfortunately.

If Tennessee Williams meets It Ain't Half Hot, Mum *is your thing, you'll love it. The audience the night I went had a rollicking good time. I didn't. Pass the chips.*

Popbitch, Thursday, 25 August 2016
Which actress at the Edinburgh Festival celebrated her great reviews by giving a special after-dark performance on the Meadows on Friday night? Apparently, her, er, vocal range was most impressive . . .

Julian on Peter
Spare a thought for Peter Milano. It was painful for him to read these reviews – even the positive ones. It hurt to see himself described as 'gnarled' and 'an old lush'.

Chapter 2

The Stage, touring news, Friday, 28 April 2017
Premiered at last year's Edinburgh Fringe, Trevor Millicent's Leopard Spots is to tour this summer and into autumn with all the original cast. Tickets are now on sale at Bath, Cheltenham, Brighton, Birmingham and Plymouth.

Jayne's diary, Wednesday, 10 May 2017
Two months stuck here at home. I've cleaned every room, sorted wardrobes, tidied the garden, caught up with Rowanne. Now I need a job, please, before I start baking cakes or decorating. Fed up with evenings at home with Dad, who never speaks.

Funny thing, though – I felt the tingle yesterday, out of the blue. A sort of buzzy feeling at the back of my neck. I've had this before. Like a premonition that something good is going to happen. Last time it happened I got a letter the next day inviting me to uni. Not that that worked out in the long run, but I've learned to trust these things. Just have to be patient now.

Jayne's diary, Friday, 12 May 2017
Taffy called, whoop! I've got a job! Dressing. Starts in two weeks.

There's a new play called *Leopard Spots* that's going on tour.

Big hit at the Edinburgh Festival last year, apparently. The dresser they had booked couldn't do it suddenly. Yippee!

Anyway, I'm pleased. Just about had my fill of being at home with Dad. Excited.

Jayne's diary, Friday, 2 June 2017
Bag packed. Dad's care package is sorted. Told him I was going but he didn't really respond. I don't know what goes on in his mind, if anything. I'd say he looked cross about it.

I'm not taking loads with me. Usual black clothes for work and a few summer dresses and tops. That sort of thing.

Found Mum's old toiletries bag in the bottom of a cupboard in the bathroom. I think I bought it for her one Christmas. Never used – she didn't go anywhere. So, I've put my bits and bobs in.

Julian on Jayne
Allow me to slide in here, if I may. Meet Jayne.

Jayne Oxley is thirty-six, and there is much to know and admire about her. Jayne is about to start work as the dresser for *Leopard Spots*. Dressers do much more than just dress. The good ones take care of the inner as well as the outer needs of their charges. They enhance every performance, stroke egos, lighten moods and pay compliments like a Michelin chef adding ingredients to their signature dish in a fractious kitchen environment. They polish the sequins, fluff up the feathers and ensure that the illusion of glamour is seen like a body stocking, whatever the sordid reality of their charges might present.

But she is so much more than that. Jayne is clever. She carries her cleverness about her person secretly, like a polished conker in her pocket or a mint under her tongue. It radiates and pulsates, all-seeing. You don't have to spend much time with her to realise Jayne is bright. Her intelligence is there in the pigment of her iris and the steadiness of her gaze. Her conversation is perceptive, and she has a habit of cutting to the chase. Some people don't bother to notice. Jayne may swim in a sea of big egos, but don't underestimate her. She can hold her own.

Jayne has the ability to enjoy life in adverse circumstances. It would be withering to say she is easily pleased, although some might see it that way. What I mean is she is a naturally happy person. There is no 'if only' or 'when' about Jayne. The sun on her face, the sausage roll in her mouth – these give her pleasure and she acknowledges the sensations. This doesn't take a conscious effort.

Jayne lives in a suburb of Wolverhampton called New Invention. The house, once gleaming and radiating contentment when her late mother was around, is now dusty and dour with her widowed father's moody presence. Fortunately, Jayne isn't there much to put up with this. She escaped. Jayne works as a theatrical dresser, ironing and zipping her way around the country on touring productions – musicals, plays, ballets.

Jayne is a principal player in this story, and we must pay attention to what she says, thinks and does. A murder is to take place and Jayne is our amateur sleuth, take note, although she has no foreknowledge of this. But it is just as well, because as we all know, the police are too busy exchanging unseemly banter on WhatsApp groups to do proper old-fashioned plod work.

Jayne has had no action on the man front for some time. She isn't bothered about this and would laugh if you asked her if she wanted a boyfriend. It might be more trouble than it's worth, she'd say. But then, it would be nice to have someone looking out for her. She finds nerdy men attractive. Glasses and beige slacks. They hide a strong sex drive, she thinks. All that obsessing over *Star Wars* or online gaming or *Taskmaster* means they have feelings and thoughts other than porn and booze.

She'd had such a boyfriend at university, called Allan. The theatre design course at Birmingham University had been going well, but then she left to look after her mother and Allan found someone else within a week.

People make assumptions about dressers like Jayne – that they are retired dancers or failed actors. No one, surely, would choose *dressing* as a career? They think dressers are people who just want to be involved in showbiz at whatever cost, no matter how paltry the wages. Jayne knew all of this, but she didn't mind. She was hiding in plain sight. Being a dresser was her destiny, her escape. She had a particular talent for it. Attention to detail, a calming presence and no real interest in financial rewards. She had worked out the limits of money as a means to happiness some time ago. Money bore no relation to life satisfaction and that was a fact.

Jayne's mother knew what she was worth, as mothers do. As she lay on her hospital bed she reached out and stroked Jayne's hair, blinking slowly.

'I won't worry about what will happen to you. I've never worried about you. You can look after yourself.'

'Can I?' said Jayne doubtfully. She felt that her mother was signing off, tying up loose ends. Saying goodbye.

She rested her hand on Jayne's shoulder and pulled her closer.

'Don't stay at home, will you? Get away from your father. He'll manage fine without you. Don't do what I did.'

'But what shall I do?'

'Oh, you can do anything. But you're a late bloomer, so time is of the essence.'

So, after the cancer took her mother, Jayne did as she instructed. She went back to university. Then, in her second year, her father had a stroke. No one else could look after him so she abandoned her education once again, packed her bags

17

and returned to Wolverhampton to do her solemn duty for her now mumbling and incontinent dad.

'I'm never going to get away now,' she thought. Her elbows tingled, indicating an imminent eczema flare-up.

Her parents' relationship had been, for many decades, one of mutual antagonism, and it soon became apparent to Jayne that the expectation was for her to recreate that role. It was as if it was too late for her father to change his relationship with any woman, be it wife or daughter. Despite his compromised abilities, or maybe because of them, he mooed his disdain.

Jayne's lightbulb moment came when she sat one evening in her mother's chair. Her father, in his usual place, now furnished with a motorised 'rise and recline' armchair, was on the other side of the kitchen door. As had been the custom when her mother was alive, this door was left open. Aha, thought Jayne. This was so they didn't have to look at each other or engage. No eye contact, no contact of any kind, in fact. The lightbulb flickered and went out. What could she do except accept her lot?

After ten years of marriage and the arrival of Jayne and her younger sister, Sara, her mother had an affair with a married neighbour. When this was discovered, she ran away with him and was denied any access to her daughters by their angry, vengeful father. When the affair fizzled out, she came home to resume her motherly duties – but not her wifely ones. Mother and father lived in a tense, glowering union that science may one day reveal to be an incubator for cancer like the one that finally claimed her.

For others trapped in Jayne's situation their fate might have been sealed, their life laid out like a funereal shroud. There might seem to be no escape.

But Jayne's intelligence was to save her: her thoughts were her own and she savoured them for their insight, serenity and optimism. This may be her situation now but she would not be smothered or defeated by it. A way out would be found. She remembered her mother's advice, and after three years the need to escape overpowered her.

She had worked as a dresser briefly at the Birmingham panto during the Christmas break, and after a few phone calls, she was invited back there to work on visiting musicals. Her sister watched over her father in the evenings.

The taste of freedom was so delicious that she wanted more. Not just evenings – her whole day, her whole life. Her mother's words ringing in her ears she began the arduous task of contacting social services and getting a care 'package' in place. Three visits a day. Her dad would be all right. He'd have to be. If he was cross and irritable, that would be normal for him. Happiness wasn't something he was familiar with, before, now or in the future. But, for Jayne, happiness was within her grasp.

A national tour of *The Rocky Horror Show* wanted her services. Jayne packed her bags and left, and had a wonderful, joyful time. One tour led to another. She was dependable and efficient, and word got around. Wardrobe mistress Taffy Evans took her under her wing and from one job to another. Taffy was tiresome and a tad eccentric sometimes, but they rubbed along fine.

She loved her new life. Not in a euphoric way. But quietly and sincerely. She enjoyed being in a different city every week, looking around, taking it all in, sitting on benches in shopping centres and eating her sandwiches. Jayne was content.

She wondered if she was too easily pleased; after all, it wasn't a well-paid job and there was little chance of promotion. But she had already established that money didn't interest her much and she wasn't troubled by ambition. She enjoyed having a sense of purpose, being a cog in the wheel – a small but vital part of the show. Most of all, she loved feeling free.

Note: I am very grateful to Jayne for letting me rifle through her personal diaries. Without them, there would be so many gaps in this book. On the readers' behalf, I sent her a Greggs gift voucher; she was thrilled.

Jayne's diary, Saturday, 3 June 2017

All Dad wants to do in the evening is watch *The Chase*. There's a channel where it's on constantly.

This is what he does when I'm not there.

After two episodes, he threw down the newspaper and asked if there was anything else I wanted to watch. Sometimes, in the interest of my sanity, I'll choose a drama or documentary, but this never goes down well.

Eventually, we returned to *The Chase*. It's like a drug. Nothing else will do. I thought to myself: Just another hour. Just another hour of Bradley saying 'Time to face the Chaser . . .'

But it's hard.

'On what part of the body is the cranial cavity?'

The contestants are having a lovely day out, at least.

The morning will be better. I'll greet him in the kitchen, lay the table and give him his porridge. We can talk about the weather, and then he'll go to the lounge with the *Telegraph* and I can get the bus to the station and escape.

I'll always hate *The Chase*. It is a time warp of misery. Relentless.

'Good luck with the wedding. But right now you have been caught by the Chaser.'

'Five attempts to push back. Two executed.'

Chapter 3

Text messages between Hermia Saunders and Miriam Haughton

H: *Hey! What great news! We're off on the road. The old gang back together again.*

M: *Yes. Luckily a TV project I've been pencilled for has been postponed so I am able to join the tour. Only five lines, but hey-ho. Three more than my last job.*

H: *I'm so glad.*

H: *That sounds wrong! I mean it wouldn't have worked without you.*

M: *Sweet of you. As long as we can keep Peter in check we'll survive. You know he tried to kiss me on the last night in Edinburgh?*

H: *No! What did ya do?*

M: *I kneed him in the goolies quick-sharp before he made contact.*

H: *Good work! He can't help it though. He'd chat up a streetlight.*

M: *Charming.*

H: *I didn't mean – oh, never mind.*

Jayne's diary, Sunday, 4 June 2017, Bath

Journey here took three hours, which wasn't bad considering I don't drive very fast and there was lots of traffic for a Sunday. Digs OK, I suppose. Single bed, own bathroom. Landlady quite posh. Has a pet parrot and a pug called Damien. Likes theatre. Was hoping for an actor, not a measly dresser, lol. Asked if I'd like to invite the cast back for supper one night. I said I hadn't met them yet! Awks.

Walked to the theatre to see how long it takes (25 mins) then had a sandwich in Greggs. No TV in my room so listened to some music on my headphones and unpacked. Googled the people I'm working with on this play. Seem OK. Hard to tell. Not exactly nervous but I hate this part of a job where you don't know anyone or if it's going to be all right or not. It's like the first day at school.

Jayne's diary, Monday, 5 June 2017, Bath

First day! Spent most of the day in the wardrobe department on third floor sorting things. Silk tea dresses for the ladies and endless hotel wear for Simon: waiter garb, chef's whites, spa uniform and security guard outfit. All extra-large, I noted.

Taffy in one of her bossy moods. Inspected my ironing and tutted. Met some of the actors. One called Hermia seems really nice and friendly. American. They can be a bit insincere (mind you, so can anyone!) so will reserve my opinion. Offered me a dab of aromatherapy oil behind the ears. I was too polite to refuse.

The other one, Miriam, has a rather sour smile. I think I saw her in an episode of *Doctors* once, but I can't be sure. The 'star', or so he thinks, is Peter Milano. I knocked on his door and he shouted 'Who?' in a really loud actory voice. When I told him it was me with his costume, he told me to leave it outside as if he couldn't be bothered with me, so I haven't actually met him yet. Dreading that.

Simon Gaunt – the comic who's a proper star – is just as you'd expect. Big, warm smile, no airs or graces. Not at all posh.

Stage management just grunters. Lol.

Went to Greggs to get a sandwich then got told by Taffy that I couldn't eat it in wardrobe in case of mice so went to green room. They were all in there talking but no one spoke to me so I stared out the window most of the time. Had a quick look at Peter Milano. Big, booming voice. Seems self-important and, I'd say, a little prickly. Clearly handsome once but sagging a bit now.

Ken Thomas's blog, Monday, 5 June 2017

Well, what do you know? Despite my dire prediction, *Leopard Spots* proved to be such a success that a national tour has been announced. There's fancy.

My fellow critics were much kinder than little old me and sprinkled it with stars like they were confetti at a royal wedding. Perhaps I had a headache the night I saw it? I certainly had one afterwards.

Anyway, the cast must be thrilled. Packing their faux Louis Vuitton suitcases as I type, no doubt. Remember, ladies – what happens on tour stays on tour . . . From what I hear through the scurrilous grapevine of theatrical gossips who text me *constantly*, plenty of prophylactics and perhaps a family-size tube of lubricant wouldn't go amiss. And some budget vodka? Apparently, there's little difference between the £6 supermarket offering and Grey Goose. According to . . . no, I mustn't say.

It is only fair that I see it again at the earliest opportunity. It previews at the Theatre Royal, Bath, from this month. As luck would have it, I shall be in that fair city that very week, mincing around in my new Jane Austen bonnet.

The reader will be thrilled to know that I have purchased a front-row ticket and will be sitting as comfortably as one can in those quaint old-fashioned seats, a sharp pencil hovering over my trusty notebook. I shall report back asap unless something unforeseen happens. Like I get a better offer. As if! Wish me luck. I may need it.

Text messages between Peter Milano and Ken Thomas
P: *Give it a rest you bitter, twisted old trout.*

K: *Peter! Mio bel tesoro! How lovely to hear from you. But surely you should be rehearsing your role rather than reading my light-hearted musings? As I recall, your performance might benefit from a little polishing. Remember to play to the gallery. That's if there is anyone up there, of course. I understand ticket sales are inexplicably slow.*

P: *How about I pay you to stay away?*

K: *What method of payment did you have in mind, you naughty boy?*

P: *This grudge you have against me has now gone on for decades, you realise?*

K: *Grudge? I've no idea what you mean!*

P: *You're a vicious, vindictive pervert. You disgust me.*

K: *I love it when you talk dirty.*

Jayne's diary, Tuesday, 6 June 2017, Bath
Watched a bit of the rehearsal this afternoon. The play is very funny. Especially Simon Gaunt – and that's without an audience. Because they did it before in Edinburgh, everyone seems to know what they're doing. More or less.

Hermia's character is weird – away with the fairies. Miriam quite intense and over the top. Peter – well, it's hard to tell. Seems quite irritable.

The director, Trevor Millicent, is the one with the nerves. He wrote it too, so you can tell it's his baby. He's got this habit of rubbing the top of his head, which is bald, when he's not happy. I notice he does this more whenever Peter comes on. Lots of angry scribbling in his notebook too. Peter has lots of hair BTW. Thinning on top but lush compared to Trevor. Lol.

Jayne's diary, 10 p.m., Tuesday, 6 June 2017, Bath
Nothing much to do this evening so I've been investigating this Peter Milano. Best to know what you're dealing with, as I sense he might be a tricky one. Google has been very informative. He's 62 and on his second marriage to someone called Katheryn, who isn't in showbiz.

Gosh, he was handsome once! Nearly became a Hollywood star in the 1980s. Now everything has sagged but he seems blissfully unaware. On the surface, anyway. He doesn't dye his hair, and it's that rather yellowish grey. He dresses casual but classy, expensive Savile Row shirts with button-down collars under a cashmere sweater. Gold cufflinks. Beige chinos with an Italian leather belt.

He sucks in his stomach if he thinks anyone's watching. I've noticed, too, that he has the habit of hopping gently from one foot to another, rather like a tennis player awaiting the ball from his opponent. The body language of someone ready for action. Keen. Alert. Or so he likes to think. I heard him telling Miriam that he's just had a health check and he's in tip-top condition. She didn't look impressed.

Letter to Peter's GP from his wife Katheryn

Dear Dr Simpson,
Please forgive me for contacting you directly. I know you conduct-ed a health check on my husband, Peter, recently, and I wanted to mention something that has been bothering me, which I doubt came to light during your consultation.

I'm not quite sure how to describe it except to say that Peter has been extremely moody and bad-tempered for the last six months or so, and I am concerned about his stress levels. I wondered if anything came up in the tests that might account for this? It's very unlike him, and I have to confess I'm more than a little worried. He's always been so cheerful and optimistic. But not lately.

I would appreciate your discretion and quite understand if this breaches patient confidentiality, but as his wife, I obviously have his best interests at heart and I'm feeling a little helpless right now.

Many thanks,
Katheryn Milano

Fun facts: Jayne Oxley
Jayne's mother gave birth to her in the back of a taxi on her way to Wolverhampton's New Cross Maternity Hospital.

Fun facts: Bath
Bath exists because of the emergence of three natural springs in the heart of the city that deliver over 1 million litres of mineral-rich water every day. Uniquely in the UK, the mineral water is hot – it rises to the surface at a constant temperature of at least 45°C.

Soaking in hot springs can be a great way to naturally detox your skin. Thanks to the high amount of silica in the water, it can also soften rough or dry skin. Plus, the mineral content of sulphur springs has been shown to help persisting skin conditions such as psoriasis, acne and eczema.

Chapter 4

Ken Thomas's blog, Wednesday, 7 June 2017
And the award for the most pretentious, condescending twaddle ever to appear in a programme goes to . . . Trevor Millicent! I reproduce it in its entirety here so you may barf along with me. It's enough to curdle milk!

Programme notes for *Leopard Spots* by author and director Trevor Millicent

As a playwright, the creative process is often fraught with agonies and frustrations, but Leopard Spots *seemed to almost write itself. The burden of the task in my gifted hand was not, on this occasion, too heavy to bear.* Leopard Spots *had been incubating in my mind for some years, of course, and when my imagination was fully dilated it slid into the Moses basket of dramaturgical destiny with the merest twinge. More of a sigh than a contraction.*

It has been said that the precision and power of my writing owes much to Terence Rattigan and Noël Coward, but in this piece, I must acknowledge a debt to Joe Orton too and perhaps a nod to Oscar Wilde and even dear Ben Jonson.

On the surface, Leopard Spots *is a love story with a twist. But by setting it in an exotic wilderness I have deftly incorporated subtle references to colonialism and even nineteenth-century slave culture, which I hope the more educated members of the provincial audiences will not fail to notice.*

What might appear to be simple entertainment, an amuse-bouche for the weary theatregoer, in fact has much more to offer. Woven into the script are the names Melpomene and Thalia – wearers of the sock and buskin, symbols of comedy and tragedy in ancient Greek theatre.

The presence of a leopard, both feared and revered, similarly represents the yin and yang dilemma of human existence. Is it a benevolent god, malevolent agent or both? Symbolic of strength, courage and determination, a sign of royalty for some, purveyor of death and destruction to others.

Nature in all its magnificent glory may take our breath away, both literally and metaphorically. Co-existence and tolerance are the keys to survival, for big cats and humans. For all the hilarity and laughter in the play, this is the profound wisdom the characters in Leopard Spots *strive to grasp. The storeroom in the play is, of course, a metaphor for human knowledge. But no amount of wisdom can save you from nature should you break the rules.*

I hope you enjoy the entertainment on some, if not every, level.

I mean. Really? Fuck me pink, what a load of tripe.

Julian on Ken

There is something about people like Ken that is simultaneously awful and fabulous. He revels in his nastiness and is energised by his own vitriol. What has happened in his life to make him so negative and bitter? He can't always have been this way. I sense hurt. The child within, dismayed by some act of cruelty that he didn't deserve but which has scarred him. He has never talked about his upbringing, despite some occasional probing from me. But if we assume something abusive in a grim northern setting then the mists may begin to clear a little. The sadness is heart-breaking. But to be so consistently waspish, so engulfed by a dour and rancid view of the world makes him, in small doses, a source of entertainment. There is a sort of fizzing energy about people like that. They can't help it, after all. They have to live with the hand life has dealt them and make the best of it. His wit still survives, despite everything. I am drawn to him, thrilled by the vicious sparks of nastiness, and grateful, perhaps, that I am not him.

But after a few hours in his company, my skin begins to prickle. With Ken it might not all be talk. What might he be capable of in his darkest moments?

Leopard Spots, plot synopsis
Act One

The open-air reception/bar area of the Hotel Folly. Faded grandeur. A lazy ceiling fan buzzing. Veranda upstage, lush tropical greenery. Marwood Weston sits at a desk doing the accounts and tutting.

Hotel Folly is a crumbling colonial-style lodge situated on a remote rocky ridge somewhere hot and wild. Visitors are rare, and manager Weston is surprised by not one but two unexpected guests. A married couple – him considerably older than her – called George and Geraldine Taylor arrive late one morning looking somewhat dishevelled, claiming they have been touring the region and their driver, Melpomene, has left them here for the day while he drives to a nearby town to get the car radiator fixed.

The manager does his best to make them welcome, serves breakfast and attends to George's unexplained bruises.

The only other resident is a sad, mysterious American woman, Miss Simpson, who has been there for several months allegedly writing her memoir. There is a whiff of a younger Norma Desmond about her. The three have drinks together and chat awkwardly. Meanwhile, it slowly becomes apparent that Weston is the only member of staff on duty, comically trying to be manager, concierge, waiter, barman, chef, gardener, masseur and chambermaid – sometimes all at once.

As more drinks are taken on the terrace and the crumbling state of the Taylors' marriage becomes clear to all, Miss Simpson alludes to a predator that lurks in the hotel grounds.

Lunch arrives and Miss Simpson deftly throws her steak tartar into the garden when no one is looking.

We hear the sound of purring.

The Taylors are drunk and fractious. Geraldine decides to go to the spa and Weston assumes the role of masseur to attend to her. George attempts to flirt with Miss Simpson, who bats him away like an annoying fly. She reveals she is an heiress, her father having once owned an emerald mine in a remote region of South Africa. This makes her even more attractive to George, who helps himself to more drinks. Geraldine and Weston return, and clearly something has occurred between them.

Miss Simpson is rude and withering to a giggling, possibly post-coital Geraldine, who asks for more cocktails. Perhaps Miss Simpson considers Weston to be her property? George suggests they take their drinks into the library to cool down. The Taylors leave.

We hear a car pull up and park. Miss Simpson leans over the balcony. Perhaps it is Melpomene, the Taylors' chauffeur? She tells him to wait 'over there'. She watches as we hear the growl of a big cat, a roar and then a scream. Miss Simpson smiles and strokes her neck.

The Taylors rush back to the veranda. Weston, as a security guard, goes to investigate. More disturbing noises and a gunshot. Weston staggers back up the steps, clothes torn and bloodied.

Fun facts: leopards
The leopard of Panar was a male leopard reported to be responsible for at least 400 fatal attacks on humans in the Panar region of the Almora district of Uttarakhand, northern India, in the early twentieth century.

Leopard Spots, plot synopsis
Act Two
The basement storeroom of the Hotel Folly. Very plain and dimly lit. Piled high with crates of drink. A small card table in the middle. One small, barred window upstage left, a metal door downstage left. Rifle propped up beside it. Miss Simpson stands by the window. George and Geraldine sit at the table, drinking wine.

Weston, his arm bandaged, says this is the safest place for everyone. A wounded leopard is a very dangerous beast. He's got the taste for human flesh.

'Maybe *she*,' points out Miss Simpson.

The Taylors have another row, and Geraldine tells Weston wants to leave. She dissuades her and their row is resolved by a passionate embrace. Weston's cook, gardener and barman – all the staff – have disappeared one by one over the course of the previous weeks. He now realises why: the leopard has taken them all. They must hope he/she is badly injured enough to die. But how will they know? None of them can leave. They open a bottle of vintage whisky.

George accuses Weston of dallying with his wife in the spa and hits him. During the fight, Miss Simpson opens the door and ushers Geraldine out. When they calm down George and Weston realise she has gone. We hear a scream. Miss Simpson smiles secretly.

Leopard Spots, plot synopsis
Act Three
George breaks down. He tells them the story of his marriage and his complicated past but is interrupted when we hear the leopard prowling around outside the storeroom, hungry for more. A flash of leopard skin appears at the window.

The men cower in fear, but Miss Simpson starts to sing. A strange, haunting lullaby in an unknown language. The leopard begins to purr, and we see a paw reach towards her through the bars of the window. Then it slinks away.

'She is calm now. Her stomach is full and her mood has changed. She will go somewhere and sleep.'

George points out that her stomach is full of his wife. And as for her mood change . . . what is it they say about a leopard never changing its spots?

Miss Simpson explains that she knows this leopard. She raised her as a cub, years ago. 'Her name is Thalia. She has gone rogue and become a maneater, but she understands me. I came to stay here because I knew she was in the area.'

Weston: 'I saw she had a collar on.'

'Yes. It's dirty now, but it's something I gave her. It's an emerald necklace. Priceless. My parting gift when she was released back into the wild.'

George, drunk, turns on Miss Simpson. He breaks a bottle and holds it to her throat. Weston tries to calm the situation, assuming his security guard role.

There is a sudden powercut. A cacophony of noise. By the time a lamp is lit, George has gone. Weston lies helpless on the floor. Miss Simpson stands, holding the emerald necklace to her throat as she makes her final triumphant speech. As she lowers her hands we see they are covered in blood.

Fun facts: Trevor Millicent
In 1994, Trevor wrote and directed six episodes of *Coronation Street*. He was sacked after Betty Williams (Betty Turpin) complained about him being 'up himself' to the producers.

Chapter 5

Kitty Litter WhatsApp Group Chat

H: *Hey guys. Thought a WhatsApp group for us poor actors might be a good thing. We might need somewhere to let off steam away from the prying ears of the 'creatives', if you know what I mean?*

S: *Thanks Hermia. Is it for having a larf or discussing the nuances of our performance?*

H: *Whatever we wish to discuss, Simon!*

S: *I'm here for the gossip and larfs.*

P: *Well, you wouldn't have much to say about the art of acting, would you?*

S: *What's that supposed to mean, Peter?*

M: *Well, that didn't take long to turn into a bitching session, did it?*

H: *Now then, boys. Miriam's right. Play nicely!*

Jayne's diary, Wednesday, 7 June 2017, Bath
Helped Miriam with her hair for half an hour during lunch break. She was really pleased and called me a 'poppet'. She wanted it in a Marcel wave, but I didn't know what that was, so did some curls on the side and a bit of a quiff on the top which made her look thinner. She talks a lot.

Told me all about her mother who brought her up on her own and is now in a care home and how she worries about her. Early onset dementia.

I told her about my mum, the cancer and how I live in Wolverhampton with my grumpy dad. Tried not to make it sound too depressing, so mentioned my nephew and how I collect him from school, and we do baking and stuff. She laughed. She would love a nephew or niece, she said. She's not married. 'Not with this life,' she said. 'Who'd have me?' Lots of actors are married, I told her. You never know. She liked that.

Later, Peter Milano stopped me in the corridor and said: 'You're prettier than you think you are, you know' and winked at me. I don't know what that's supposed to mean. How does he know what I think? I've marked his card and if he tries it again, I shall put him in his place.

Julian on Miriam

I have admired Miriam's work for years now. She has a certain poise about her as an actress that I like. There is always a lot going on behind the eyes, a boon in an actress. She carries herself grandly, whether in a comedy or serious piece and she always delivers, in my opinion. She is often cast as a posh, educated type of woman, like a thirtysomething Patricia Hodge, with whom she shares a similar porcelain-skinned, heavy-lidded beauty.

When I had my own (albeit ill-fated) sitcom in the late 1990s, I asked for her to be cast as my neighbour who lived in the upstairs penthouse. Sylvia was a camp, cynical, chain-smoker who popped in occasionally to give a caustic monologue about her ex-boyfriend, who she was very possibly stalking. She was everything I'd hoped for: vicious but full of pathos.

Popbitch, **Thursday, 8 June 2017**
Which D-list actor is such a letch in rehearsals that his code name amongst the female members of the company is 'doorknob'? This is due to his habit of pressing his engorged member against them at every opportunity.

Jayne's diary, Thursday, 8 June 2017, Bath
Miriam saw me picking my skin in the green room and winced and sucked her teeth. She didn't say anything but shook her head. I was embarrassed because I didn't even know I was doing it. Later she put her hand on my shoulder and apologised. 'I used to have that problem, too,' she said in a whisper. 'Try Lotriderm cream. Worked for me.'

I've tried that. Nothing works. It flares up when I'm nervous.

Thought I might go for a 'healing' bath in the spring water here but it's too expensive for the likes of me. £40! I'll just have to suffer. Lol.

Haven't checked Tinder since my last date in Birmingham, months ago. The guy didn't even turn up. Sucks to be him. I think my profile photo is a bit serious, so I tried to lighten things up with my bio: 'Hi-de-hi! If all men are pigs, I'm in the mood for a bacon sarnie.' Which might have been a mistake. Anyway.

Bath is a different city (and smaller than Brum, so less competition) so I logged on and had a look. Not sure dating apps are good for my self-esteem. The whole business depressed me a bit, so I didn't stay for long. A bit like my last date. Ha.

Anyway, there's a guy called Spud on the crew who has caught my eye.

Jayne's diary, 10 p.m., Thursday, 8 June 2017, Bath
Literally bumped right into Spud as I turned a corner on my walk home. I was a bit flustered, and we both did awkward

apologies. I'd dropped my Sainsbury's bag and he picked it up for me. Tampons and cottage cheese fell out, of course. Mortified when he picked them up. He sort of grinned. I thought later it was like a scene from a Richard Curtis film.

Julian on Spud

It's me again. This is embarrassing, but I'd better be honest. I've lived a full life, as anyone who has read my autobiography (still in print, I believe) will be able to confirm. I have encountered Spud on a number of occasions. Years ago.

But there are times in life when people you meet in passing, who seem of no particular interest, then later resurface in a more significant role. Had I assessed Spud more carefully in those first casual run-ins, might I have spotted some pointers to what lay ahead for him? He was an attractive youth, although monosyllabic and world-weary, even then. I can see, with the power of hindsight, that he was probably troubled and easy prey for those with sinister intentions. But of course I couldn't have known then what the future held for Spud. I doubt I could have done much to stop what fate had in store.

Julian on Jayne

So Jayne got to know the actors and crew she was working with. She jotted down her thoughts and musings in her diary not knowing that there was to be a murder. But she would be grateful, in a few weeks, that she did. For it would fall to Jayne to work out who the murderer was, and these early assessments of those around her would prove invaluable.

Chapter 6

Kitty Litter WhatsApp Group Chat

H: *Any thoughts on today's rehearsal?*

M: *I thought it went well and is coming along nicely.*

P: *It would help if some of us learned their lines.*

S: *I have an awful lot to learn, if that's directed at me.*

P: *Touchy these comics, aren't they?*

S: *I'm a comedian AND an actor, thank you very much.*

P: *That's a matter of opinion.*

H: *Guys, please! It isn't going to help the production if we are spending our energy negatively.*

M: *Quite. We must behave like grown-ups.*

H: *As actors, we should remember how lucky we are to be working.*

S: *I agree. And in a BIG HIT PLAY. Some people spend years limping around the provinces playing crap in draughty theatres to a few dozen sleepy pensioners. We should be grateful.*

P: *Some of us honed our craft in the provinces. Ask Rula Lenska.*

S: *I'd rather not.*

Trevor Millicent: notes for archive

It is interesting the effect that casting a comedian in the play has on the others. They don't like it. Feel their 'craft' is somehow sullied by the cross-pollination of genres. This is just what I intended to happen. Seething fury below the surface adds nuance. If only I could get more of it.

Fun facts: psychodrama

Psychodrama is a structured form of therapy in which a person dramatises a personal problem or conflict, usually in front of a group of other therapy participants.

Julian on what happens backstage

Who you get to know on tour largely depends on your 'track'. This means where you move around during the show, depending on what is required of you.

Jayne, as a dresser, saw all members of the cast briefly when she delivered costumes to their dressing rooms before the show and collected the laundry after. That is how her relationship with Miriam evolved. But Peter, his flirting having come to nothing, soon indicated that his clothes were to be left hanging outside his room; post-performance his shirt was tossed disdainfully in the hallway for collection, so there was rarely an encounter, awkward or otherwise, to endure. Behind every diva is a desperate desire for importance, in my experience. I've worked with – no, I daren't say . . .

Other aspects of Jayne's routine required her to wait in the wings to help with a quick change for some actors or pass them props. As everyone, cast and crew, are repeating the same routine for every performance, it is these incidental encounters that build up, minute by minute, day by day, to an organic familiarity. Standing close together in a darkened stage wing you may nod or smile to begin with, but you can't, unless determinedly stony-faced, ignore the human that is stood in such close proximity. There is the added factor of the performance happening just a few yards away that is your shared focus.

Senses are sharpened, heartbeats raised and conversations whispered.

As a tour progresses and nervous tension recedes, these snatched conversations stray into areas more intimate than how the play is going or what the audience are like that day.

Jayne's diary, Friday, 9 June 2017, Bath
Quite the cheery chat with Simon during tech rehearsal. He has a lot of changes which I have to sort for him: he wears a linen suit for his first scene but has to change outfits to portray a chef, gardener and butler. Then, as the plot develops, just pink polka-dot boxer shorts and, finally, a ripped and stained security guard uniform. He doesn't half lark about and make me laugh. Very rude and funny. Asked me if I trained at KwikFit.

He said that he's used to being centre stage, alone, with a microphone in his hand and measuring his performance by the strength and number of laughs. This 'theatre lark' was a whole new world. He said Trevor had tried to make him more 'actorly' but didn't understand how you knew if the punters liked you or not if you didn't get a laugh.

He's performing all the time, I realised, even during a quick change. I'm his audience and he's watching for my reaction.

He's a bloke, if you know what I mean. Told me his career as a stand-up had sprouted from having a laugh in the pub with his mates. It was a short hop from making the lads guffaw at his dating disasters to entering an open mic competition in the very same bar.

Ten years down the line that's still his appeal, even if he is a huge TV star headlining big theatres with his one-man tours. He still wanders on stage wearing jeans and T-shirt and carrying a pint. He's got a ruddy complexion. Quite porky round the midriff. Talks about his wife – reality TV starlet Laura Porter – a lot. And his kids.

I've seen the DVD of his last tour, *Geezer in the Freeza*. All about how unsuited he is for fatherhood, the devil-possessed toddler tantrums of his two-year-old, cleaning sick from a car seat, quickie sex, lads' nights out – that sort of thing. Funny.

Apparently, Trevor had watched him on *Live at the Apollo* on TV and instantly knew he was the right person to star in the play. Everything fell into place: he wrote *Leopard Spots* within weeks, imagining Simon as the hotel manager, writing the dialogue in his rough-around-the-edges south London voice. That's what I read, anyway.

Once finished, he sent the script to Simon's agent who saw its potential and encouraged his client to accept. The rest, as they say, is history.

'It's these matinees that I can't get my head round,' he said to me. 'It's packed out there! All old folk with white hair. You can see their glasses glistening and hear them unwrapping Murray Mints. What are they doing here?'

'Come to see if you're any good,' I told him. 'And from the sound of it, you're not too bad.'

'But in the middle of the afternoon?'

'They like to get home in time for the early evening news.'

Letter from Trevor to Simon
23 March 2016

Dear Simon,
Please excuse the intrusion of this letter; I know how busy you must be so I will be as brief as possible.

Congratulations on the success of your Netflix special. I, along with the millions of viewers, roared with laughter. You have a down-to-earth quality to your performance that I greatly admire.

In my opinion, this is a rare and unique gift. No one else can do what you do. It is simply gold dust.

In the days after watching your show, I felt compelled to begin work on a new play called Leopard Spots, *which I'm happy to say is now complete. I wrote the central character with you in mind. I think it is one of my best plays and I am very much hoping you will be willing to consider it.*

I shall contact your agent, of course, but felt a personal approach might bear fruit sooner. If I say so myself, I feel this could be a very exciting venture for you.

I do hope you will consider it. Feel free to contact me at your earliest convenience.

With admiration,

Trevor Millicent (RSC, National Theatre, etc.)

Julian on Trevor

Excuse me, but I feel I must say something here. Far be it from me to plant doubts in the reader's mind, but I rather doubt the sincerity of Trevor's letter. This is because he sent me a remarkably similar missive some five years earlier by email. Trevor said he'd written a play with me in mind called *The Man With the Swollen Head* and would I possibly consider reading it, etc. Full of flatteries and promises of theatrical success. It was rubbish and I politely declined. If I was any good at computers, I'd find it on my hard drive; it will be there somewhere. But take my word for it.

And then, when all this happened, I was in the Groucho club chatting to Rylan and he said *he* had once been sent a script by Trevor Millicent, written specifically for him, blah, blah, etc.

Half an hour later, Sue Perkins came in and told us the same thing! We had a good laugh about it. Either Millicent is a prolific writer, repeatedly inspired by light entertainment types, or he just tries his luck.

Attaching a 'name' to a script is one way of attracting producers and getting a project off the ground. There's no law
against it, I suppose, but honestly, these showbiz sharks! You
can't trust anything anyone says these days.

Jayne's diary, Saturday, 10 June 2017, Bath
I was sewing in the wings during the dress rehearsal while
Simon was doing his big scene.

'I'm sorry,' Miriam said to Hermia, 'but there's no *depth* to
it. I know he's funny and he's a darling, but he's just playing
himself, let's face it.'

I don't think Hermia likes bitching. 'None of us would be
here if it wasn't for him,' she said. Quite snappily. 'I don't agree.
Anyway, he's perfect for the part.'

'Mmmm,' said Miriam. 'Maybe you're right. He's just *acting*
shallow for the role,' she said with a snort.

Chapter 7

Jayne's diary, Sunday, 11 June 2017, Bath

Hermia seemed very on the brink today. Surely no one could be that relentlessly on edge? Actors – proper actors – are nearly always riddled with insecurities: about their last performance, their next one, being liked, getting a job, changing agents. Being judged for every performance, when it comes, doesn't help. And being 'vulnerable' seems to be a prized characteristic in their line of business.

Today Hermia was quivering with vulnerability. Like a baby bird when their skin is so thin you can see all their internal organs pumping away. As if her soul was exposed to the elements, writhing in torment. I couldn't bear it, so I asked her if she was OK. Shouldn't have, really, as it all came tumbling out in a rush.

'I am in such pain, today,' she told me. 'Bless you for noticing. The years of rejection in this business . . . audition after audition, screentests, call-backs, read-throughs, all followed by complete radio silence. Have you any idea what that does to an actor? I am scarred by it, and for some reason, those scars have all opened up today. I'm stressing. I'm suffering emotional flashbacks and they are hard to cope with.' I'm good at changing people's outlook; I do it for myself all the time, so I had a quick think and told her how I saw things.

'Life has a funny way of sorting things out for you, I find,' I began. 'As if all that happens is directed by a higher force. Wasn't it that suffering that made you so perfect for the role of Miss Simpson? No one could have *acted* so damaged a character. Everything you've been through shows in your face, in your every gesture on stage. You're using it to your advantage now. It's sheer genius, Hermia,' I said as a final flourish.

Hermia stroked her forehead and mouthed a silent 'thank you', her eyes brimming with tears.

'I guess "no pain, no gain" is what you're saying, honey?'

'Exactly,' I said, anxious to bring what had been a rather intense conversation to a happy conclusion.

'And one success invariably leads to another. Just as the opposite is true. You've done your time in the doldrums. Now your star is on the rise. Just you see.'

Julian on Hermia
What Jayne's ruminations fail to incorporate is Hermia's claim to be an emotional psychic. Either she forgot, or Hermia hasn't divulged this information yet. It's a wearing condition to cope with, and the gifted few must guard against tuning in to all and sundry as this may cause overload. Hermia does her best in this regard, but it is fair to say that the pained expression, the quivering and the vulnerability may be due as much to this burden as it is to her professional failures.

A terrible affliction, in my opinion. As if life wasn't hard enough.

Fun facts: Hermia
Hermia is a girl's name of Greek origin. Meaning 'messenger', it comes from the same roots as Hermes, the Greek messenger god, but the name is probably best known as a character from

Shakespeare's *A Midsummer Night's Dream.*

Kitty Litter WhatsApp Group Chat

P: *Simon – are you really intending to play the big scene at the end of Act 1 like that?*

S: *Excuse me? Like what, exactly?*

M: *Stop it, Peter.*

S: *No, I'd like to hear his thoughts.*

H: *Oh God.*

P: *It's a very moving soliloquy. Or it could be.*

S: *Oh really? Congratulations on your new job as assistant director.*

P: *Don't take offence, dear chap. I thought this was our actors' forum where we could discuss such things off the record.*

S: *Discuss away, old-timer.*

P: *Not if you're going to reach for the smelling salts every time I try to be helpful.*

M: *I'm going to bed.*

S: *Well?*

P: *You're playing it for cheap laughs when really it is tragic.*

H: *Rehearsals are the place to try different things out, to experiment, surely? We will all perform better if we support each other.*

P: *I appreciate your attempt at diplomacy, Hermia, but in the past I have used my wealth of experience to help younger actors find their best performances.*

S: *Tell me about your wealth.*

P: *Very well. You're going for laughs because you need the reassurance of a reaction from the audience. It's all about your ego. I suggest you try acting it instead. Let the text do the work. Your gurning and leering at the audience just cheapens it. You are in danger of turning a dramatic climax into a lowbrow* Carry On *scene.*

S: *Zzzzzzz . . .*

Trevor Millicent: notes for archive
Simon showed me the WhatsApp conversations that are going on 'secretly', or so they think. Peter is coming to the boil nicely. I just need to add some sugar to the water.

Fun facts: sugar water
In the UK, distinct from many other jurisdictions around the world, prisoners have a legal right to have kettles provided in their cells. However, an unfortunate side effect of this is that boiling water is readily available for assaults on inmates and staff. One particular mechanism of assault common to the prison population is burns involving boiled sugar solution, referred to as 'prison napalm'.

Chapter 8

Jayne's diary, Tuesday, 13 June 2017, Bath
Guess what? Spud is on Tinder. I swear it's him. Uses the name Harry. Picture is a bit arty. Face not clear but photo shows some kind of gothic tattoo with a snake on a bicep. Spud is covered in tattoos.

Profile says he's 35. About right. Looking for 'mature'. That could mean a number of things!

No chit-chat with Spud. Just grunts if you say hello. But at the same time, you're very aware of his presence.

Jayne's diary, Wednesday, 14 June 2017, Bath
I'm definitely interested in Spud. He's moody and mysterious. I'm going to try giving him a meaningful smile when I get the opportunity. It worked in the library that time.

Jayne's diary, 2 p.m., Wednesday, 14 June 2017, Bath
Spud just looks right through me. Oh well. His loss.

I noticed that Hermia made two cups of coffee in the break then gave one to Spud without saying anything. Wonder if they know each other better than I thought?

Jayne's diary, 7 p.m., Wednesday, 14 June 2017, Bath
Trying to ignore Spud but finding it difficult. There's a bit in the show where we both have to be in the same wing waiting for a cue. I can't help inhaling. A girl's got to breathe, after all. Hard to describe his smell. Definitely no aftershave or deodorant going on. Musty but quite sexy. I think he sleeps in his T-shirt.

Jayne's diary, Thursday, 15 June 2017, Bath
Plucked up the nerve to swipe right on Spud's Tinder pic. Gave me a little flutter, anyway. Tried the vegan sausage roll at Greggs. Yummy.

Hermia definitely targeting Spud, IMO.

'One of the plugs in my dressing room is a bit dodgy. Do you think you could come and have a look at it?' she said today. I wouldn't be surprised if 'plug' is American slang for your snatch. Lol. Surely there's nothing going on?

Thinking of getting a tattoo. There's a place called Think Ink I pass on my way to work every day. I've been looking in the window and trying to decide. A daisy, maybe, for Mum. But where to have it? I think my heart, but I'm not getting my baps out for a stranger with a needle in his hand.

Fun facts: spud
By the early seventeenth century, the word spud was used to refer to a digging implement: a sharp blade, mounted on a staff or handle, for cutting through clots of soil and roots.

Jayne's diary, Friday, 16 June 2017, Bath
Got an alert on Tinder. Not one but two matches! I nearly jumped out of my skin.

First guy is called Robin. My type. Cute. Tall. Lives in Bath. Not looking for anything serious. Big ticks all round.

Second guy is this Harry, who I reckon is Spud.

49

I'm not responding to either straight away. Rowanne says you mustn't look too keen. After all, I'm a busy woman working in the glamorous world of show business. If and when I have time for a little romantic dalliance, I'll let them know. Lol.

I think I'm addicted to the vegan sausage rolls. Had three today.

1.15 p.m. Tinder exchange between Robin and Jayne
R: *Hey*
J: *Hi*
R: *How's it going?*
J: *All good with me. How about you?*
R: *Bit bored. At work.*
J: *What do you do?*
R: *Estate agent. You?*
J: *Working backstage at the Theatre.*
R: *That's cool.*
J: *I guess. Sold any houses today?*
R: *Not yet. I've got a nice semi at the moment, if you're interested?*
J: *I'm not looking to buy a house.*
R: *I'm not talking about a house, am I?*
J: *Oh, I see. Awks.*

10.30 p.m. Tinder exchange between Jayne and Spud
J: *Hi*
S: *What?*
J: *Just saying hi.*
S: *Why?*
J: *Let's forget it, shall we?*

Jayne's diary, Saturday, 17 June 2017, Bath
Felt a bit uncomfortable at work after last night's Tinder

rudeness from Spud. Rowanne says I shouldn't though. He 'liked' my profile, we were a match. A chat is the next stage. Maybe he was in a bad mood. Seems to be his natural state.

Fun facts: estate agents
People who can make a personal connection, are engaging and get along with everyone are well-suited for a career in real estate. If you're the type of person with whom others are comfortable and like being around, it will help you grow in this career.

Jayne's diary, 11 a.m., Saturday, 17 June 2017, Bath
Was in the green room waiting for the kettle to boil before the half. Spud came in, saw me and immediately turned around. He stopped at the door and rolled up the sleeve of his T-shirt on the left arm. There it was. The tattoo. Snake and all. He sort of smirked at me and jerked his head up before rolling it down again.
    'Do you want anything?' he said quietly in a husky voice, and left, making a funny noise exhaling through his teeth as he went. Baffled. Rowanne says maybe he's playing a game. He wants you to know he definitely is Harry. Now what? Gave me something to think about, I guess. What a knob, though.

Jayne's diary, 11.30 a.m., Saturday, 17 June 2017, Bath
Decided not going to get a tattoo.

Tinder exchange between Robin and Jayne
R: *Hey*
J: *Hi*
R: *How's work?*
J: *Busy. Previews going on and extra rehearsals during the day.*
R: *Sounds tense.*
J: *A bit. How about you?*

R: *Buyin' 'n' sellin'.*

J: *Well, that's good, I guess.*

R: *You get tomorrow off?*

J: *I do.*

R: *Wanna meet up for a coffee?*

J: *Could do.*

R: *Great. I'll think of somewhere.*

Fun fact: Harry 'Spud' Grimshaw
As a young man Spud burgled a house in South Kensington and stole a Patek Philippe watch worth £23,000, which he sold in a pub later that day for £100. He only realised his error when an article about the theft appeared in the next day's *Evening Standard*.

Jayne's diary, 6 p.m., Saturday, 17 June 2017, Bath
An hour before curtain up, Miriam decided her dress wasn't right for her character. In quite a strop.

'It's all wrong! Very few people can carry off horizontal stripes. Unless they have an eating disorder.'

Nothing I said made any difference.

Quite petulant, she was. Nerves, probably. I said I'd go and speak to Taffy, who marched straight in there with a determined expression.

'I haven't got time for this,' she said through gritted teeth.

Apparently, Miriam took it off in front of her and threw it on the floor. I was told to iron it and take it back in, by which time she'd calmed down a bit, but her lip was trembling. I paid her some compliments, said I'd always thought she looked great in the dress, how flattering it was, what a good actor she was – all that sort of pep talk. She looked at herself in the mirror as I spoke, and I could see the confidence rising.

'You're sure I don't look like a deck chair?'

'Not in the slightest,' I said. 'And if you did, it would be a very classy deck chair on the beach at St Tropez.'

'Maybe you're right,' she murmured.

They're very insecure these actors. Full of self-doubt. I guess it comes with the job. Being judged all the time. For their appearance. Especially women. We all want to be liked, don't we?

Texted all this to Rowanne.

Keep catching Spud looking at me. He whispers into his mobile phone in the wings a lot during the show. I'd get the sack if I did that. He smokes a vape.

Text exchange between Jayne and Rowanne

R: *Got some goss for you.*

J: *Oh yes?*

R: *Mmmm. Good gossip too. Heard through the grapevine about the dresser that you replaced on* Leopard Spots.

J: *Oh yes?*

R: *Had some sort of fling with Peter Milano, apparently, and it all went a bit Pete Tong.*

J: *Is that why she dropped out.*

R: *Yes. But here's the interesting thing, though: It wasn't a she, it was a he.*

J: *Blimey!*

R: *I know. Good, isn't it? Just goes to show . . . you never can tell.*

J: *And there's me thinking it was unusual to have no gays in the company. Lol.*

Jayne's diary, 10.30 p.m., Saturday, 17 June 2017, Bath
Went to the pub with everyone. I had a lemonade. Sat with Taffy and Miriam.

Trevor sat in a corner with Peter, who was giving him notes

on his performance, I think. Lots of finger jabbing and squaring up to each other.

'Just look at them,' said Miriam, sneering slightly. Miriam always wore full make-up offstage. You could see where the foundation stopped and her neck was darker than her face. She wore a chunky gold necklace and matching earrings.

'They're like a couple of extras from *Peaky Blinders*,' said Taffy.

'Many a true word . . .' said Miriam. 'They have history, you know. Were at RADA together years ago. Trevor was an actor back then.' She sipped her sauvignon blanc and stared thoughtfully into the glass.

'I've noticed some friction,' I said.

'Bold of you,' said Miriam, a little indignantly. I suppose it was bold. Dressers aren't supposed to air their opinions, but I thought, off-duty in the pub, I might be allowed to make an observation.

'What do I know?' I said, attempting to make myself and my comment insignificant. I think Miriam likes everyone to keep in their place. She sensed my discomfort and her expression softened. 'You know all sorts of things, I'm sure,' she said, clearly implying that she had no interest in any of my pearls of wisdom.

'Hard to imagine them as young 'uns,' said Taffy.

'Perhaps they fell out over a ball game all those years ago and never settled their differences,' I said.

'Maybe,' said Miriam, seemingly surprised that I had spoken again. She finished her wine, picked up her big cream faux fur coat and slung it over her shoulders, ready to leave.

'Maybe not.' She stood up, bowed slightly at us by way of goodbye and moved her crocodile skin handbag. 'I think the only ball game those two ever played together involved a billiard ball inside a sock.'

Alone with Taffy, I asked her about the previous dresser who I replaced.

'Gordon. Only a young lad. Very fey.'

'Why did he leave? I heard it was about Peter, which is a surprise.'

'Well, yes. These things go on though.'

'I guess it's none of my business.'

'The sordid details I don't know. But Gordon was a bit of a lost lamb, always trying to latch on to people. Too much eye contact, if you know what I mean.'

'But Peter? A married man in his sixties?'

'I think Gordon thought he was Catherine Zeta-Jones.'

Taffy laughed, a little sadly.

'Silly boy.'

'Yes, well. He wasn't a very good dresser, more to the point. Then after whatever happened happened, he started crying all over the place.'

'Was it just a one-night thing, then?'

'I don't know. But I don't think Peter was planning to leave his wife and kids and run away with Gordon, let's put it that way. He was probably just flattered by the attention. And there wasn't anyone else after him. That's men for you. Things did calm down again, and I offered Gordon the job on the tour – I felt it was only right and proper – and he accepted. But now he's fallen in love with a shop assistant in Birmingham and dropped out.'

Jayne's diary, 11.30 p.m., Saturday, 17 June 2017, Bath
Hermia gave me a lift home to my digs as it was raining. She's one of those people who claims to find joy in unusual things. Rain. She loves it. She asked me if I was psychic. I said I didn't know. She's an emotional psychic, she said. She knows what people are feeling.

'Are you all right?' she asked me as I got out the car.

'Yes, but are you really all right?' She gave me a look as if to say I wasn't telling the truth. *Really* all right? I thought I was *really* all right but now I'm not so sure. There's no small talk with Hermia; she goes right in there. But in a positive way. I don't think she's a lesbian, judging by her shoes.

Chapter 9

Jayne's diary, Sunday, 18 June 2017, Bath

Went on a Tinder date this afternoon. I don't get many matches, so I wasn't exactly excited. More pleased, I'd say. An estate agent called Robin.

We met in a pub near the theatre. He didn't have a suit on – it's Sunday so he was in jeans and a T-shirt with a leather jacket. He had a thin face with a sexy twitch in his cheek. I thought he was gorgeous, but I couldn't tell what he thought of me. There was a sort of 'Oh, well. We're here now' tone to his voice, but then a half smile, as if he was playing a game. He asked me a lot of questions about my job.

Wasn't very forthcoming about life as an estate agent. When he started fiddling with his phone and telling me how busy he was tomorrow, I thought he was paving the way for a quick exit. But no. Got another round of drinks in.

'What are your hobbies?'

'I mean, like stamp collecting? No one has hobbies anymore, do they?'

'Why can't actors dress themselves?'

I had to explain about quick changes and all that.

'I'm not zipping up their flies or tying their shoelaces!'

'Aren't all actors druggies?'

The conversation limped on. 'What's your favourite food?'
'Greggs.'

He laughed, even smiled a bit, but then he looked away. There's something about him I really like.

Fun facts: Robin Kowalski
Robin achieved twelve A* GCSEs at school and four A* A-levels. He was expected to go to university but decided against it.

Jayne's diary, Monday, 19 June 2017, Bath
Got a message from Robin asking if I wanted to meet up this afternoon for some no-strings fun. I was surprised. I think he was, too, when I said yes.

I met him outside some flats and he said I had to pretend I was a buyer. I wasn't sure if this was roleplay or in case someone was listening. Anyway, I went with the flow and rather enjoyed pretending to be someone I wasn't: a wealthy young commuter, I decided. Once I was in character, I felt rather empowered. Suddenly it was *Carry On up the Estate Agents*.

'Nice bathroom,' I said. 'Is there an extractor fan in case it gets steamy in here?'

We ended up having sex in the bathroom, standing up. No kissing. Quite frantic, as if someone was about to come in and we had to be quick. It's a weird thing to say, but his body smelled horsey. Like straw and leather.

Afterwards, we both just laughed as we sorted our clothes out. Wasn't sure if it had actually happened or not, but I've got a bruise on my lower back from the porcelain, so it must have. Lol.

Fun facts: no-strings fun
An NSF relationship is one in which two people carry on a purely physical relationship with one another: there is no emotional connection between them.

One of the pros of having a no-strings-attached relationship is that while you get to enjoy a physical connection with another person, there's no sense of obligation or commitment.

The nature of no-strings-attached relationships often leaves many individuals feeling used, emotionally wounded and unvalued, leading to negative emotional experiences in the long run.

Jayne's diary, 6 p.m., Monday, 19 June 2017, Bath
Miriam was in a chatty mood so I stayed in her dressing room for a while as she put her make-up on. She wears one of those towelling turbans to keep her hair out of the way.

She asked me if I thought her foundation was the right colour. I said yes, even though I think it is a bit too light.

'It's Tom Ford,' she said. I looked out the window as I thought this Tom was outside but then I saw the name on the bottle.

'Are you seeing anyone back home?' she asked me.

'Oh, no. Just as well as I'm never there.'

'Shame,' she said. 'You're still quite young.'

I was confused as she must only have been a few years older than me, but I suppose I didn't want her feeling sorry for me, so I said, 'I had a date with a guy called Robin.'

I suppose my giggle gave me away.

'I see,' she said regally. 'And shall I assume it was a . . . fulfilling occasion?'

'Oh, well. You could say that. I've got a little light bruising below the waist. Ahem.'

'Jayne!' She put down her make-up brush and said, 'Well good on you for meeting your womanly needs so vigorously . . . Your secret is safe with me, my dear.'

Which was all fine except my secret wasn't safe with Miriam, was it? She must have said something about it to Spud because when I passed him in the wings later he gave me a knowing

59

look. I could feel myself blushing, but I didn't say anything. Pardon me for trying to have a bit of fun. And how dare Miriam!

Jayne's diary, Tuesday, 20 June 2017, Bath
Was quite tight-lipped with Miriam today. During the interval, she pulled me into her room and asked what was wrong. Told her about Spud but she swore on her mother's life that she hadn't said a word to anyone.

'He's a strange one,' she said. He apparently spends a lot of time listening at closed doors, eavesdropping on private conversations. Likes to think he knows everyone's business. Did I want her to have a word with him?

'No,' I said. 'Please don't make it any worse.'

Gone right off Spud now. It's always the quiet ones you have to watch. As for Miriam, I don't know if I believe her or not. Certainly won't be confiding any more secrets. Either she betrayed my confidence, she lied, or Spud has some sort of extra-sensory perception.

I'll save my juicy secrets for Rowanne from now on.

Jayne's diary, 10 p.m., Tuesday, 20 June 2017, Bath
Spud was quite friendly today. I'm so confused. Offered me a packet of crisps. Just shoved it under my nose in the green room.

'What flavour?' I asked, a bit flustered.

'Sniff it and see,' he said. Was he trying to flirt?

Anyway I sniffed. 'Cheese and onion?'

'Wrong. Sausage,' he said with a kind of half grin. Then sauntered off without giving me one! Funny man.

Now I'm wondering if I misunderstood his look. Could it be he was saying something else? Perhaps I was projecting. Anyway. Whatever it was I've decided to move on. It's press night tomorrow, so all hands on deck.

Then, late at night, my phone pinged. A Tinder message. From Robin. Saying: 'Just so you know, that Spud fella is bad news. Leave well alone.'

Bizarre. Too tired to even think about it right now.

Chapter 10

Press night, Wednesday, 21 June 2017
Group email from Trevor
Subject line: Our journey together

As we begin our *Leopard Spots* journey together, I thought it
might be a good moment for me to say a few words. I'll be saying
these words 'live' as it were, before our dress rehearsal, but it
occurs to me that some members of the crew might be otherwise
engaged at that time, and I feel it's important to include EVERY-
ONE. We are a 'family' after all. We are inter-dependent, all of
equal standing. In it together and in it to win it!

As we go along, I'll be jotting down my thoughts and observa-
tions about this great adventure, and I'll be sending these to you
(to do with as you will!) every week from now on. Motivational
Mondays, I like to call it. I've no doubt you'll find them useful.

So, here we go. Together we have created something unique
and wonderful. The play is reborn since Edinburgh. It has de-
veloped and evolved. It is beautiful and perfect. It is one of
your jobs to keep it that way.

Leopard Spots needs to be the most important thing in
your lives for these weeks. Everything, from the moment you
open your eyes in the morning needs to build towards the

performance. You must be at peak physical and mental condition. Nothing else will do, because trust me, I will know. The audience will know. Eat and drink sensibly. Get eight hours of sleep a night. Think calm and happy thoughts. This play is like a beautiful, pristine swimming pool. What happens if you turn up below par? Hungover? In a bad mood? With negative energy? Then you are pooping in the pool. Miss a cue? That's a poop in the pool. Get your timing wrong? A poop in the pool. Don't let that happen. Don't you be the one to poop in our pool. Promise me. Promise yourselves.

Touring is tough: it can become a pressure cooker if we aren't careful. Support one another. Be kind. You are bound together by this play. The little, petty irritations that may build up over time? Let them go. It happens, it is human nature. But dismiss them from your consciousness. They'll get in the way of our work here. The work is what matters most. I might even say it is *all* that matters.

Most of all I want you to remember that you are artists. This is a role like no other in our society. We are the ones who elevate the human experience. We transfer the mundane to the divine. The best job in the world. The people out there, the audience, look to us to make life worth living. That is our role. Laughter. Tears. We engage their emotions. There is no other job like it. Artists! So use your artistry, your privilege, your power. Nurture and feed the talent that you carry. It is precious. A gift from the universe.

I am incredibly proud of what we have created. I am in awe of each and every one of you, from the actors to the props, wardrobe, stage management. Dressers, even. Everyone. I acknowledge and respect your hard work. It is, I promise you, worth it. Now is when we claim our reward. This is an incredibly powerful and transformative piece. Give it your all, all night, every night, and the sky is our limit.

Finally, I want to thank you. I know it will take its toll. But we are artists and this is what we do. And we do it bloody well. From the bottom of my heart, thank you.

Kitty Litter WhatsApp Group Chat

S: *Quite the speech. He'd make a good evangelical preacher.*

H: *Don't poop in the pool.*

M: *If I'd known how important and time-consuming this was going to be I'd have asked for more money.*

S: *Too late now.*

P: *I didn't listen to it. Same crap they used to force-feed us with a RADA.*

H: *You were rather obviously fiddling with your phone during Trevor's speech.*

P: *Speech? More of a monologue. He likes the sound of his own voice, but that doesn't mean I have to. Anyone coming to the pub for a quick half before we do this crap?*

S: *I'm up for a cheeky livener, Peter. Shall we meet there?*

P: *Oh. OK. Yes, let's meet there.*

M: *Not me.*

H: *I'm going to do some deep breathing.*

Text messages between Peter and Katheryn Milano (interval of Bath press night)

K: *Whoop! Going Brilliantly!*

P: *Thanks, darling. Audience a bit hysterical. I sometimes wonder if they get rent-a-crowd in for these nights and pay 'em to wet themselves laughing.*

K: *You're brilliant, that's all.*

P: *Your seats OK?*

K: *Not really. I'm sat next to the dreadful Laura. She's asking if I know any London pied-à-terre flats in Knightsbridge. 'I take it you'd like to be close to a tanning shop,' I said.*

P: *You didn't!*

K: *Well, yes, I did. She was fuming, but I can't stand her. Cheap tart. Has no one told her you're not supposed to clap after every line Simon utters?*

P: *I could hear. Very distracting and interrupts my flow.*

K: *I bet. But never mind that. Just concentrate on the play.*

P: *Not easy with Ken bloody Thomas sitting in the front row with steam coming out of his ears.*

K: *Rise above. Do your job. Truly, you are smashing it.*

P: *See you after.*

Text messages between Peter and Katheryn Milano (after the show)

K: *Bravo. Best I've ever seen you. Seriously dazzling.*

P: *It would be rude to disagree with you.*

K: *Hurry up and come to the drinks thing. It's dreadful.*

P: *Just getting my slap off.*

K: *Word of warning: Ken's here. Drinking from a flask. Looks pissed and dangerous.*

P: *Great.*

K: *Laura now wants a riverside penthouse overlooking Tower Bridge. She's also been to the loo and her pupils are like saucers. I made a point of wiping a little white powder off the side of her nose with a tissue. 'The paps are out in force,' I said to her. 'It would be a shame if your little habit made the headlines instead of the play, wouldn't it?'*

Text messages between Simon Gaunt and his wife, Laura

L: *I'm flirting with a twenty-year-old waiter, Babes. If you can't find me at the party, I'll be out the back by the bins giving him a blowy.*

S: *That's my girl. Doing a quick interview and I'll be there.*

L: *Oh, and Katheryn's keen to sell us a London bolthole for a snip.*

S: *Anything for my Laura.*

L: *Can you get us some coke? Running low here.*

Jayne's diary, Wednesday, 21 June 2017, Bath

Press night. This is the important one where we must all be on top form and make no mistakes. The good and the great are watching, not to mention all the reviewers from newspapers, magazines and online bloggers.

Everyone was very quiet beforehand, saving their energy. Concentrating.

Thankfully it went really, really well. Great audience. Big laughs. Standing ovation. Party afterwards and Trevor made another speech about how we'd all done him proud and how marvellous the play is. A bit rich, seeing as he wrote it. He said we're all equals, everyone playing their part for the greater good or some such carry-on. I glazed over a bit.

There were a lot of people. Peter's wife, Katheryn, in a chintzy frock. Professionally speaking, I didn't think it worked for her. If I'd been her dresser she would have worn a navy blue trouser suit, maybe with a white bow blouse.

Simon's wife, Laura, in more of a handkerchief than a dress and wearing more make-up than Boy George. The theatre management was there, and who knows who else. I was given one free ticket so Rowanne came, and I smuggled her into my digs after. She was agog to hear all the gossip. Normally I leave these parties early before they get messy, but Rowanne wanted to stay. It all went off . . .

Some man, I think he was from the press, had far too much cheap white wine and started being loud and rude to Peter. I saw him being removed from the premises by two barmen, one either side, kind of carrying him by his elbows. Peter gave him the middle finger as he passed.

But that wasn't the half of it. It was quite a night. Alcohol doesn't half loosen people's tongues. And sharpen them. Glad I don't drink.

I thought Simon and Peter didn't really get on, but it seems I was wrong. They were outside the loos chatting intently.

'How much longer?' Peter was asking.

'You're gonna get it, mate,' reassured Simon. 'Keep your fucking hair on!'

It all goes on, doesn't it?!

Meanwhile, Rowanne got cornered at the bar by a well-oiled Trevor. She didn't even know who he was, but he spilled the beans about how he should have been a star actor, not a director. He had more talent in his little finger than Peter Milano had in his whole, bloated body. He'd wiped the floor with him at RADA.

'Why did you employ him, then?' Rowanne asked innocently and Trevor just tapped the side of his nose and smiled bitterly.

We left the party when last orders were called, and in the alleyway outside, Miriam and Spud were walking up the road together. He must like older women.

Row and I stayed up half the night whispering in my room and giggling about it all like teenagers.

Ken Thomas's blog, Thursday, 22 June 2017
High drama at the Theatre Royal, Bath, last night – but sadly not on the stage. The talent on display there was more akin to a school nativity play, but more of that dirge later. *Leopard Spots* has begun its national tour. What a treat for the nation!

Sadly, as any seasoned hack will tell you, it's one thing to triumph at the Edinburgh Fringe, the annual gathering where lefty luvvies meet to tell each other how wonderful they are and where a 'hit' may have more to do with cocaine consumption than a successful creative endeavour, but quite another to replicate that momentary rapture in less refined, drink-addled circles . . .

Leopard Droppings (as I prefer to call it) left me cold in Edinburgh, and despite my pashmina shawl and merino wool leggings, I was shivering with boredom in Bath, too. I feared I might be slipping into a coma, but it was really just my mind and body employing a survival mechanism, similar to a grizzly bear's torpor in the early stages of hibernation.

Forgive me, I was in no state to take notes and my memory of those hours is mercifully vague. But I can inform the reader that my dormant state was triggered not by lack of sustenance or winter chills but by the appearance on stage of Peter Milano. The second he lumbered on, gurning and leering at the audience, like Wayne Rooney at a grab-a-granny night, my eyelids became heavy and my heart rate slowed almost to a stop. He is propofol on legs.

Why does anyone employ him? He's never been any good. I grudgingly concede that there was an air of rugged attractiveness about him in his early days – if you'd had enough to drink. But the same might be said about my ginger tom and you wouldn't pay good money to see him now, toothless, riddled with cancer, his nether regions dotted with piss-soaked furballs.

So, *Leopard Droppings* droned on as I snored, like *Countdown* in a nursing home TV lounge, until I was woken by the polite applause and the sound of Bath pensioners wheezing with relief as they got onto their bunioned feet. (Clearly, the curative powers of the hot springs are overrated.)

Desperate to salvage something pleasurable from my trip to Somerset, I felt duty-bound to attend the after-show party. The rather miserable soirée was populated mainly with Bath theatre club members keen to mix and mingle with the cast, the main benefit of their annual subscription unless you count 'early-bird' tickets for shows like the one we had just endured. Friends and relatives of the cast air-kissed with all the sincerity of Donald Trump taking his oath of office.

Simon Gaunt's anaemic wife, who has clearly eaten nothing but rice cakes and laxatives for the last six months, asked for a ('large') Malibu and coke. The waiter politely told her only wine and beer were free tonight. She told him to put it on her husband's tab. He doesn't have a tab, she was told. He does now, she said. You can take the girl out of Essex . . .

Peter Milano's wife stood apart, talking into her mobile phone. Closing the deal on a mock Tudor house in Chester for someone with more money than taste? If so, the tinkling laughter and lowered eyes seemed inappropriately flirtatious. Who knows? I wouldn't want to spread rumours. But you will be familiar with the old saying: 'What's sauce for the goose is sauce for the gander'.

There was the usual meagre buffet of curled sandwiches and questionable canapes, while slim-hipped waiters in bow ties carried trays of cheap, cloudy prosecco the colour of a urinary tract infection patient's sample. Just as well I had brought my own refreshments in a handy, deceptively capacious hipflask.

Fun facts: press night
On 5 September 1887, a fire broke out in the backstage area of the Theatre Royal, Exeter, during the first night of *The Romany Rye*. The fire caused panic throughout the theatre, with 186 people dying from a combination of the direct effects of smoke and flames, crushing and trampling, and trauma injuries from falling or jumping from the roof and balconies.

Ken Thomas's blog (continued), Thursday, 22 June 2017

When the cast finally meandered in, flushed from their stoical exertions and wearing what only touring theatricals consider 'best', they were besieged by theatre club devotees. Phones flashed, programmes were signed and compliments graciously accepted.

Most generous with her wan smiles and flourishing signature was Miriam Haughton. A word to the wise: wrap-around dresses aren't always the best choice for the fuller figure. There's a lot to be said for an ethnic print smock, I thought to myself.

But then, dear reader, things took an unexpected turn. Here, at last, comes the drama I promised you. The drama without which no blog of mine would be complete.

I must steady myself to accurately recall the indignity of what befell me. I state the bare facts and do not, for once, enhance the essential truth with waspish sentiment or roguish attitude.

So. There I was, present at the 'party', perusing the dreary, cheaply framed posters on the wall with my critical eye and preparing for a low-key departure.

Disdainful, if not homophobic, stares from Katheryn Milano were beginning to make me feel uncomfortable and my single room suddenly seemed a more inviting prospect.

I made myself comfortable in the gents and was threading my way nimbly through the honking crowd when suddenly I was grabbed from behind.

Peter Milano, clearly possessed and intoxicated, was babbling incomprehensibly, his face a twisted mask of hatred. Fearful for my safety, I did what was necessary and screamed for help. What I got was two sturdy security men frog-marching me out of the premises and dumping me on the pavement like a bag of refuse. Dignity, had I none!

Well, let me just state here that this will not be the end of the

70

story. My legal team is on it. My injuries have been assessed and photographed and my PTSD is ongoing.

This sorry incident will cost Mr Milano dear, of that you can be assured.

Chapter 11

Popbitch, **Thursday, 22 June 2017**
Who's been a naughty boy? Which comedy legend has been
caught red-handed stealing material from a little-known new-
comer's set? Flattering as it was to hear his jokes repeated in a
three thousand-seater arena, the newbie would rather like some
financial reward . . . Cough up!

Metro, **Friday, 23 June 2017**
Headline: Q&A with Simon Gaunt

Best-known for his hilarious stand-up arena tours and many
appearances on the telly, Simon Gaunt's latest venture sees him
trying his hand at acting in the hit play Leopard Spots, *which is*
touring the country for the next six weeks. We caught up with the
funny man just after press night in Bath.

> *Metro: The play is hilarious. How did you come to þe involved?*
> *Simon: Thanks! Well, as soon as I read the script, I knew I had*
> *to do it. Trevor Millicent, who wrote and directed it, had me in*
> *mind, apparently, so it's kind of written in my style.*
> *M: Amazing. Did you know each other, then?*
> *S: No, that's the funny thing. He just happened to see me on TV*

doing something and thought bingo!

M: *The character you play is called Marwood Weston, and he has to rush around being lots of different people in the hotel. It's a tour-de-force for you. Where did you find the inspiration?*

S: *I've always loved John Cleese, and when I mentioned this in rehearsals, Trevor laughed. Marwood is John Cleese's middle name and he was born in Weston-super-Mare. So he had that in his mood board all along. There are lots of little clues like this in the script, all there to help you as an actor, pointing the way. I love that.*

M: *Do you think you'll do more acting now you've got the taste for it?*

S: *Definitely. If anyone will have me! I think stand-up will always be my first love but if the right thing came along I'd be up for it.*

M: *What about Shakespeare?*

S: *Nah, too many long words, innit?*

M: *Tell us about the people you are working with. Are you having fun?*

S: *I'm having the best time. They're all so brilliant and amazingly generous and kind. It's a real joint effort, with everyone there to support each other. Peter Milano – I've been such a fan all my life and to be in a play with him now – it blows my mind. How did that even happen?*

M: *You really bounce off each other on stage.*

S: *That's the thing with this sort of comedy. It's like a game of tennis. We all depend on each other to make it work and hopefully that shows. Miriam and Hermia, too. I'm in awe of their talent.*

M: *Definitely. The play turns dark towards the end. How are you finding the serious bits?*

S: *I love how it does that. I'm not going to lie, I found it daunting at first. I'm so used to getting laughs that sudden silence threw me a bit. But Trevor taught me to trust the text. And I might not*

73

be able to hear the audience response when it gets tense, but I can feel it. They are holding their breath.

M: I certainly was! Congratulations and I'll let you go and have a well-deserved drink. Thanks for talking to us.

S: Cheers!

Simon Gaunt in Leopard Spots *continues in Bath then Cheltenham, Brighton, Birmingham and Plymouth until the end of August. See the* Metro *review on page 19.*

Fun facts: Simon Gaunt
While on a lads' holiday in Magaluf when he was twenty, Simon had a tattoo drawn on his thigh that reads 'Large doner kebab, yoghurt, mint, no salad and extra chips, gracias'.

Julian on Trevor Millicent
Trevor directed me in a production of Edward Bond's *The Sea* when I was at drama school. Bit of a comedown for him after his earlier success, but never mind. He's good. Old school. Likes to sit around for a couple of weeks discussing each character's back story. Bit of a bully.

I remember he made me do one line over and over again. About fifty times, until I 'got it right', in his opinion. I think that's when I decided I wanted to be a comedian rather than an actor. A self-contained entity, pleasing myself, talking about myself, not at the mercy of a bossy director. Especially him. Lovely.

Notices outside the Theatre Royal, Bath

Not to be missed! *** *The Daily Mail***
A theatrical masterpiece! *** *The Guardian***

Extraordinary ***** *The Times*

Voicemail message from Simon to Peter
'Hi, Pete. I've had Bernie on the phone and he's going ahead with the investment opportunity. He said we have to move fast or we'll lose it. Word has got out, and some big money guys from Miami are going to take the lot if we don't get in there. He can hold off for 24 hours. No more. He reckons a 200 per cent profit within a month. Minimum! Like I told you, this is the real deal.

I've done it five, maybe six times now and Bernie knows his stuff. It might sound too good to be true but it ain't! It's how things work these days. Money makes money, if you've got the cash. It's all above board. I know barristers who are in on it, MPs, doctors, you name it. I'm bringing you in on this as a mate, OK? I'm putting £100K in this time, I'm not mucking about. You in for £50K? I've got all the bank details, but we need to do the transfers first thing tomorrow. Sharpish. Then we just sit back and wait for the dosh to come flooding in. Hey presto, happy retirement!'

Text exchange between Peter and Simon
P: *The eagle has landed. Money sent 11 a.m. Does Bernie send me any paperwork or receipt?*

S: *Brill! Bernie will be in touch. He's on a plane to Saudi right now, so out of contact. Keep your money transfer certificate safe. That's all you need. Congrats, mate. You've deffo done the right thing.*

Text from Katheryn to Peter
K: *Can you tell me what's happened to the £50K missing from our bank account?*

Chapter 12

Jayne's diary, 7 p.m., Sunday, 25 June 2017, Cheltenham
Nice short drive to Cheltenham, which seems like a very smart place. Big houses and lots of green space. Found the rough bit, which is where I'm staying. Lol.

I'm with a family and it looks like they've just hoiked the teenage son out of his room and put me in. I guess they've changed the sheets but there's no wardrobe space and I'm looking at posters of rappers and footballers on the wall. Smells of feet, so I've opened the window. Never mind. It's only a week and I've got an ensuite.

Jayne's diary, Sunday, 25 June 2017, Cheltenham
We're all sold out. Everyone loves the show and reviews are glowing. If only the punters knew what the atmosphere was like backstage. Toxic!

There are sharp words and haughty departures, teeth are sucked and complaints made about this and that. I think I'm the only happy one, so I find myself trying to hide my natural cheerfulness in case it looks suspicious. Ridiculous state of affairs. Misery always seems pointless to me. Self-indulgent. Maybe I'm a shallow person? Lol.

Here I am spending my time with a rather strange, dysfunctional group of people. Simon seems preoccupied, Miriam worried about her mother, Peter pompous, Hermia full of some inner turmoil, Taffy stressed and Spud – well, Spud has never been known to show a flicker of a smile – at least he is consistent.

He's messaged me a couple of times on Tinder with emojis, if you please, but I haven't answered. I mean, how do you respond to an aubergine, a frost crystal, a weird cloud or a smiley face with its tongue hanging out?

I don't know, and I guess it is just more of his silly games. I don't quite have the heart to block him though. I don't much like him but there is a spark of something which I know would probably be a bad idea to ever investigate. Rowanne calls it 'fizzy knickers' syndrome. Lol.

I spent my day off having a final wander around Bath before I came to Cheltenham. I find myself gazing into the window of several estate agents, wondering if it's where Robin works. There is no sighting of him. I walk around and then I'm outside the flats where we had our furtive sexual encounter. I smile to myself and laugh.

Fun facts: Cheltenham
Apart from the horse racing, there are more 'festivals' in Cheltenham than you can shake a festive stick at: Cheltenham Literary Festival, Jazz Festival, Science Festival, Music Festival, Film Festival, Cricket Festival, Food and Drink Festival.

Anyone for bunting?

Group email from Trevor
Subject line: Motivational Mondays 2
Congratulations everyone on our brilliant opening.

I am in awe of you all. You are so, so talented. And not only that, but what I've seen this week is how your individual talents all mesh together to create a stunning whole.

77

Now we know where the laughs fall, we can – and you are already – hone and polish our performances. Everything is there: pace, rhythm, light and shade. I just want to push you slightly more, if I may, from brilliance to exquisite genius, no less!

This play is undoubtedly a hit. We know that already. There seems every likelihood that it will play for many years all around the world. Your performances are the seminal ones that everyone will remember. They will be fixed in people's minds forever.

This is a groundbreaking play. You are the foot soldiers, conquering uncharted theatrical territory. We may have just opened, but I hear on the grapevine that the Olivier selection committee is making some very interesting noises.

Jayne's diary, Monday, 26 June 2017, Cheltenham

Trevor's email, though! Hilariously delusional. All is a bed of roses, apparently. He conveniently ignores that backstage is seething with trouble and the actors have steam coming out of their ears! Lol.

And what about that fracas at the party with Peter confronting that journalist?

It's the talk of the wardrobe department but Peter is pretending it never happened. His complexion looks a bit grey and he seems to have put on a few pounds. Comfort eating – I wouldn't blame him.

The reviews are pinned on the noticeboard for everyone to read, and while Simon gets called 'genius' and 'remarkable', Peter is 'reliable' and 'endearingly pompous'. All positives, but hardly thrilling if you're Peter.

Don't think Miriam is overcome with delight: Hermia was widely praised as 'dreamy' and 'otherworldly' while one paper called Miriam 'matronly'. She's swanning around with a pained expression on her face. Actors! Thought about sulking 'cos no critics said how well-ironed the costumes were but I don't think anyone would notice if I did! Lol.

Kitty Litter WhatsApp Group Chat
    S: *Morning, everyone. Loving Cheltenham.*
    H: *It's dreamy.*
    M: *As are you, according to* The Stage.
    H: *Am I? I don't remember.*
    P: *I've played this theatre a thousand times. The public here know me and appreciate my craft.*
    M: *Will you be keeping in that amusing popping sound we heard during the last night in Bath?*
    P: *What are you talking about?*
    M: *I think it might have been the sound of a button from your waistline.*
    S: *It flew across the stage. Genius!*
    M: *It's a hazard though. I could have slipped on it.*
    P: *We wouldn't want any mishap to befall matron, would we?*

Jayne's diary, Tuesday, 27 June 2017, Cheltenham
Trevor is still here, hanging round like a bad smell. Says he's still got some 'fine-tuning' to do. This seems to be all about Peter's performance. Keeps calling him in for extra one one-on-one rehearsals. 'We're nearly there,' he said to him today.

Peter sighs a lot, accusing Trevor of contradicting his previous instructions. But he has no choice, so does as directed, but it is never right – always too much or too little. This afternoon, Peter had enough and threw his script on the floor and stormed off, calling Trevor a 'fucking control freak'. He then sat in the green room eating a whole packet of Bakewell tarts.

Rowanne thinks it's an outrage. Usually, the director leaves everyone to get on with it after the first week and everything settles down. Not with this play though.

Jayne's diary, Wednesday, 28 June 2017, Cheltenham
Yet more rehearsals for Peter today. Trevor told him to try doing the whole thing in a Scottish accent!

'It might help,' he said, sounding doubtful.

I asked Taffy why Trevor keeps picking on him.

'He seems intent on destroying the poor man's self-confidence.'

'Ah, well,' said Taffy, closing the door so no one would overhear.

'I think I have a clue what this is all about.'

Taffy has heard (from a source she wouldn't divulge, but I think it's another actor she worked with) that there has been a grudge going on for many years. Trevor and Peter were both at RADA together back in the late 70s.

'Really good friends they were, shared a flat together and the odd girlfriend, too. Always playing pranks on each other.'

Taffy had seen a photo of them when they were students: Peter handsome, with shoulder-length hair while Trevor was slight and receding.

'Anyway, they both graduated and were signed up with a top agent and were all set for glittering careers. They got their first job together, playing minor roles in rep at the Royal Shakespeare Company at Stratford for a year.

Trevor was the better actor, apparently, but Peter was more confident and ambitious. He did everything he could to get noticed, ingratiating himself with all and sundry, flirting with anyone who might be useful and hanging out with the top brass, networking and all that. Trevor quietly got on with it, learning his craft and biding his time.

'Peter got his way in a production of *Romeo and Juliet*, cast as Count Paris, a fairly meaty role with a fight scene; Trevor had to make do with the bit-part of Balthasar who doesn't have any lines until Act 5. For a laugh one day, Trevor told Peter the matinee was cancelled so Peter went to the cinema with a girlfriend. Caused a lot of trouble and the understudy had to go on last minute.

'Peter got his revenge a week later when he locked Trevor in his dressing room, and he missed his cue. When he finally got out, he rushed on stage, breathless and upset. The audience laughed uproariously, and he fluffed his lines and generally made a disgrace of himself. Peter thought it was hilarious, but Trevor got the sack, became afflicted with terrible stage-fright and never acted again. Peter never apologised.

'Trevor left showbusiness and spent twenty years licking his wounds, plagued by insecurity and working in bars and restaurants while Peter's acting career went from strength to strength.

'Trevor finally got his revenge, by writing a play about a vain, unscrupulous actor who will do anything for fame, easily recognised as Peter although he always denied this.

'*Who Are You and What Do You Want?* made Trevor famous and respectable at last. It ran for two years and transferred to Broadway. It may or may not be a coincidence that Peter's star began to fade around this time, along with his looks.

'Casting his old enemy in this new play is a curious thing to do under the circumstances. Quite Shakespearean, in a way. Was it a way of finally making peace or a chance to humiliate Peter, twist the knife and shatter his confidence just as Peter once shattered Trevor's?'

Blimey. It's amazing what goes on, isn't it? I ate a whole tube of Pringles while Taffy told me all this. Felt a bit sick after.

Trevor Millicent: notes for archive
Cheltenham is where I really started to put my 'plan' into action, where it became more than just a fanciful daydream. I have to say the enjoyment I got from seeing Peter suffer was deeply satisfying. I had him on the rack and I was turning the handle. Payback time for Trevor at long last!

81

Chapter 13

Jayne's diary, Friday, 30 June 2017, Cheltenham
Well, that was unexpected. Got a text from Robin to say he was in Cheltenham to view a flat for work and asked if I was free this afternoon.

Met him outside Greggs. Went for a walk along the river. He didn't talk much. I told him about all the goings on at the theatre and how odd everyone is. He grunted sympathetically.

I chatted away merrily.

'What's this flat like that you're selling in Cheltenham?'

'Two bed, two bath. Balcony.' I wondered if he was going to take me there for another role-play session. I wouldn't have minded. I think I've had a bit of a thing about bathrooms ever since last time. Always look around working out the various sexual possibilities. Sink, bidet, shower screen? If this turns into a full-blown fetish I'll have to get counselling. Lol.

Robin must have read my mind: 'Current owners still in residence. We can't go there.'

'Oh, right,' was all I could think to say.

'But I've got the keys to a garage that's up for rental,' he said and gave me a sort of sideways smirk.

'Garage?' I said. He took my hand and said, 'It's this way.'

We walked there in silence and I couldn't help wondering what sort of estate agent he really is. Flats in every city? Garages for rent that he just happens to have the keys for?

Anyway, we got there and it was a row of posh garages behind a block of mansion flats. He shut the door and put the light on. Just a few gardening tools and old pots of paint neatly arranged on some shelves. I began to question what I was doing there. This could be a scene from one of those crime documentaries you see on Channel 5.

But Robin smiled at me and pulled me towards him. He looked so handsome that I melted. We kissed.

I didn't realise until we'd finished that we'd had sex against a lawnmower. I've got grass and grease stains on the back of my skirt, which I'm going to have to soak in Vanish. Lol. But I must say I have no objection to these unusual locations for friskiness. Sort of dogging-lite, I suppose.

Afterwards, he treated me to a Greggs, and what do you know? I saw Peter leaving just as we arrived, holding a huge bag of pastries and a look of determination on his face that implied he was going to eat the lot himself.

Fun facts: Greggs
There are over 2,400 Greggs in the UK. The bakery sells around 2.5 million sausage rolls every week or around 140 million a year.

Jayne's diary, Saturday, 1 July 2017, Cheltenham
Show's going well. Even the matinees are sold out. But, of course, the better things are going front of house, the more tense it is behind the scenes.

Miriam was outraged because Peter burped during their kissing scene and says she nearly threw up.

Simon changed his delivery of a line and Hermia was

83

completely thrown by it. Lots of fierce whispering in the wings and door slamming in the interval.

Apparently, 'important people' were in this evening, although no one tells me what that means. Important to who? Themselves, no doubt.

'Investors, producers, love,' Taffy explained to me. 'This play is putting bums on seats, isn't it? Those men in suits can smell money like a cat with cream, that's what it's all about.'

Robin texted:

R: *How's things?*

J: *All good, thanks. Where shall I send my laundry bill?*

R: *Sorry about that. If it makes you feel better my jeans are ruined, too.*

J: *Where are we going next time? There's a rubbish skip round the back of the theatre by the bins.*

R: *I'll bring my step ladder.*

Jayne's diary, Monday, 3 July 2017, Cheltenham

Peter is in a particularly arrogant mood. Every spare moment he is in Simon's dressing room, but the conversation stops as soon as I enter.

'Would you kindly knock in future?' he said to me.

Well, I did knock. Not my fault if they didn't hear me.

I tried to shrug it off, but he clearly wanted to put me in my place.

Later Simon passed me in the corridor and said, 'You ok, darlin'?'

I just nodded.

'I had a go at Peter for being so rude to you. It's not on.'

'Oh, you needn't have. I'm used to it with actors!'

Simon shook his head. 'I can't stand bullies. It won't happen again,' he added with a wink.

So that was kind of him. Who knows what Peter's problem is.

Maybe it's the reviews? Simon definitely got more praise than Peter. You'd think he'd forgotten about them by now. I don't think I'd read them if I was an actor.

Very sweet of Simon to be concerned about me, though. What a nice guy. He's the only one who doesn't take it all too seriously.

Miriam in quite a tizz when I went in to fix her wig. Sat there biting her lip and screwing up a tissue in her hand. I couldn't just ignore it. I don't trust her after the Spud business, but we had a show to do and I wanted her to be focused and calm.

'Everything OK?' I asked.

'My mother has had a fall in the care home.'

I felt a wave of sympathy for Miriam, despite her faults. I know how preoccupying it is when you're worried about something, especially your mother.

She needed to talk about it. Talking is always a good thing. I put on my counsellor hat and told her I understood all too well, having cared for my mum during sad times. It didn't take long for Miriam to explain the situation.

Her mum used to be an actress. Never married. Had 'difficulties'. Got the impression she had a difficult childhood although she didn't once allude to that or criticise her mother. Clearly adores her. She now lives in a posh care home where she gets proper psychiatric support. I think those places cost a fortune. Anyway, she had a fall on Sunday and Miriam rushed down there. Face all bruised and a bit confused.

'It upset me so much. I just want to wrap her in cotton wool and look after her.'

Miriam got her phone out and showed me some photos of her mum as she was in her prime. Alice Haughton. So glamorous! Blonde bob, sitting on a motorbike. Proper star. She was going to be in a remake of *Charlie's Angels* apparently, but then she got pregnant when she was twenty-three.

'So beautiful!'

'Wasn't she?' Miriam sighed.

Couldn't she have carried on working, though?' I asked. It was the 1980s, after all.

'She didn't, somehow. Everything stopped. It wasn't the shame of being unmarried – she'd have coped with that, I think. More like post-natal depression, which people didn't understand back then.'

I was wondering what sort of childhood Miriam had and who looked after her. Then she showed me another photo of her poor mum as she is now. Terribly sad. Not just fragile but . . . the eyes: frightened and lost. Made me realise how important it is to enjoy life while I can. You never know what is going to happen. I didn't try to jolly Miriam along. I mean, what can you say? I sensed she just wanted someone to listen while she talked and I'm good at that.

Eventually, it became apparent that it would be appropriate for me to say something. 'It was a very different situation with my mum, but I know that pain – seeing someone you love so vulnerable. It's so hard.'

Miriam squeezed my hand and she definitely seemed calmer and less fraught.

And she was great tonight. Really magnificent.

Jayne's diary, Wednesday, 5 July 2017, Cheltenham
Robin came round to my digs this afternoon for 'a cup of tea'. Meant we actually had sex horizontally for a change. That's progress! He did a bit of kissing in the heat of the moment.

As we lay there having a postcoital rest, as you do, I pointed out the marks on the ceiling that have been bothering me.

'Is that cobwebs or black mould?'

I thought with his property knowledge he'd know the answer. But he had no idea. Surely, they're trained in these matters?

Never mind. We're off to Brighton next, so I expect that's the end of things.

Ken Thomas's blog, Wednesday, 5 July 2017
No surprise – I am off sick this week, so no theatre expeditions to report. My arms are seriously bruised and I'm advised not to go anywhere crowded in case I'm bumped into by some inconsiderate brute. My PTSD is also off the scale.

I'm also distraught because my cat, Marcel, had to be put to sleep. He has been my constant companion for the last nineteen years and I don't know how I am going to cope without his comforting presence. The flat seems so lonely and desolate. To make matters worse, due to my injuries I was unable to hold him in my arms as the vet put him to sleep. I could only stand and watch through a veil of tears. Damn Peter Milano.

RIP Marcel.

Chapter 14

Julian on Brighton

Now our travelling players move on to the south coast, to Brighton, where a blow on the front is available to anyone who might want it.

The place is alive with the gays, which is fine if you like that sort of thing. Personally, I think a bit of a cull might be in order. I suggest they kettle all the old gays on the Isle of Wight. Then stop the ferries so they can't come to the mainland spreading their UTIs and eating all our Murray Mints.

My editor (a dreadful woman who wears a beanie hat and lives in a throuple in Cobham) is getting a bit anxious as there hasn't been much blood and gore yet in this book. But it is coming, dear reader. The general idea is that you are currently fully engaged trying to work out:

a) Who the victim is going to be?

b) Who is the murderer?

It's not so much a whodunnit as a 'who is gonna do it and to whom?'

A jolly ruse might be to write down your predictions on a piece of paper then pop it in a safe place and see if you're right when you get to the end of the book?

Anyway, help yourself to snacks. I'm rather keen these days

on sesame pretzel thins (baked not fried, 86 calories per serving). Or if you're near a Portuguese deli, I can't recommend the 3D's Bugles (*sin gluten*) highly enough.

Fun facts: Brighton
Keith Waterhouse once said: 'Brighton looks as though it is a town helping the police with their enquiries.'

The Brighton Argus, Thursday, 6 July 2017
By Jane Chan.
Headline: A chat with with Peter Milano

Theatre fans are in for a treat this week as legendary heartthrob Peter Milano stars in Leopard Spots *at the Theatre Royal. We spoke to the star and asked him if he was looking forward to coming to Brighton.*

'Of course!' *Peter exclaimed, the silky tones instantly recognisable even down a crackly phone line.* 'I'm delighted. It is the most wonderfully, vibrant city. And the Theatre Royal is glorious. So looking forward to bringing this wonderful play to you all there.'

Leopard Spots *began life at the Edinburgh Festival and is now on a sell-out national tour. Many superlatives have been written about it, but what can we expect?*

'It's a fascinating play. Clever, funny, unexpected. Some people come more than once, I'm told. There's so much to absorb in it.'

The play is set in a hotel somewhere tropical. Tell us a little about your character.

'I play George Taylor, a heavy-drinking, unhappily married man who, together with his wife, stops off at a rather strange hotel for a few hours while his car is being fixed. But he never leaves. Well, I don't want to give the plot away.'

And how is it sharing the stage with funny man Simon Gaunt?

89

'To take on a role like that with no acting experience is very brave. Very brave indeed.'

The reviews for his performance seem to be glowing?

'Yes, I think we've all been surprised how kind the press has been, on the whole. It's been a steep learning curve for Simon, hasn't been easy for him, but you know, he's on stage with a group of very experienced thesps and we are all rooting for him every night and ready to catch him should he fall.'

Kitty Litter WhatsApp Group Chat

M: *Nice* Argus *interview, Peter.*

P: *Thank you.*

S: *Glad to know you think I'm brave.*

P: *What I really think of you after what's happened would not be printed in a family newspaper.*

S: *Have another doughnut, Peter. I'm worried you're wasting away.*

Jayne's diary, Monday, 10 July 2017, Brighton

The Theatre Royal is lovely but could do with some TLC backstage. Taffy is fuming about the damp, the smells and the mice.

I've got a huge room in a big flat in Adelaide Crescent, overlooking the gardens. Older gay couple, ex-musical theatre types. Very sweet. Made me a sandwich when I got here. Quick bus ride to the theatre.

Miriam had a face like thunder. Like a tsunami.

Her mother, I think.

Jayne's diary, 7 p.m., Monday, 10 July 2017, Brighton

With all this tension in the air I suppose an eruption was inevitable sooner or later.

They'd all just finished vocal warm-up and were in the corridor leading to the dressing rooms. I was ironing in wardrobe with the door open because of the steam, so I could see and hear everything.

Miriam was telling Hermia the latest about her mother, how she was still quite shaken but better than she was. Her voice was getting a bit quivery, and Simon put his arm around her and said, 'Don't worry, she'll be right as rain in a few days.'

'Mind if I squeeze past?' said Peter, a bit snippily.

'Dunno mate, can you? Stand back everyone – extra-heavy load passing through!'

Peter lost it. He froze for a second, shouted 'Oh, piss off you fucking con man,' and punched Simon in the face. Hermia screamed, Miriam yelped.

Simon grabbed Peter's throat and the pair of them fell to the floor wrestling like a couple of schoolboys. Taffy sprang into action at once, shouting, 'Stop this, the pair of you!' just as Trevor rushed in from the stage and separated them.

'This is not acceptable,' Trevor said sternly and sent them to their dressing rooms.

I had to go and dab Simon's cheek with TCP. He was OK. Thought the whole thing was a laugh.

Then I went to Peter's room to put a plaster on his knuckles. He was quite shaken and, I think, sore. He wouldn't make eye contact. Seething, still. I felt sorry for him. Such an undignified scrap.

When I went to Miriam's room a bit later, Hermia was there. Both pale and pouty. 'Equity should step in,' said Hermia decisively.

'How can I be expected to act under these circumstances?' asked Miriam. 'It's not *Peaky Blinders* for goodness' sake.'

Despite all this they managed another good performance. Simon's face looked a bit swollen, and Peter had a bit of a limp, but I don't think the audience would have known about the backstage drama.

Chapter 15

Jayne's diary, Tuesday, 11 July 2017, Brighton
Yesterday's fisticuffs have had an interesting effect. After the show Peter and Simon couldn't leave the building fast enough.

'Off to lick their wounds,' said Taffy. We went to the pub and Hermia and Miriam joined us.

'Well,' said Miriam, sitting down in a cloud of Chanel N°5. 'Aren't boys silly?'

'Men behaving like boys,' corrected Taffy.

'Ridiculous that they can't just discuss their differences in a civilised manner,' tutted Hermia. Then she turned to me. 'Are you OK?' with an intense expression.

'Oh, I'm fine.'

'But are you? Really? You're a sensitive girl, I think, and exposure to a sudden eruption of male violence can be traumatic.'

'Jayne is no stranger to male eruptions,' said Miriam, which I thought must be a reference to Robin, but it was funny, so I laughed. What a thing to say! Then she asked me if I fancied a drive out to the country tomorrow.

'Fresh air and maybe a cream tea? Meet me outside the theatre at midday.'

Jayne's diary, 6 p.m., Tuesday, 11 July 2017, Brighton

Turns out the drive to the country was actually a visit to see Miriam's mother, whose care home was in Redhill, not too far away from Brighton.

After our conversations concerning her mother, I felt it was an honour, in a way, that she wanted me to meet her. She was even more spruced up than usual, wearing a flared long-sleeved floral dress, full slap and designer sunglasses. Her red Alfa Romeo was spotless, gleaming in the sunshine. She was friendly and relaxed, and although I still had misgivings about her and decided I had to be careful what I said, Miriam was clearly in a chatty mood.

'As you know, my mother has issues,' she told me as we drove along.

'Don't we all?' I said.

'True. It's amazing I'm as sane as I am,' she said. 'Given the upbringing I've had.'

'Was it just you and your mum?'

'Yes. Mostly. I had an imaginary friend to keep me company. Children are very good at surviving.'

'True.'

'My poor mum hasn't had it easy.'

'What about . . . I know it's not my business.'

'My father? Dead. That's all I've ever been told.'

'I'm sorry.'

'So am I. But it's difficult to be sorry about something or someone you know zero about. I'm guessing he must have been the sane one, though. Never mind.'

The care home is called Summer Breeze, a cheerful, low-rise building in red brick with a ramp leading to the wide glass entrance and friendly staff who tell Miriam her mother is in her room and having a good day.

Miriam checked her appearance in a mirror in the corridor

93

before we went in. Her mother was sitting by the window, a blanket over her knees.

Alice's face, yellowish with fading bruises, lit up when she saw Miriam. She looked blankly at me to begin with but smiled when Miriam told her I work in the theatre with her.

'I was an actress, you know, wasn't I, Mirry?'

'A very good one, I hear,' I said.

'Jayne is a dresser, not an actress,' Miriam pointed out.

Alice looked at me. 'Didn't you have the right legs?'

I laughed.

'I didn't, no. But I prefer to be backstage, anyway.'

I remembered I had a *Leopard Spots* programme in my handbag that I was going to post to Dad. I took it out and gave it to Alice.

'Here. You might like this to read.' Alice took it and peered at the cover, not much interested.

'I'll have a look later.'

'Let's have tea. I brought a walnut cake,' said Miriam briskly. 'You're getting better, then?'

'Head, shoulders, knees and toes. Knees and toes,' said Alice, then rather suddenly fell asleep.

'Ah. This happens,' Miriam whispered to me with a shrug.

So, we drank our tea and ate our cake in silence. Before we left Miriam nudged her mother gently.

'We're off now darling,' she says.

'Ah, yes. Nice to meet you – Joan, wasn't it? Come and see me again, won't you?'

There was less chat on our drive back to Brighton and Miriam put the radio on.

As we arrived back at the theatre Miriam's mobile rang. It was the care home. Alice had become very agitated. Something had upset her.

Text exchange between Robin and Jayne

R: *Wassup?*

J: *In Brighton. Nice. How are you?*

R: *All good. Work a bit quiet.*

J: *Wish I could say the same.*

R: *Happy families?*

J: *More drama off stage than on it.*

R: *Lol*

J: *I think of you whenever I go to Greggs.*

R: *About five times a day, then?*

Jayne's diary, Wednesday, 12 July 2017, Brighton

I don't know where to begin about today . . . At the half, when I went into Hermia's room with her costume, I saw that her coat was on the floor, so I picked it up and hung it on a hanger for her. It smelled of weed. That really strong, pungent smell. She could have just passed someone in the street, I thought.

I didn't say anything, of course, but she was sitting in front of the mirror staring at herself, giggling.

'How are you today?' I asked as breezily as I could.

She slowly turned to me and her eyes were completely blood-shot. Looked rather glam still, in a Marianne Faithfull sort of way.

'*Why, it's hotter than a hoar house on nickel night,*' she said in an exaggerated Southern drawl, then laughed hysterically.

'I'll open the window,' I said. 'Get some air in.'

'*I'll tell ya summin' else, Miss Jayne,*' she carried on in this weird voice. '*Tarnation! I'm as hungry as a hog. Couldn't fix me some corn bread and sweet potato pie, could ya?*'

I tried to laugh, to show I knew she was joking, but she didn't stop. '*Hungry as a howg!*'

I went to the green room and stole one of Peter's Bakewell tarts for her in the end.

Hermia then did the whole play in this weird accent and was late for an entrance because she got disoriented and couldn't find the stage.

When Peter complained to Trevor in the interval, he was told that 'an actress of Hermia's calibre is perfectly within her rights to look for new depths to her character'.

'I see,' said Peter. 'Then you won't mind if I come on as Tarzan tomorrow?'

'Any attempt to improve your performance would be more than welcome, dear chap,' said Trevor witheringly.

I texted Rowanne who said it sounded like Hermia was stoned today and said there was a thing called 'the munchies'.

Fun facts: cannabis
Cannabis smells like 'skunk' because of one of its components: myrcene. Myrcene is in lots of other highly fragrant plants, such as bay leaf, mangoes, hops and thyme. Different strains of marijuana can contain more or less myrcene.

Marijuana strains that smell fruity or skunky may have more sedative effects.

Jayne's diary, Thursday, 13 July 2017, Brighton
Hermia invited me to meditate with her in her dressing room between shows. Lol. Didn't want to be unfriendly, but I politely declined. Said I couldn't as I had sinusitis. Don't know why I said that. She sort of snorted, and I saw a flash of sourness cross her face for a second.

'Just thought it might be good for you, Jayne.' She was looking at the eczema rash on my wrist.

'Maybe. But I've got the laundry to do,' I said, trying to be polite but keen to get away. I'd only nipped in to get her clothes.

'Always rushing about, aren't you?'

'Yup! Busy, busy!'

She sighed. 'Oh Jayne. You ought to take more care of yourself. Don't you know that just five minutes of guided meditation is proven to improve focus, self-compassion, mood, immune function and quality of sleep?'

'Mmmm,' I said.

Hermia turned back to the mirror. 'You want to get away, I can see that. You spend a whole day with Miriam, but just five minutes with me is unthinkable? Go.'

I somehow felt forced to apologise. 'I'm sorry, but—' I began.

'You can go,' she said coldly. 'But be careful around Miriam. She may not be as nice as she appears to be.'

That was enough. I left without saying anything else. Is she really jealous because I spent an afternoon with Miriam? Why? And what was that warning all about? Every day in this company is like tiptoeing through a minefield!

Text exchange between Robin and Jayne

R: *Wassup?*

J: *I'm eating some coconut macaroon Hobnobs.*

R: *Sounds good. Hope you're steering clear of that Spud?*

J: *I'm not sharing the packet with anyone, if that's what you mean.*

R: *I think you should keep away from him.*

J: *You don't have to be jealous of him.*

R: *It's not that. I've heard some bad things about him.*

Fun facts: Hobnobs
The name Hobnob comes from the verb 'to hobnob', which means to spend time being friendly with someone who is important or famous. Others claim the name comes from two words: 'hob', suggesting home-cooked on a stove, and 'knobbly', referring to the biscuit's texture.

Popbitch, **Thursday, 13 July 2017**

Which lucky theatre company is blessed with its very own in-house dope peddler? While several actors are only too keen to take advantage of these recreational enhancements, there is a problem for one. How to square spending cash on gak when you really ought to be paying back the loan to your co-star? Quelle dilemma!

Chapter 16

Jayne's diary, Friday, 14 July 2017, Brighton
Simon asked if I knew where Spud was and could I ask him to pop in and see him.

'He's a good kid,' he said with a wink.

Discovered Spud asleep on a chair in the wings. I found myself sneaking a look at him before I woke him up. His long legs were splayed out and his crotch area looked, er, generous. His head was resting on his left hand. Asleep, with no 'attitude' about him, he looked boyish and innocent. Beautiful long eyelashes. Was just about to clear my throat to wake him up when he suddenly stirred and opened his eyes. Still half asleep, he blinked at me.

'What you doing?' he asked groggily.

'Er, Simon wants you,' I mumbled.

He sort of sneered at me as if he knew what my thoughts were then got up and ambled off towards the dressing rooms. So embarrassing!

Jayne's diary, 10 p.m., Friday, 14 July 2017, Brighton
Saw Spud coming out of Hermia's room, looking a bit dishevelled and stuffing several £20 notes into his back pocket. Rowanne says maybe he's a gigolo. Is that what he does? Sadly, my savings are exactly zero. Lol.

So sweet. Every night when I get back to the digs, the land-lords have left me a plate of food in the hot drawer. Risotto tonight. Lovely. Never eaten that before. Miriam's smiles starting to give me the ick.

Fun facts: risotto
Risotto is rice cooked in meat or seafood stock and seasoned with parmesan cheese or saffron. When preparing a risotto, do not wash your rice. You need all the starch to achieve the creamy taste. Add a little water at a time, stirring constantly.

Julian on showbiz
I need to break something to you. Showbusiness friendships tend to be a tad shallow. On tour, away from home and thrown together with a random selection of people, you might form liaisons of temporary intensity for the duration of the tour. Mostly, these evaporate as quickly as they began once the contract is over and you all go your separate ways. Sometimes the WhatsApp chats continue for a while, left on your phone like leaves in a corner, until they turn to dust.

I was at a party once and someone started speaking to me cheerily as if we were old chums. Eventually I asked if we'd ever met before. He looked hurt.

'Yes. We shared a flat for a month at the Edinburgh Festival last year,' he said. I had no recollection. I only hope I didn't sleep with him.

Jayne assumed Miriam's rather sudden friendship advances were of this genre. They had nothing in common whatsoever, apart from the fact they were working on the same production. Age, class, interests: there was no reason to suppose they would be friends. But it became apparent that Miriam wanted to get to know her. Liked her, even, for some reason. She started smiling brightly whenever they encountered each other, complimented her and engaged her in benign conversation. She called her 'dear' and slipped her a daily chocolate bar and tipped her well over the odds in cash at the end of every week. When Jayne delivered Miriam's wig or costume to her dressing room, Miriam would pat the chair next to her and tell her to sit for a moment.

'Have you had a good day, dear? How are you enjoying the delights of Brighton?'

Maybe she was lonely, Jayne thought. Or perhaps just kind and maternal. But she hadn't noticed Miriam courting others in this way. Then there was something else.

For all the cheery chat and concerned questioning, Miriam seemed somehow insincere. There was deadness behind the eyes that didn't match the apparent interest she was showing in the lowly dresser. It felt calculated and left Jayne feeling uneasy. She took to saying 'Can't stop, I'm afraid' when told to sit and chat during her delivery rounds, but Miriam overruled her.

'They can wait. Sit down for a second and tell me how you are today. So kind of you to come with me to visit my mother.'

But the conversations were stilted and fidgety, and even though these enforced chats were instigated by Miriam she seemed distracted and her interest fake, like a mother's feigned admiration for her child's artless drawing.

Jayne's diary, 1 p.m., Saturday, 15 July 2017, Brighton
Don't know what Miriam is up to. It was like the Spanish Inquisition today.

'Tell me about your family . . . Have you got a boyfriend? Do you enjoy cooking, my dear?' I mean, who cares? We're having so much eye-contact I find myself studying her eyes. Hazel. Quite wide apart. Needy!

I've noticed that these seemingly casual chinwags seem to focus more and more on Peter.

'How's Peter today? Have you seen him?'

'What time does Peter arrive at the theatre usually?'

'Does Peter go out between shows or does he bring a sandwich in with him?'

All delivered with an airy casualness, but my answers listened to with great alertness and a knowing nod of the head.

So, I've stopped waiting to be asked and started offering little snippets of Peter trivia to Miriam without prompting, knowing it would please her and avoid the tumble-weed moments of our previous enforced chitchats.

Maybe she fancies Peter? I can't think why.

Fun fact: Miriam Haughton
Miriam was born with a foot disorder known as brachymetatarsia, where the fourth metatarsal bone on both feet does not grow proportionally with the other toes. It hasn't caused any problems in terms of function, but she is self-conscious about it, will not wear sandals and it may be why she has never married.

Jayne's diary, 11 p.m., Saturday, 15 July 2017, Brighton
Things got stranger still today. Miriam wanted to know if Peter had a hairbrush in his room. I said yes, I thought he did.

'Why do you ask?'

'Well, it's his birthday soon. I thought I'd get him something useful.'

'Er. Right.'

He'd rather have cakes, I thought to myself.

Miriam smiled brightly at me. 'Don't tell anyone, will you dear?'

I tried to smile back but only managed a brief twang of my lips on one side. 'I won't,' I said. Miriam then swung round to face me and reached across to grip my forearm.

'The thing is, I want to get him a brush he'd like. You know how fussy men can be. Do you think you could slip it into your pocket and bring it to me during that long scene in Act 2? Then I can have a proper look.'

She made it all sound so urgent. I mean . . . a hairbrush?

'Um,' I said, pulling my arm free. 'I'll try, but I'll be busy getting ready for Simon's costume change, won't I?'

'It'll only take a moment,' said Miriam decisively, as if that was the matter settled.

'But I'll have to put it back, too. I don't think there's time.'

'Don't be silly!'

'OK then,' I said flatly. I dislike being manipulated, even over something as trivial as this. I might be a lowly dresser but I've learned over the years to stand up for myself. I remembered dressing one particular actress, not unknown to the public, who expected me to remove her bra for her. Just stood there and raised her arms. You might get that sort of service on a soap opera, but it's not part of my job description. Sort out your own boulder holder.

'I don't do bras,' I said firmly. There had been an awkward silence and then the actress sniffed and did it herself. Give them an inch and they take a mile. Stealing Peter's hairbrush, even for a few minutes, wasn't something that I felt comfortable about, and I wasn't going to do it. If I did, who knows what other furtive errands it might lead to.

In the end I had a bit of a brainwave. I slipped into Peter's dressing room during Act 2 as requested. But instead of taking the hairbrush, I took a photo of it on my phone. Three photos, in fact, from various angles. That would give her the information she required.

Miriam was standing there waiting when I got to her room.

'Yes?' she said anxiously.

'Yes,' I said. I pressed a few buttons on my phone and held it up for Miriam to see.

'It's plastic. Tortoiseshell effect. Probably from one of those gentlemen's grooming shops in London.'

Miriam stared at me, not even looking at the photos.

'No! You stupid girl. Why didn't you bring it to me?'

She was so cross that for a moment I thought she was going slap me.

'This'll do, surely? You can see what sort of brush it is.'

Miriam exhaled sharply and rolled her eyes.

'Why can't you just do what I ask? Is Peter's room unlocked?'

'Yes, but—'

Miriam pushed past me and stomped down the corridor and around the corner towards Peter's room. I didn't hang around. This was all too weird. It was only a bloody hairbrush. Why was it so important to see it, for God's sake?

Jayne's diary, Sunday, 16 July 2017, Brighton

Miriam still in a strop cos I wouldn't bring her Peter's hairbrush. I mean . . . really? All too cloak and dagger for me. All this for a bloody birthday present, she said.

But guess what? I just googled Peter. His birthday is six months away. WTF?

Went to Waitrose. That's a first. They've got a competition on: I could win a holiday to Australia. I needed a Waitrose Points card number to enter. Nice wander round the aisles. Twelve quid for a honey and mustard salad dressing, though! I bought a single lemon.

Chapter 17

Express, Sunday, 16 July 2017
Cats, London Palladium, no stars. By Ken Thomas.
Headline: Tomcat Titchmarsh needs spaying

What were they thinking? Well, Alan Titchmarsh is a staple of cosy Sunday morning TV so I can see why casting him as a grizzled old moggy curled up by the fire seemed like a good one at the time. But sadly, his Bustopher Jones is about as much fun as ringworm.

Bless him, though. It's not his fault. His image is so seared into our collective consciousness that our brains can't accept him being anything else. With his funny palm tree hairstyle, he'd make a better house plant than a cat.

There are other people in this ill-conceived venture, of course, doing their best to create an entertaining feline world. Dancers danced and pranced, some West End Wendy shrieked 'Memories'. But their efforts are wasted. We come away with only one memory that may well be more correctly classified as a recurring nightmare: Alan Titchmarsh dressed in fun-fur. My eyes!

The Stage, Monday, 17 July 2017
By Kim Bhatia.
Headline: The claws are out in theatre world

Leopard Spots, *the Trevor Millicent play starring Simon Gaunt, is to get a four-week run in the West End, beginning on Tuesday, 29 August. The London Palladium has become unexpectedly vacant following the dire failure of the recently opened modern revival of* Cats, *starring Alan Titchmarsh. After scathing reviews and scant ticket sales, the producers made the 'difficult decision' to pull the plug just two weeks after its ill-fated opening. The gap will now be filled by the hit comedy, currently on tour. Tickets now on sale.*

Julian on *Cats*

In the interest of balance, I'd like to add that I enjoyed the show so much I went twice. I'm a big fan. I've read all of Alan's saucy novels and I'm addicted to *Love Your Garden*, a show in which terminally ill people get their back yard ruined while they're out at a hospital appointment. If that's not entertainment, I'd like to know what is.

Kitty Litter WhatsApp Group Chat

H: *Whoop! We're going to London, folks!*

M: *What an unexpected thrill.*

P: *It's a big old barn to fill, the Palladium.*

S: *I hear the star dressing room is very luxurious.*

P: *And some distance from the others, which is great.*

H: *Well I am very excited.*

M: *We all are, really.*

H: *No more provincial digs.*

S: *Apart from Peter's little snipes.*

H: *I think it's time we all pulled together for once.*
S: *About the only thing Peter can pull these days, eh? Fnaaar!*
P: *Shut up, barrow boy.*

Ken Thomas's blog, Monday, 17 July 2017

I've just been sick in a bucket. Is my medication causing me to hallucinate? *Leopard Droppings* to transfer to the West End? There must be some mistake, surely? Haven't I suffered enough? Monstrous.

Jayne's diary, Tuesday, 18 July 2017, Brighton

So that's who the important people who came the other week were. Big time producers plotting our ascent to theatrical success. This will soothe everyone's egos, surely? Well, no. Not everyone. Hermia is in tears as she doesn't think she's worthy. Simon's muttering that comedy gigs are much better paid and the producers will have to cough up. Taffy says she won't believe it until she gets a contract. Meanwhile, she had a tour with Celia Imrie lined up and how is she supposed to get out of that? Miriam doubts she can stand another four weeks of being 'married' to Peter and his rancid breath.

The four weeks at the Palladium is just the beginning, according to Peter. The news has put him in such a good mood he's even quite chatty with me. He sees another transfer, to the Duchess or the Garrick, he said. 'Pull this one off and we could all be making hay for the next three years,' he said, rubbing his hands together.

'Big house, the Palladium,' I heard him bellow to Simon as he passed by. 'And your cut will be coming straight to me!' Simon scowled at him.

I wonder if I'll get paid more in London?

Text exchange between Robin and Jayne

J: *Guess what? As soon as the tour finishes, we're doing four weeks at the London Palladium!*

R: *Can I come?*

J: *If you want.*

R: *Great. I'll wear one of my cheap suits.*

J: *Best offer I've had today.*

Trevor Millicent: notes for archive

Conceiving and directing a play is one thing, but guiding its progress through the swamps and foothills of the theatrical landscape to help it achieve its ultimate potential is quite another. *Leopard Spots* is my beloved child and I think it is fair to say we are coming through the difficult adolescent phase, plagued by stroppy behaviour and unfortunate dermatological outbreaks, and we are soon to glide into our adult prime. With me at the helm, I feel quietly confident. Watch out, London. Watch out, Peter.

Chapter 18

Julian on Birmingham

We have to give massive thanks to Birmingham for launching chocolate onto the nation's palates. But on the other hand, they are also responsible for inflicting heavy metal music into our ears, so I guess it's swings and roundabouts.

The Midlands accent is a curious one, which even I, a proper showbiz type, have trouble with. I only managed to reproduce it properly once, but I was underwater in a jacuzzi at the time. (I'll spare you the details, but it was at a gay party in the 1980s, and as I recall, several Aston Villa footballers were involved. What I actually said isn't recorded for posterity, which is just as well, frankly. Probably something to do with forming an orderly queue.)

Jayne is sentimental. I know this because I've been to the cinema with her several times to watch cheesy romcoms and she cries obligingly when prompted while I sigh with annoyance at the emotional manipulation of it all.

Once, when we were having tea in a café, she showed me the little embroidered pouch that she carries everywhere with her in her handbag. Inside are things that would mean nothing to anyone else but are of great significance to her: a cracked marble, an old bus ticket, a little brown acorn. These are keepsakes from the past. The marble, a gift from Rowanne when they were at primary school, the bus ticket from her last trip to hospital to visit her mother, and the acorn she picked up from under a tree when she and Robin went for their silent walk. She told me that on long bus journeys, she would sometimes open the pouch and think, misty-eyed, about the significance of each object.

So, to return to Birmingham, her own patch, was a thrill for her, and she glowed with joy as she walked the familiar streets to the Alexandra Theatre, where *Leopard Spots* was to spend the penultimate week of the tour.

Less thrillingly, she could also stay at home, commuting the short journey to the centre of Birmingham. She felt reassured to see her father, still sat in his chair complaining. It was nice to hear people who spoke with her own twang, and her own accent became thicker by the day.

Best of all, she got to spend time with Rowanne, who was working backstage at the Birmingham Royal Ballet, just down the road at the Hippodrome.

Jayne's diary, Saturday, 22 July 2017, Birmingham
A suspected case of tour blues for Simon today and I find myself feeling sorry for him. Because he's a comedian, he thinks he has to be funny all the time. But really he doesn't need to bother with me.

He could just be real, if he wanted. When I went into his room with his costume before the show, he was looking at his phone.

'All right, Jayne? You bostin'?' he said with a big grin, but his shoulders were slumped. I recognised that his attempt at a Brummie accent was meant to be funny.

'I am, bab,' I said.

'Hey, seen my T-shirt? I bought it this morning.' He stood

up to show me. It said in big letters: 'I'm fat but I identify as skinny. I'm trans slender.'

'You silly sausage,' I said.

'Guess what today is? My eldest boy's birthday. He's five.'

He showed me a video Laura had sent him of the party.

There were loads of kids jumping around with balloons and music. 'Quite a big do, then,' I said.

'Yup. The theme is superheroes. Hired a whole restaurant for the afternoon,' he said proudly. 'They've got Spider-Man, Superman, the Incredible Hulk and Barbie. Jellies, ice creams and a cake in the shape of the Joker.'

'Wow! I think I got a Troll and some plasticine if I was lucky!'

'Laura doesn't do things by halves.' Clearly not, judging from the diamante boob tube and matching tiara she was wearing in the video.

'That's just the lunch. Then a coach is taking them all to the London Eye.'

Must have cost a fortune, I thought. I could see sadness in his eyes, despite the jolly tone of the conversation.

'Shame you're not there,' I said.

'Yes, it is,' he said quietly. Then he closed his phone and clapped his hands together.

'Got to earn a crust though! My public awaits!' But he wasn't fooling me. Simon is not a happy man. Happy people are in short supply here, let's face it.

I didn't win the Waitrose Australia holiday. Bloody cheek. No doubt some posh divorcee in a twinset and pearls is packing her matching suitcases right now. I hope she gets cramp on the flight.

Text exchange between Hermia and Miriam

H: *Hope you're not too shocked by last night.*

M: *Terrible hangover. I'm still processing. Or trying to.*

H: *It's a lot, I know.*

M: *A cooling-off period might be a good idea.*

H: *We got through three bottles of red!*

M: *Hmmm. What we discussed . . . It mustn't go any further. OK?*

H: *Absolutely. For now, anyway.*

Jayne's diary, Monday, 24 July 2017, Birmingham

Hermia and Miriam both rough as you like.

They had a girls' night in, apparently. I did the rounds with some paracetamol and a damp flannel for Miriam, whose hands were shaking so much her eyeliner was all over the place.

'Would you be a dear and nip out to the shop for some Lucozade?' she asked in a quivery voice.

Hermia winced on stage whenever anyone raised their voice so, of course, Peter was even louder than usual, booming out his lines deliberately.

'Childish and unprofessional,' Miriam sighed in the wings.

Fun facts: red-wine hangovers

Tannins are shown to trigger changes in serotonin levels and release lipids known as prostaglandins, both of which can induce migraines. Wines with high tannin levels will make you more thirsty and more susceptible to dehydration. In general, red-wine hangovers are worse than the ones you get from drinking white wine.

Jayne's diary, Tuesday, 25 July 2017, Birmingham

Got to work and Taffy was chatting to a tall young man wearing all black. I got the feeling I might have been interrupting a private conversation. Silence fell as soon as I walked in and he looked me up and down.

'Hi, you must be Jayne?'

'Yes. Hello.'

'This is Gordon,' said Taffy. 'Your predecessor in this job.'

'Ah, yes. Hello, Gordon. Pleased to meet you.'

Gordon was very thin and given to pouting. His hair was grown into a long fringe dyed blond. He wore a baggy black coat and big platformed boots.

Given what I knew about his history with Peter, I was surprised to see him backstage.

'I'm not after your job, don't worry,' he said. 'Just popped in to see Taffy, my old partner in crime.'

'Ah, I see!' I said. He had rather intense eyes. 'You living in Brum now, then?'

'With my other half. We've got a little love nest in Bordesley Green. Perfect, it is.'

'Lovely,' I said. But I could think of better areas to live in.

'Nathan and I will come and see the show. Will make a change to see it from out front. I still know all the words. Brilliant, isn't it?'

'Er, yes, I guess it is.'

'I want front-row seats. I've told Nathan all about it and he's gagging. Then we'll go out on the town. Come with us if you like? We get free entry to all the clubs, you see. Everyone loves us.'

'I bet,' I said, for want of something else to say. 'I'd better get on. Lovely to meet you, Gordon.' He pursed his lips and gave a rather stagey bow.

'I'll deliver these, Taff,' I said, wheeling the costume rail into the corridor.

Interesting. Gordon, so badly wronged by Peter during some brief, sordid affair now mincing about backstage! What if Peter bumped into him unexpectedly? He wouldn't be happy.

Actors are very sensitive creatures and a shock like that

might cause an on-stage wobble, or worse.

But fifteen minutes later when I returned to wardrobe, Gordon had gone.

Taffy was busy with the wigs and shook her head.

'That was tricky. Gordon just waltzed in. Knows the stage door man from the Nightingale, apparently.'

'Bold of him,' I said.

'Game playing. Looking for more drama, I'm sure of it.'

'What if Peter had come in?'

'Don't! He's rarely here before the half, but I was fully aware of the risk. I said we had a lot to do and I was sure he understood and showed him the door.'

'Supposing he hangs around outside for a bit?'

'Well, I can't help that, can I? If the chickens come home to roost, it's nothing to do with me.'

Fun facts: Gordon Griffiths
Gordon can swallow a banana whole without chewing it.

Text exchange between Robin and Jayne
J: *Hello from sunny Brum.*

R: *How's tricks?*

J: *Very happy. I can wander around the Rag Market, I've got my best friend to see and I get to sleep in my own bed.*

R: *Alone?*

J: *So far.*

R: *Shall I come and visit?*

J: *I'll see if I can squeeze you in, shall I?*

R: *Fnaaar.*

Fun facts: Birmingham Rag Market
Open four days a week, the Birmingham Rag Market provides

market shopping at its best. It's home to 350 stalls and 17 perimeter shops, selling a massive and diverse range of goods. The Rag is renowned for the extensive range of fabrics it has to offer, in addition to other goods.

Chapter 19

Birmingham Mail, Thursday, 27 July 2017
Headline: *Leopard Spots* actress plunges through stage

A performance of Leopard Spots *at the Alexandra Theatre had to be abandoned last night following an accident on stage. Actress Hermia Saunders suffered a broken forearm when she fell through a trapdoor that had unexpectedly opened.*

Ms Saunders was taken by ambulance to the Queen Elizabeth Hospital on Mindelsohn Way, where doctors attended to her and a plaster cast was placed on the injury.

A spokesperson for the Alexandra said the trapdoor, which hadn't been used for years, had malfunctioned during the first act of the popular comedy and a gap had appeared into which Miss Saunders stumbled. Following treatment, she was discharged and was resting at her hotel. She was said to be shaken by the incident but otherwise doing well.

Hermia Saunders plays the part of a wealthy American heiress in Leopard Spots *and her lively, charismatic performance has been widely praised, with the* Birmingham Mail *calling it 'riveting, subtle and nuanced'.*

Leopard Spots *is due to continue its run at the Alexandra for*

*the rest of the week. Ticket holders are advised to check with the
box office.*

Kitty Litter WhatsApp Group Chat
S: Poor old Hermia. Looked white as a sheet.

M: Gone into shock. As you would. How could that have happened?

*P: I was playing to the upper circle. As we were taught at
RADA. No idea.*

M: It could have been fatal! Anyone know how far she fell?

*S: I had a look down there once the audience had gone. About six
feet, I'd say. It's not usual, is it, for the stage to suddenly open up
and swallow an actor like that?*

P: It could have been me!

S: Doesn't bear thinking about. At your age.

*M: Well, I'm not being funny, Peter, but if you'd been following
the usual blocking it would have been you. That spot is right where
you normally stand.*

P: Someone was watching out for me.

S: St Zimmer, patron saint of pensioners.

P: Shut up.

M: What happens now, anyway?

*P: We sit on our arses and wait to see how long she has to take
off. I always said it was a stupid risk not to have understudies.*

*S: No one could possibly come close to your performance, though.
Apart from Nigel Havers, perhaps.*

P: Never heard of him.

M: I suggest we all club together to get Hermia some flowers.

Jayne's diary, Thursday, 27 July 2017, Birmingham
Went to see Hermia and took her a vegan sausage roll (Greggs'
finest). She was sitting surrounded by flowers and joss

sticks. She's a bit sore but taking paracetamol and some anti-inflammatory pills. She looked quite dazed, but then she often does.

'I'll be fine. It's just one of those things, honey,' she said. 'The funny thing is I don't usually move down-stage centre for that bit. It's not how we are directed. But Peter, as he does, suddenly changed things around and I thought I'd better fill the space, so I wafted over. Next thing I know it's all gone dark, and I'm covered in dust!'

No one has a clue about how the trap door could have opened. It's operated by a mechanism under the stage, and I don't understand how it could spontaneously open like that.

'There's a lot of talk about the theatre ghost,' I said jokingly, but Hermia took me seriously. She nodded.

'I've sensed it. And between you and me, I had one of my psychic twinges the day before. Something evil was in the building.'

Not Gordon, I hope? Lol.

Fun facts: plaster cast care

Keep arm raised on a soft surface, such as a pillow, for as long as possible in the first few days. This will help any swelling to go down.

Do not get your plaster cast wet as this will weaken it and the broken bone will no longer be supported.

Plaster casts can make skin feel itchy but do not poke anything down it as this can cause a nasty sore and lead to infection.

Kitty Litter WhatsApp Group Chat

H: *You guys, honestly! The flowers are divine. How did you guess yellow carnations are my favourite?*

Julian on yellow carnations
Each to their own, I suppose. But can yellow carnations really be anyone's favourite? I find them mean and spiteful. The general public is sometimes moved to present me with posies as an expression of their admiration, but please be advised, although grateful for the gesture, such offerings will, I'm afraid, be destined for the bin. And here's why . . .

Fun facts: yellow carnations
While they are incredibly pretty, yellow carnations don't have the happiest meaning. Symbolising disappointment and rejection, yellow carnations are best to send to someone you need to say sorry to. They're also acceptable to send in times of sympathy.

Jayne's diary, Friday, 28 July 2017, Birmingham
No understudies with this show, of course. Hermia still a bit shaken up, so tonight's performance is cancelled. Spent the morning catching up with Rowanne. Went for a look round the shops and had a burger. So lovely to gossip. She was all ears about Robin. 'Maybe he's the one,' she said. Lol. Then I got a text from him.

Talk of the devil. Soon as he found out I was free, he took the afternoon off work and jumped on the train. Keen!

There's something very romantic about waiting at a railway station for your man to arrive. Like *Doctor Zhivago*. Lol. He looked really handsome weaving his way towards me through the crowds. When he saw me and smiled, I felt a lovely shudder.

We went to the Broadway Bar & Grill because Robin was hungry and they have a carvery. He was ever so chatty this time.

'Good job it wasn't you that fell through the hole in the stage,' he said, squeezing my hand.

119

'I know,' I said. 'You'd have to find a new girl to visit.'

'Yup. I don't want damaged goods. So how did it happen?' I told him no one really knows. Some old stage trapdoor suddenly gave way.

'Weird,' he said. 'Who was around at the time?'

'Well, we all were. Doing the play, weren't we.'

'Hmmm. Where was Spud?'

'Spud? I don't know! Doing whatever Spud does during the performance. Technical things.'

'I've heard he's dodgy, that's all.'

'But you've never even met him! Just because you've heard some Bath gossip.'

'True. But he's trouble, apparently. And when something like this happens, I can't help wondering.'

Then he asked loads of other questions. Were people jealous of Hermia's good reviews? Who can't be accounted for at the time of the accident?

In the end I said: 'Oh shut up, Miss Marple, and finish your chips.'

He came back to New Invention.

Introduced him to Dad, who looked amazed to see me with a bloke.

Couldn't really have sex in my box room with Dad next door so we improvised in the conservatory. Lol.

Jayne's diary, Saturday, 29 July 2017, Birmingham
Hermia back on stage with her plastered arm in a cashmere silk scarf sling. That was my idea. Found something that looked expensive but wasn't (Rag Market, naturally). She did so well. Bravo for only missing two shows. Trevor made another of his speeches during warm-up about what a trouper Hermia is, and how professional.

The trapdoor mechanism had disintegrated with age, he said,

but had now been secured. Most unfortunate. Then he emphasised, rather pointedly, how important it is everyone sticks to the original blocking or the 'choreography' of the 'piece' becomes 'muddy'. This was clearly a dig at Peter who stared into space looking bored.

'Is he never going to leave us in peace?' he said to me after. I gave a sympathetic smile. Seemed appropriate. I think he's started speaking to me as I'm the only one left who he hasn't fallen out with.

Heard Miriam call Spud 'a blithering idiot' under her breath. Why, I wonder? Was he responsible for the trapdoor business? I've really no idea. Happy families, as usual.

Extra rehearsal called to change bits due to the sling.

Text exchange between Robin and Jayne

R: *Got home without incident. Thanks for last night.*

J: *The conservatory seems very quiet without you.*

R: *Have the windows un-steamed yet?*

J: *My dad wanted to know why the cushions were on the floor . . . I blamed the cat.*

Birmingham Post website, Sunday, 30 July 2017
By the news desk.
Headline: The show must go on!

Actress Hermia Saunders was back performing last night despite breaking her forearm in a freak accident onstage on Wednesday.

In her dressing room surrounded by cards and flowers from well-wishers, the 33-year-old Leopard Spots *star told the* Post: *'Everyone has been so kind. I'm quite overwhelmed. I shall go on tonight wearing a lovely sling. I'm in a little bit of pain but Doctor Theatre, as they say, will soon make it go away.'*

The brave star fell through a loose trapdoor during a performance and was treated at Queen Elizabeth's Accident & Emergency department. Paying tribute to the doctors and nurses, Miss Saunders said: 'They were all so wonderful and caring. I couldn't have had better treatment anywhere in the world, and I'm American! I shall be writing to them personally to thank them.'

The cause of the dramatic accident is still being investigated. 'It seems it was just an old, rusty contraption that suddenly gave way. A bit like my arm,' joked Hermia.

Some details of the play have been altered to accommodate her injury. 'I'm supposed to open a bottle of wine at one point, but we've switched from bottle opener to screw top. Luckily, our wonderful director is on hand to redirect little things like that.'

Trevor Millicent, who also wrote the play told us: 'Hermia's fall gave us all quite a shock. There are no understudies on this show, so we are enormously grateful to her for coming back to work so soon. She has shown remarkable fortitude and professionalism. She is coping so well, not only with her injury and discomfort but with the changes we've had to make. Everyone is rallying round, doing what is necessary.'

Leopard Spots continues its run at the Alexandra Theatre until Wednesday.

Chapter 20

Jayne's diary, 7 p.m., Sunday, 30 July 2017, Birmingham
'What's wrong, Peter?' I asked, his body convulsing with sobs. He was barely coherent. He said, as far as I could understand, that his performance in the play was terrible, that he'd made a balls-up of his life, ruined everything and there was nothing he could do to make it better. I didn't understand then what he meant.

'We're all making a mess of our lives,' I told him, because it's true. 'No one really knows what they're doing.'

'But I have done terrible things. I'm an idiot. A disgrace. All in pursuit of something I never really wanted. Not truly. I just thought I should have it all. There were happy times,' he said, wiping his eyes. 'Now I am a joke. Past it.'

I asked him why he was torturing himself with these negative thoughts. He was a respected actor, loved by the public and in a hit play.

'This damn play,' he spat. 'It's like I'm doing it all again. Every night I have to face my past and it's killing me.'

Ken Thomas's blog, Sunday, 30 July 2017
Great news from Brum. I couldn't be more thrilled. The evil spell I cast on *Leopard Droppings* is bearing some very satisfying

fruit. The dreadful American actress Hermia Saunders (no, I've never heard of her either) fell through a trapdoor and broke her forearm. But that's not the best bit. With her arm in a cast, it is beyond her (very) limited acting capabilities to slap and punch the pickled old fart Peter Milano in the climactic fight scene. So guess what has replaced those feisty acts of combat? She SPITS at him! In the face! Oh, happy days. How she must enjoy that. I do hope she has a spot of bronchitis so she can gob a big, green oyster on his vile, wrinkled visage.

It seems there is a God, after all. Tempting to go and see it again just to witness that moment and lead a rowdy cheer from the stalls. I've always been a punk at heart . . .

Kitty Litter WhatsApp Group Chat

S: So, my line after I come back on the veranda – 'I'll fix you a drink. Something to take the taste away' – has always, ALWAYS got a laugh. But not the last three nights.

M: Yes, I noticed that too.

P: Regional variations in what folks find amusing?

S: No. Something else.

P: I can't imagine. Do tell.

S: You know perfectly well.

P: Can't think what you mean old chap.

S: I listened out tonight. Right where I say 'taste' you've been making a subtle guttural sound, drowning out that word and killing the laugh.

H: Peter!

P: It's my acid reflux. Causes catarrh. I'm just clearing my throat.

M: Oldest trick in the book, you old rogue.

S: Well, two can play at that. Dust mites are playing havoc with my sinuses, mate. Might need a good clear out during one of your lines. We'll see.

P: There might be other things affecting your sinuses, perhaps?

Jayne's diary, Sunday, 30 July 2017
Strange, fishy smell in the green room. Apparently Spud has some new wacky vapes. Tuna flavour. I mean? Really? He's got others. Roast chicken and garlic. Anyway, he was told off for vaping indoors. Not that he'll take any notice.

Alice Haughton
Alice featured in a twelve-page *Vogue* fashion spread in 1981, photographed by Helmut Newton.

Jayne's diary, Monday, 31 July 2017, Birmingham
Lovely time with Rowanne yesterday. We mainly talked about work. Hers seems relatively normal compared to mine. Ballet dancers are all too busy stretching their G-strings to get up to mischief, she says.

Hard to sum up this week. But I'll try. The acclaim seems to have gone straight to Hermia's head. First the glowing reviews, then her accident and all the subsequent attention, followed by her gracious return and enough bouquets to fill a florist's shop. She's started wearing dark glasses for her arrival at the stage door and nodding at anyone who wishes her well, as if to say: 'I know; I'm a star!'

Miriam is constantly on the phone to her mother talking agitatedly in a loud whisper or looking furious about something or other. There's real fire in her eyes. Maybe she's jealous of Hermia? Got a chip on her shoulder about something, that's for sure.

Spud smells of weird vape flavours and is skulking around, disappearing into Miriam's room. Maybe because her room has access to the fire escape where he can smoke to his heart's content, but that's the kind explanation. Others might possibly come to the conclusion that there's something 'going on' between them. That thought gives me the ick. Robin says Spud is a drug dealer. Perhaps he's stocktaking in there? Lol.

Peter and Simon are at each other's throats like a couple of rabid rottweilers. Jealousy? I don't know. Squaring up to each other. Simon's wife, Laura, seems to be the one spending all the money from what he's said in passing to me. Clothes, jewellery, cars, whatever. She's out of control with credit cards. The happy, carefree Simon Gaunt you see on the telly is a long way from the worried-sick-looking lad I see every day. I feel sorry for him. Honestly, it puts me off ever getting married.

Taffy seems to have adopted the weird goth boy Gordon who had a thing for Peter. Texts him all the time, meets him between shows.

'He's having a hard time,' she says. 'Boyfriend trouble.'

What's it got to do with her? Maybe she's just a caring person. Unlike me. She's always asking me about Robin and how things are going. I mean, I like her, but she's one of those people who likes to get involved in other people's turmoil.

If you ask me, that's what it is with Gordon. He's only too happy to spill the beans. I read a magazine article about how some people are 'victims' and others are 'rescuers' and how they seek each other out to fulfil a need and confirm their role. Something like that. It's never a good idea to tell work people too much, in my opinion. Keep it bright and breezy, that's what I try to do. But, it isn't easy with this company.

Then there's Trevor with his delusions of grandeur. He thinks his play is the greatest thing ever written. Every word is sacred. I mean, I'm glad the play is a success, and don't get me wrong, it works really well and the punters go home happy. They have a laugh. Get their money's worth. But Trevor won't let it settle.

He's tinkering constantly, getting all worked up if the slightest thing changes. I'm just a dresser and I know nothing, but surely you have to let things breathe a bit? Peter gets the brunt of it, and I can see it's driving him nuts. Trevor told him off for putting his hands in his pockets during a scene the other day. When you know you're constantly being watched like that it must give you the jitters. It would me.

If Peter knew when he was at RADA that his larking around would have consequences this far in the future, he might have thought twice about it.

I'd say Peter is a bit depressed. His wife seems to have him on a tight leash and, let's face it, he doesn't get the attention he used to from the ladies. There were lots of dalliances, late-night naughtiness, apparently. By all accounts he used to take his pick. Now, if ever I go to the pub after the show, he's sat by himself with a pint, looking around hopefully for someone to talk to. Must be very difficult when you used to be a looker. Not a problem I've ever had to worry about, of course. Lol.

Best thing about this week, apart from Rowanne, has been Robin. You know something is happening when you get butter-flies just seeing their name come up on your phone. Me! With a fella! Who'd have thought. He'll probably dump me tomorrow, knowing my luck. Lol.

Chapter 21

Julian on Plymouth
Ah, Plymouth, where the streets are full of seamen – making it well worth the journey.

There is a novelty post-war pedestrianised city centre, which I'm sure seemed a good idea at the time, but there are yards of yawning pavement between one side of the street and the other, which for an ageing homosexual riddled with tendonitis means a comfort break on a (dubious) public bench is essential between the purchase of my smoked salmon sandwich from M&S and my perusal of trinkets in Claire's. I don't think they thought this through.

Jayne's diary, Sunday, 6 August 2017, Plymouth
I didn't trust my old banger to get me to Plymouth so left the Honda on the drive at Dad's and accepted Miriam's offer of a lift in her Alfa Romeo.

I was a little nervous about spending so many hours with a woman I had come to regard as rather peculiar but didn't feel I had much choice. A train ticket would have cost me a week's wages.

'That's a nice top, dear,' she said when I arrived with my suitcase.

'Thank you.'

'Such a pity the shop didn't have your size, though.' Charming.

We set off mid-morning for the five-hour journey along the dreary M4 and M5. As Miriam wouldn't accept any petrol money, I stocked up on drinks, chocolate and sandwiches. I could see that Miriam was still preoccupied, frowning and biting her lip as she drove, irritated by any vehicle that, in her opinion, impeded our progress for even a few seconds.

Once we passed Bristol, the Sunday traffic eased, and with it, Miriam's mood; she seemed more inclined to chat.

'Let me know if you need us to stop for the loo,' she said.

'I'm fine for now, thank you. Would you like a Jaffa cake or a sandwich? I've got all sorts here.' I rustled the carrier bag as if to indicate the delights within.

'Just some water,' said Miriam. 'I'm trying to lose a few pounds before the Palladium.'

'Will there be another press night?'

'Of course. The nationals – and they are going to be harsher this time. Not to mention photos and probably daytime TV. Although I expect Simon and Peter will be first choice for that. I may get *Drivetime* on BBC Radio London, if anything.' She sounded rather bitter.

I passed her a bottle of still and then we lapsed back into silence for a few miles.

'It'll be nice to be by the sea,' I said.

'Yes, dear,' answered Miriam. 'And Plymouth is a lovely, well-run theatre. Dressing rooms with windows and a water dispenser in the corridor. Just such a long way!'

We listened to Radio 2 for a while until Miriam turned it off with a suck of her teeth. 'I wonder why Michael Ball does that peculiar laugh all the time? It's not a proper laugh. It's just a strange cackling noise from the back of his throat. Very odd.'

My tummy rumbled so I opened a tuna-and-sweetcorn sandwich. Miriam accepted an apple.

'It was lovely meeting your mum,' I said between bites.

'Mmmm,' said Miriam.

'Must have been nice seeing her when we were in Brighton.'

Miriam seemed to be considering her response before she spoke. 'Well, yes,' she said. 'As you know, I worry about her constantly. She is old before her time. A pity she can't be out and about enjoying herself more, but the dementia . . . I sometimes feel it is all my fault. She gave up so much for me. But I know that I'm not half the actress she was. We both know that is true.' Miriam bit her lip.'

We lapsed into silence. I looked at the hands gripping the steering wheel and could see that Miriam's eczema was back, red and angry. Mine, for now, was dormant.

Jayne's diary, 7 p.m., Sunday, 6 August 2017, Plymouth
Staying in the Hoe. Bay window room overlooking the sea. Fridge and microwave. Very nice, apart from the seagulls squawking. They depress me a bit – don't know why.

Fun facts: Plymouth Hoe
Sir Francis Drake played bowls on Plymouth Hoe in 1585 before setting sail to fight the Spanish armada.

In 1620, the Mayflower set sail from Plymouth to America carrying the pilgrims who founded the modern USA.

Plymouth Herald, **Tuesday, 8 August 2017**
By Sally Lifton.
Headline: *Leopard* roars into Plymouth

Heads turned at Plymouth City Airport yesterday when comedy star Simon Gaunt flew in by swish private jet. The funny man's stylish arrival comes ahead of his week-long stint in the hit comedy Leopard Spots *at the Theatre Royal, starting tonight.*

Accompanied by Laura Porter, his glamorous wife, and their two young children, he was then whisked to the five-star Boringdon Hall Hotel and Spa, where the family will live it up in style during his stay.

Happily posing for selfies with fans, Mr and Mrs Gaunt took time to speak to well-wishers in the arrivals lounge before heading for their blacked-out limousine.

'He was so lovely and really down to earth,' said fan Maureen Hartley. 'I'm definitely going to see him in the play even though it's not the sort of thing I'd usually bother with.'

'What a gent,' said her husband, George. 'I recognised him straightaway. His wife is great, too. It's not often you get to see people off the telly in real life.'

It is thought the star had his family with him for a week in the sunshine. Fans should no doubt look out for Laura, a keen shopper, at the city's famous waterfront boutiques.

There are just a handful of tickets left to see the play this week before it heads for the London Palladium and its West End debut at the end of August.

Text exchange between Peter and Simon

P: *A fucking private jet?*

S: *Got to keep the missus happy.*

P: *I'm furious.*

Jayne's diary, Tuesday, 8 August 2017, Plymouth
Peter's National Express coach broke down on the M5 and he had to spend three hours waiting for the AA. Only just made it in time for the show. Not in the best of moods. I took him a

cupcake, but I don't think it helped. He didn't eat it.

Fun facts: Plymouth
Early in 2008, 'Mad Jack', a twelve-pound lobster thought to be at least 100 years old, was caught by local fishermen and now lives 'in retirement' in the Plymouth Aquarium.

Jayne's diary, 10 p.m., Tuesday, 8 August 2017, Plymouth
We've got Hermia with a broken forearm, Miriam having a nervous breakdown about her mum, Simon with his entire family camped out in his dressing room, Trevor prowling around backstage still barking notes at people, Peter breathing fire and now Taffy is in tears.

And I can't say I blame her. Guess who has followed us to Plymouth? That peculiar Gordon boy.

'He was at the dock door at the back of the theatre when I arrived this morning. I was trying to be kind to him in Birmingham. And now this.'

'What did he say? Why on earth is he here?'

'Oh, Jesus. Another drama. Had a row with Nathan or something. Needed to get away. I said, look Gordon, you can't come here looking to cause trouble. He just laughed and said it was a free country and he just wanted some fresh sea air.'

'It's not your fault,' I told her.

'Feels like it, somehow. Anyway, I told him he couldn't hang around here. I was very firm.'

'But he's not the sort to take no for an answer, is he?'

Jayne's diary, Wednesday, 9 August 2017, Plymouth
Taffy got a call to say that Gordon had been admitted to hospital and was seriously ill on a drip. I assumed he'd taken a few junior Disprin as a cry for attention, but no. He's got food poisoning. But it gets more bizarre . . . when Taffy asked him

what he'd eaten he said he slipped into the theatre during the performance last night and went into the green room. He hadn't eaten all day and helped himself to whatever he could find. What was it? The cupcake I gave Peter. Rancid, out-of-date butter icing, I guess. So, somehow, this could all be my fault . . .

Jeez.

Going to sleep now and maybe I'll dream about Robin. Sigh.

Chapter 22

Popbitch, Thursday, 10 August 2017
Which actor found himself broken down on the hard shoulder of the M5 this week? In a hurry to get to Plymouth's Theatre Royal, what did he do? He rang 999 and demanded the local constabulary come and pick him up quick sharp. Things didn't go the way he wanted: the police were apparently otherwise engaged doing mundane things like, er, policing. And yes, his famously seductive tones were overheard saying the classic line 'Do you realise who I am?' and the rather less popular 'I pay my rates!'

Text exchange between Robin and Jayne
R: Hey. How's it hanging in the Hoe?

J: I think I may have accidentally poisoned someone.

R: Er . . . excuse me?

J: I bought a cupcake for Peter. It was on discount but it looked all right. Anyway, he didn't eat it and it was left lying about in the green room. Then this boy Gordon ate it. He ended up in hospital. Ever so sick, he is.

R: What was in the cupcake?

J: I think it must have been in the shop window in the sun all day and the butter cream curdled.

R: You wouldn't end up in hospital though.

J: He did. On a drip and everything.

R: I don't believe this. Sounds like something dodgy is going on to me. Maybe someone tampered with it?

J: You're always looking for a sinister angle, you are.

R: I think you might be in bad company, that's all.

J: I wonder myself sometimes . . . You might be right about Spud selling drugs.

R: Told you. Steer clear.

J: I don't even take a paracetamol. He's in and out of everyone's room this week. Must be the sea air.

R: I heard he has quite the selection.

J: Where did you hear this?

R: My mate is a policeman. They're watching him.

Jayne's diary, Thursday, 10 August 2017, Plymouth
I've got a new job as a nanny. Lol. Laura has got into the habit of dropping the kids off in wardrobe about 4 p.m. while she and Simon go for pre-show dinner. Teddy is five and Evita is three. She doesn't ask or anything, she just flings the door open and shoos them in.

'In you go! Auntie Jayne will give you a biscuit if you're hungry.' Then she turns to me and says, 'Gluten-free for Evita, please,' then she's off.

Taffy is fuming, but I like children. They're no trouble, really, although Evita isn't potty trained yet. Hugo did a drawing for me. Looks like a stick insect. 'Who's that?' I asked. 'Mummy,' said Teddy. Clever boy. She needs all the dinners she can eat from the look of her. I can't imagine being that thin. Lol.

She's here all the time, like she owns the place. On matinee day, as well as the children, she brought in a bag of rather pongy laundry and handed it to me. 'A boil wash would be great,' she said. 'Just pop them into our room when they're ironed. I'll be

135

in the green room. I've got a pedicurist coming, so if everyone could stay out for half an hour that would be great.'

Miriam was very indignant today because Laura announced she was going to be an actress. 'When the kids start big school. Only West End and TV though. None of this touring shit.'

'She'll need some elocution lessons,' said Miriam with a sniff.

The only one who doesn't seem to mind her being here is Peter. 'Pretty little thing, isn't she?' he said to me with a wink. He holds doors open for her and looks her up and down like Leslie Phillips. All in front of Simon, so he might be doing it to piss him off.

Then I heard today that Peter patted her on the bum and she turned around and called him 'a dirty old letch'. Simon was about to thump him but Laura said: 'Leave it, Si; it's not worth it.' Perhaps she's auditioning for *EastEnders*?

Kitty Litter WhatsApp Group Chat

P: *Can whoever is responsible for the frightful hippy music wafting down the corridor please turn it down.*

H: *Apologies. I was meditating.*

M: *Maybe to drown out the incessant noise of your burping.*

P: *I have acid reflux, a medical condition. And while we are at it, is the incense coming from you too, Hermia?*

H: *I am trying to heal myself after the trauma of my fall. Apologies.*

Jayne's diary, Friday, 11 August 2017, Plymouth
Messy night, to say the least.

In wardrobe, Evita spilt Ribena on the floor and Teddy kept escaping and running up and down the corridor being a rhino.

When Laura finally sauntered in to collect them at 7.20 p.m. Taffy had had enough.

'We're not running a creche here, you know. Your kids have

been left in our care for over three hours. Causing chaos. It's interfering with our work.'

'Work?' snapped Laura. 'All you do is gossip all day like a couple of fish wives.'

'Oh, do we? Well, there's plenty to talk about with you here every waking hour.'

'What's that supposed to mean?'

'Think you're a star, do you, because you've got your husband's gold Amex card and have been on page 17 of the *Plymouth Herald*?'

'You fucking Welsh lesbo witch.'

'Well, that's better than being a jumped-up, coke-sniffing, talentless cunt!'

With all the ripe language flying around, I thought it best to usher the children out of the room, just as Laura burst into loud floods of tears. Simon rushed out of his room to see what was going on and charged up the corridor.

With all the mayhem, the show didn't start on time, so Trevor stormed backstage to demand an explanation and called us all unprofessional drama queens.

In the interval, Peter told Simon that if he didn't pay him what he was owed by next week, he'd tell the press about him and ruin his career. Meanwhile, Miriam was in another vile mood and said she simply couldn't bear the kissing scene with Peter for another night, and if he didn't keep his tongue to himself, she'd bite it off. Spud went into her dressing room just as I left and who knows what went on there because Miriam's mood dramatically improved and she was flushed and giggling like a schoolgirl.

Hermia was so stoned she couldn't find her way to the stage for Act Two, and when she did eventually go on, she stared up at the gods in silence as if it were a fairy grotto. How we got through it all, I don't know.

Somehow they got a standing ovation after all that. What people mistake for great acting is sometimes just a display of dysfunction. Lol.

Jayne's diary, Saturday, 12 August 2017, Plymouth
After yesterday's spat with Taffy, Laura asked me if I'd 'mind' the kids in the green room.

'I don't want to upset the old dragon again, but I need a facial urgently. Crying always leaves me looking puffy under the eyes.' I couldn't really refuse.

When Taffy heard, she pulled a face and said, 'Botox, more likely. From the look of her she's on about three pints a week.'

Miriam was holed up in Hermia's dressing room before and after the show. Are they hatching some sort of plot, I wonder? They could have just been meditating but there was something about Miriam's expression – pale and wide-eyed – that makes me think it's something else. They huddled together in the wings, whispering.

'What shall we do about him?' hissed Miriam during a scene change.

I've got an idea that it might all be to do with Spud. I mean, he's been seen emerging from both of their dressing rooms at various times looking a lot more cheerful than he normally does.

I feel I ought to warn them that they'll end up making fools of themselves, but it's not really my place to do that. They clearly don't want me involved as all conversation stops the moment they see me.

Miriam was quite bitchy with me after the show when I went to collect her dress.

'Who does your hair for you, Jayne? Is it the council?'

Chapter 23

Reuters, Monday, 14 August 2017
Headline: TV version of *Leopard Spots* stage play commissioned by Channel 4

TV production company Tiger Aspect has bought the rights to Leopard Spots *and pre-production is already underway, it has been announced. The hit comedy may form part of Channel 4's Christmas schedule.*

'I am delighted,' said writer Trevor Millicent. 'Tiger Aspect is a company I greatly admire and I'm bowled over by the enthusiasm and ambitious plans for my play.'

Leopard Spots *is currently thrilling audiences in the provinces prior to a four-week run at the London Palladium from the end of August. Casting for the TV version has yet to be announced.*

Kitty Litter WhatsApp Group Chat
P: Have we all heard there's to be a TV version of the play?
H: Amazing.
M: I've been here before. A Nell Dunn play I was in decades ago. When it went to TV, they gave my part to Kate Winslet. Bitch.
P: No, no. Not this time. We ARE the play.
H: Don't bank on it.

S: My agent knew about this a week or so ago. I was sworn to secrecy.

P: Oh. So you're cast, are you?

S: Couldn't say.

P: It's a different medium, TV. You might want to tone it down a bit. Just saying.

S: Thanks for that. If they don't cast you, perhaps you could hang around as my acting coach? Whatdyasay?

Jayne's diary, Tuesday, 15 August 2017, Plymouth

Well. Peter is all smiles. Seems to think he's going to play Tom on TV. 'I created the role of George. It's mine,' he said in the green room. Even claims to have rewritten most of his dialogue in rehearsals. 'It was crap. Total rubbish. No nuance or light and shade. Plus, there was no comedy before I added the Milano touch.' Says he'll sue if he doesn't get it.

Miriam doesn't agree. 'No TV company is going to touch him with a barge pole. He's deluding himself, the silly old fool.'

Ken Thomas's blog, Tuesday, 15 August 2017

Fabulous news, my darlings. I'm feeling much better. My wounds, both physical and psychological, are healing slowly but surely. I'm a tough old bird, after all. But there's more . . . It seems that *Leopard Droppings* will be hitting your screens this Christmas. 'Tis the season to be jolly after all, and I, for one, will be hanging out the holly and the ivy – but mainly the holly.

It will be prickly viewing for Old Father Time himself, coffin-dodger Peter Milano, as I hear he is to be replaced by none other than Nigel Havers, his arch-rival. Nigel, it seems, networked more successfully than Peter at the Channel 4 summer party. (Darn those more-ish cocktails!) Gurning in the gazebo, eh, Nige? Good for you, if that's what it takes.

Ms Milano isn't best pleased, as you can imagine, and has

been throwing quite the strop in her Plymouth dressing room, I hear. Sedation has been required, and the plastered pensioner has been seen consuming quite heroic quantities of diazepam, among other things, to deaden the pain. Could we be witnessing the death throes of an unremarkable career? I do hope so. Painful to watch but oh-so-deserved! The end can't come fast enough.

My spies tell me the only original member of the cast to make it to the hallowed elevation of the TV upgrade is the talentless Simon Gaunt. The small screen may suit him better, methinks. The smaller the better. Bring out the brandy butter. Not to mention the corn-on-the-cob. Sigh.

Wednesday, 16 August 2017
Subject: Notice to cease and desist

Dear Mr Thomas,

We write to you on behalf of our client, Peter Milano.

This letter has been served as notice of your unwarranted harass-ment activities, or the equivalent thereof, that have been ongoing in recent weeks. Therefore, you are required to cease and desist all published, verbal and physical attacks, including but not limited to:

Your online blog
Newspaper articles

If you do not cease all related acts, a harassment lawsuit will be commenced against you. The previously conducted actions are unwanted, unwelcome, professionally and personally damaging and have become unbearable.

Due to the aforementioned harm you have caused, this cease and desist shall serve as a pre-suit letter demanding that you provide us written assurance within ten days that you will refrain from further actions that could be deemed as harassment.

If you do not comply with this cease-and-desist letter within the aforementioned time period, a lawsuit may be filed in the proper jurisdiction seeking monetary damages as well as pursuing all available legal remedies for your harassment.

Sincerely,
David McGillivray LLB (Hons)

Trevor Millicent: notes for archive

It is important to tell actors how talented they are. Repeatedly. Even if they aren't. It doesn't make it real, but it fuels their self-delusion, and given this is the world they inhabit, I must do my bit to stop the walls from crumbling. Their talent is unreal. Off the scale. Mind-blowing. This makes them happy and confirms the lie they already believe to be true.

Apart from Simon, this lot are decidedly mediocre. Nature has not bothered them in that department. But this is something they need never know. It encourages them to work hard for little financial reward, thinking their time will come when the world realises what they already know – and have had confirmed by my good self.

Fun facts: talent

Talent: special aptitude – often athletic, creative or artistic in nature.

'Hard work beats talent when talent doesn't work hard enough.'
Tim Notke, a high school basketball coach

Text exchange between Robin and Jayne

R: Hey

J: *Hello*

R: *How goes it?*

J: *Madness. Get me out of here.*

R: *Nearly done in Plymouth, aren't you?*

J: *Yup*

R: *Then London's glittering West End*

J: *It needs to be glittering at those prices. I still can't find any digs that I can afford.*

R: *Ah. Well. Don't worry about that. Robin to the rescue.*

J: *Really? How come?*

R: *I know of a nice spare room in Camden. Let me make a call . . .*

Ken Thomas's blog, Wednesday, 16 August 2017
THIS PAGE IS NO LONGER AVAILABLE

Act Two
Chapter 24

Julian on the action so far

My dear reader,

I am a very caring and compassionate person – I'm known as the Marcus Rashford of the comedy circuit. So, it won't be a surprise to hear you have been in my thoughts constantly during Act One. How are you coping with all the unpleasantness I have had to put before you? I sometimes feel like a pet cat that is constantly bringing home half-eaten shrews and slaughtered baby birds to the horror of its owner. But there's worse to come. Far worse, I'm afraid.

My frightful editor is going through some personal difficulties: she has left the throuple arrangement, you'll be sorry to hear. It was all too much, apparently, and she was riddled with cystitis. She's now having a bash at solo living in a bedsit in Ipswich and informs me that Act Two is where the plot thickens and the tension rises. Everyone is a suspect and the axe is about to fall, blah, blah, blah. I expect she's right, having just completed the second act of her own steamy love life. She has some sort of literary degree that was doubtless purchased on the dark web. I dutifully take on board her editing notes, although it isn't easy to respect the word of someone who wears Paisley tights.

But, yes, it's all going to go off, like a dogging spot on the night of a full moon.

It is at this point in the story where different worlds begin to mingle.

Jayne had been my dresser in a production of *Dick Whittington* at the Birmingham Hippodrome about twelve years ago, as it happens, and we have always stayed in touch. I enjoyed her company during those seven weeks and we'd had a laugh together.

I calculated that with nine costume changes to complete over two performances a day she pulled my trousers down eighteen times. Which means, over the course of the lengthy run, she performed this solemn duty 756 times. A very bonding achievement that even my husband struggles to better.

I confess I once spat my water out in her face because I was bored. We still laugh about it now. So awful of me!

I returned to London when the contract finished, but Jayne and I kept tabs on each other from a distance. Text exchanges, mainly. When my tours took me to Birmingham, we'd meet up for coffee and a visit to the Rag Market or, on the rare occasions she visited London, we'd walk my dog in Regent's Park and laugh about life.

I've lived in Camden Town for over thirty years, so I was delighted when Jayne called.

'Guess what?' she said. 'I'm staying around the corner from you!'

Robin's brother Nathan lived in Royal College Street and it was his spare room that she would occupy. It happened to be empty after his lodger moved out and he was more than happy to have a few weeks of minimal rent to fill the gap.

I was thrilled to have her nearby – and with the news that there was a romance involved. She'd always guffawed at my enquiries regarding her love life, but a good seeing-to puts a spring in your step, I always told her. Look at the Krankies. Always cheerful.

Jayne's diary, Tuesday, 22 August 2017, London
Robin met me at Camden Town tube station and took me to his brother Nathan's house. He said he was valuing a flat in Kensal Rise and that's why he was in the area. I thought estate agents had their 'patch' and stuck to it, but he seems to be everywhere I happen to be . . . I mentioned it and he mumbled something about lack of experienced staff and he was on the 'floating' rota. Oh well.

But his brother's flat is great. I can't believe my luck! It's a nice room in the basement – my own bathroom. One of those dinky, terraced houses that are so narrow you wonder how they ever get a sofa up the stairs lol. I'd never be able to afford this on my dresser's wages so I'm feeling very grateful.

Julian lives just down the road, too, so hopefully I'll have time to visit him.

Nathan is gay and fit! He works as a personal trainer. Fridge full of protein shakes.

Likes theatre too, so was very interested in the show. I get two tickets for opening night at the Palladium so he's going to come along with Robin. Robin has the week off work so is staying too. I know – domestic bliss.

Fun facts: Camden Town
Singer Amy Winehouse lived in Camden Town for many years. First buying a flat at 2 Jeffrey's Place in 2003 then at 25 Prowse Place in 2008. In 2010, she moved to 30 Camden Square, where she was found dead in July 2011. Winehouse was strongly associated with Camden Town. Since her death, she has been titled as 'the Queen of Camden' and a bronze statue of her was placed

in Stables Market on what would have been her 31st birthday, 14 September 2014.

Email exchange between Amanda Proud (of Proud PR) and Simon Gaunt
Thursday, 24 August 2017
Morning Simon. I hope all is well. Arrangements for tomorrow's interview below. Should be a nice, positive piece. The journalist is called Henry Wilmot. He's a good writer and it should all be fun and straightforward. I'll see you there.

Amanda x

P.S. Do you want me to bring some smart shirts along for the photos?

ITINERARY: Friday, 25 August 2017
9.45 a.m. Car to pick Simon up from home address. Crawfords. They will text on arrival.

11 a.m. until 12 p.m. Photos at Proud Studios, 20 D'Arblay St, Soho W1.

Photographer: Peter Mountain.

Make-up: Madelaine Shelton.

12-1 p.m. Interview. There's a nice, quiet lounge area at the studios or we can go to the Ivy Club or Groucho if you prefer.

1 p.m. After interview we can grab some lunch if you like or a car will be standing by to take you home. Whichever you prefer.

\- - -

Ta Amanda. No, I won't want a posh shirt. Too showbiz. Going for the grunge these days. Cancel make-up too.

Sx

Email to Jayne Jones from Leopard Spot Productions, Thursday, 24 August 2017

Dear Miss Oxley,

I hope you are well.

We are currently preparing to welcome you all to our residency at the London Palladium.

Following consultation with Mr Gaunt's management, a request has been made for him to have a personal assistant at his disposal for the duration of the run. This role is part of the wardrobe department, and while it involves all the normal dresser duties with regard to Mr Gaunt, it would also include other duties, such as running errands, arranging lunch and post-show hospitality for guests and answering fan mail requests etc.

We are pleased to offer you this position, which comes with an increase of £100 per week to your current wages.

Please let us know at your earliest convenience if you wish to accept.

Best regards,

Trevor Millicent

Jayne's diary, Friday, 25 August 2017, London

Eek! Something nice has happened for a change. I'm going to be Simon's PA at the Palladium (has a nice ring to it, lol). I'll not only have to dress him but also pamper him a bit and get him chips between shows. More money too, which, I'm not going to lie, is going to come in handy with London prices. A cup of coffee is about five quid. Daylight robbery, if you ask me.

Anyway, it means I won't have to tiptoe around Miriam when she's in one of her moods or put up with Peter's rudery or Hermia's weirdness. Simon is the sanest of the lot.

I'm well chuffed. PA sounds much posher than dresser too.

I'm going up in the world! Can't stop smiling.

Text exchange between Jayne and Taffy

J: Accepted job as Simon's PA. Amazing!

T: You deserve it, girl. Bloody good at your job, as I told them.

J: Did you recommend me then?

T: I gave a glowing reference. You'd blush if you heard.

J: Thank you so much. I hope I don't let you down.

T: You'll be able to shop at Waitrose now.

J: But I do have a question. If I'm exclusive to Simon at the Palladium, who is going to do my job?

T: There's only one person who can do it who knows the show. Gordon.

J: Gulp!

Jayne's diary, 10.45 p.m., Friday, 25 August 2017, London
So, Gordon is coming to take over my old job at the Palladium. I suppose I can see why. He is familiar with the show and they won't have time to break in someone new. But blimey! That's going to put the cat among the pigeons, surely? Obviously, the management don't know about the goings on with Peter. No one is supposed to know. But it's bound to upset Peter and cause some drama. Just what he needs before an important first night. Taffy says Gordon is over all that now and will be professional. I hope she's right.

If I've learned anything during my years as a dresser, it's that your focus has to be on the actors. You have to help them give the best performance they can. You chivvy them along, keep them cheerful, make them feel confident and capable. Your own emotions and baggage must be left at the stage door. Whether Gordon knows that or not remains to be seen.

Oh dear.

Text exchange between Hermia and Miriam

H: I'm having some very strong psychic twinges.

M: Oh. Will there be ectoplasm? Should we put newspaper down?

H: Seriously. They're all about this Gordon.

M: Good or bad?

H: Bad, I'm afraid. Very bad. I am going to meditate on putting myself inside a prism of white, protective light.

M: Oh dear.

H: We must be on our guard. Dark shadows follow him around.

M: Often the way with homosexuals, dear.

Fun facts: emotional psychics

In parapsychology, the mechanism for being an empath is claimed to be psychic channelling; psychics and mediums claim to channel the emotional states and experiences of other living beings or the spirits of dead people in the form of 'emotional resonance'.

Kitty Litter WhatsApp Group Chat

P: If Simon is having a personal assistant, I don't see why we shouldn't all have one. Or is he the 'star' and we're just riffraff?

M: I think we know the answer to that.

S: Management request, guys. Nowt to do with me.

H: It's only Jayne with a new title. Hardly an entourage.

P: Will she be offering hand relief between shows?

M: Rude.

Text exchange between Miriam and Jayne

M: Congratulations, dear, on your promotion.

J: Thank you.

M: Hasn't gone down too well with Peter. Thought you should know.

J: *It wasn't my idea.*

M: *I know. I shall miss you fixing my wig and all our chats.*

J: *I'm still in the building. I haven't gone to Hollywood or anything!*

M: *Gordon has always been a worry, but I'm sure we will manage.*

Email exchange between Peter and Trevor

P: Can I just say, on record, that bringing Gordon back into the fold for the Palladium run is a big mistake. The boy is emotionally unstable for one thing and an incompetent dresser for another.

T: Done deal I'm afraid, old boy. And not my decision. Taffy's. He knows the show and that's what matters.

P: Fine. If I come on stage with my trousers on back to front you know who's to blame.

T: Try to keep your trousers up by yourself – although I know this has always been a difficult area for you. Suggest you concentrate more on your performance. I still think your opening scene could do with a bit more vim and vigour. Will call an extra rehearsal tomorrow to work on it.

Jayne's diary, Saturday, 26 August 2017, London

Can't believe I'm working at the world-famous London Palladium. I wish Mum was around, she'd be very excited.

So today is the get-in day, when lorries deliver all the set and costumes to the dock door. Lighting rig going up, lots of people doing carrying and lifting, and management types looking serious. Trevor was in the auditorium being in charge, waving his arms around and growling. No cast, thank the Lord, just the set and lighting and us in wardrobe. The Palladium is huge! Backstage is all done out like a Premier Inn. Lovely.

Simon will be in dressing room one, Peter in two, Miriam in

three and Hermia in four – actually the biggest room.

Lol.

Enjoying Camden life, apart from the junkies. But they mean no harm, I guess. Just feel sorry for them.

Nipped round to see Julian and filled him in on all the gossip. Turns out he knows most people in the cast, so I didn't have to do much filling in. He said Simon has a bit of a wideboy reputation. Can be quite ruthless and the 'I'm just an ordinary bloke' stuff is just an act.

He liked working with Peter on a tour once but said don't expect him to ever be happy with his lot. Miriam is camp, he said. He did a TV show with her years ago. Always fussing about her wigs, he remembered, but he likes her grandness. 'Like a Duchess,' he said.

Hermia is the one he only encountered once, so he wanted to know all about her. He's a fan of Trevor's plays and they met once at a BBC drinks thing, apparently. He even knew Spud, although he was vague about how. Hadn't worked together on a show or anything. But he knew him. That's all – then he changed the subject.

You find out things when you 'live' with someone. Robin's got a hairy arse like a Brillo Pad. Mind you, he's had a close look at my dimply thighs so I shouldn't judge.

We eat toast in bed and listen to the radio. He's bought a packet of condoms which he keeps in the bedside drawer. A big packet of ten.

Voicemail on Simon's phone, Saturday, 26 August 2017
'Simon, it's Amanda. I am *so* sorry. That was a hatchet job, pure and simple. We didn't see that coming and we should have. But don't worry. I know the editor of the *Mail* and I will make sure the interview never sees the light of day.'

Popbitch on Twitter, Saturday, 26 August 2017
Which comedian wants a court injunction to stop an interview going to press? Apparently it might damage his cheeky chappie image . . . oh dear!

Chapter 25

Mail on Sunday, Sunday, 27 August 2017
By Henry Wilmot.
Headline: 'Luvly-Jubly': We're Not in Romford Anymore.

*When I arrive at the Soho studio where lefty comic Simon Gaunt
is having the photos taken to accompany this piece, there is no
one there. Simon, I'm told, didn't like the set-up – too formal and
colour supplement-ish – so he took the photographer, his assistant
and his team out into the streets to capture something more 'gritty'.*

*I find them down the far end of Berwick Street, where a few
street-food vendors and market stalls remain. Not so much apples
and pears, these days, though, more avocados and kumquats, but
I guess you have to move with the times.*

*I stand and watch comedy's newest star as he threads his way
through the yuppies and instructs our bewildered photographer to
'Get this.' Simon goes behind the stall, grabs a handful of Cherokee
purple tomatoes and pretends to be selling them to an imaginary
housewife.*

*'There you go, darlin', yours for a pound. Bootiful!' His pub-
licist, Amanda, smiles proudly in the background. It strikes me
later that this scene is something of a metaphor for Gaunt himself.
His image projects the idea of a smiling, nodding cockney barrow*

boy 'avin a larf – a man of the people. But these days at least, he's elevated from all of that. He's rich, successful and riding the crest of a wave. And this isn't Romford market, it's newly gentrified Soho. The patrons are media types with Oxbridge accents. There are no headscarf-wearing housewives in sight. All is not what it seems – with Soho nor with Simon Gaunt.

But for now, it's smiles all round and vigorous handshakes and manly pats on the back as we make our way back to the studio for the interview.

'It's not me, is it?' he reasons. 'Sitting in front of a tripod on a fancy chair?' He shudders at the thought.

We settle into some easy chairs (Amanda sitting discreetly behind me). I turn on my tape recorder and he opens a can of lager. I get my first chance to observe him. He flicks his hair back and runs his palm over his forehead. He's wearing a faded grey T-shirt and rather tight jeans with some blue scuffed deck shoes. He follows my gaze.

'I could have made more of an effort,' he says and laughs. 'But if ever I dress up, I start sweating and look like a twat.'

He's sweating gently either way, I notice. 'Perhaps you've made an effort not to make an effort,' I suggest. He gives a little shake of the head then rubs his hands together as if to say: 'Let's get on with it.'

'You must be very happy with how things are going?'

He turns on his happy, smiley face.

'Amazed, more like. I mean, never in my wildest dreams did I think I'd get anywhere in this business. I'm gobsmacked. Truly.'

'How did you imagine your life would turn out?'

'Just . . . something ordinary, I suppose. My old man's an electrician. My mum works at Marks & Sparks on the till. You know? I wasn't clever at school. I was popular 'cos I made everyone laugh, but that was at the expense of any education. I wasted all that. Couldn't concentrate.'

I ask if that makes sense now, given his success as a comedian. Maybe school was his training ground?

'It was. Very addictive business, comedy. But I was disruptive, and I regret that now, I really do. I mean, for the kids that wanted to learn having me sitting at the back, arsing around during the lesson, it was wasting their time. The teachers were too busy trying to control me to teach.'

He wasn't exactly expelled at 16, but he was asked not to return.

According to the biography kindly given to me by his publicist, Gaunt spent the next four or five years working on building sites and generally being a lad about town, kicking his heels and getting up to mischief before finding himself in a pub that happened to have a comedy open mic night. His mates more or less pushed him on stage, and he was an instant hit.

Except that isn't quite the full story. And Simon Gaunt isn't his full name either. Back in the days of his youth he was better known as Simon Gwent. And a rather misspent youth it was, too. He may have spent time on building sites but he was more likely to have been stealing anything he could get his hands on than being on the payroll.

Gwent and his gang were notorious in the Dagenham and Basildon areas, and we aren't talking about light-fingered teenagers pilfering sweets and bottles of pop and getting into the odd scrap along the way: over several years they graduated from theft and muggings to robbing corner stores and small-time protection rackets.

It was a violent attack on a pub landlord in Epping in 2001 that landed Gwent and his cohorts a six-month stretch in a young offenders' institution. All of this seems to have been conveniently whitewashed from his past. And no wonder.

Albert Pritchard, the landlord of the White Swan told the Mail on Sunday *that he still remembers that night.*

'It makes my blood boil to see that thug on the telly, making

millions and swanning about like Mr Nice Guy. Simon and his pals wrecked my pub. Furniture smashed, windows broken. I had cuts and bruises, my arm broken. I don't know who swung the blow that knocked me across the room, but Simon was right at the centre of it, egging everyone on and kicking things off. They thought they were the Krays, or something.'

Lisa Clark, Simon's girlfriend when he was nineteen and mother of his estranged daughter, Phoebe, told us she lived in fear of him during their turbulent relationship.

'He was volatile. Nasty. I never knew if he was coming home with a bunch of flowers or a boot full of stolen goods. If I said anything he'd punch a hole in the wall. I've got nothing nice to say about Simon. He might have been young but that doesn't excuse his behaviour. He's never paid a penny towards his daughter. I took him to court multiple times, but then I gave up. I'm glad he's not part of our life anymore. I've moved on.'

When asked about his upbringing, Gaunt smiles and seems to have nothing but happy memories. 'I was a handful, but Mum and Dad did right by me. I was well loved. A secure kid. I mucked about at school, and of course they heard about that, but we stick up for each other. Family is very important, innit?'

'What about your teenage years, after you left school?' I ask.

'Just normal,' he answers with a blank look. 'Typical Essex lad, I guess. A few scraps and scrapes. Bit of a charmer with the ladies, you could say. Just normal.'

I raise an eyebrow. 'What did you get up to?'

'Oh, you know,' he shrugs, wiping his forehead again.

'Actually, I do know,' I said. 'I've done some digging, Simon.'

I hear Amanda fidget behind me and clear her throat.

'I've been talking to Albert Pritchard, who was the victim of an attack by you and your friends, and Lisa Clark, the mother of your child who you haven't seen or paid maintenance for in eleven years.'

'That's enough,' said Amanda. 'I think we'll wrap it up there.'

'I think Simon should answer my questions. The public has a right to know.'

Gaunt marched out of the room with an expression that left me in little doubt about what he'd like to do to me.

It's fair to say we all have a past and have done things we aren't proud of. But when you're in the public eye you have to be careful about the secrets you hide.

There's a steely determination about Gaunt that he doesn't want the public to see. A twitch of the jaw, a coldness in the eye. Much as he claims to be a beer-drinking Jack the lad who fell into comedy purely by chance, these newly uncovered facts cast doubt on his version of events.

How did he think he could get away with it, I wonder?

Chapter 26

Jayne's diary, 1 a.m., Sunday, 27 August 2017, London
About midnight my phone started pinging. It was Taffy sending me a link to a newspaper interview with Simon. Completely shocked. It starts off quite cheerful, but you can tell the journalist has something up his sleeve, then it turns into an exposé about his past – gang fights and abandoned child! I don't always believe everything I read but this will cause ructions, no doubt. There's another side to Simon, it seems.

Just when I was expecting a period of happiness and joy because we are at the Palladium. Silly old me!

Text exchange between Laura and Simon
L: *I can't believe I'm reading this shit, Simon. Young offender? You've got an 11-year-old daughter? Did you not think of telling me? WTF?*

S: *It's all false, babe. I've been set up.*

L: *Why didn't you tell me this was coming?*

S: *We thought it was getting blocked.*

L: *How am I supposed to show my face at Sugar Hut after this?*

S: *We need to set up some photos of us together. Lovey dovey stuff. Maybe take the kids to Legoland.*

L: *That shithole? Not even Sharm El fucking Sheikh? Going to bring your long-lost daughter along, too?*

S: *Babe, we'll talk about this later. We need to stand together and it will go away, I promise you.*

L: *It may not be the only thing that goes away.*

Text exchange between Peter and Simon

P: *Who's been a bad boy, then?*

S: *I guess I have. I was ambushed. Lawyers are on it.*

P: *I wouldn't be surprised if this doesn't get you cancelled.*

S: *The* Mail *is scum and everyone knows that.*

P: *Your cheeky barrow boy image is in tatters, mate.*

S: *Publicist is launching a charm offensive. Hopefully we can ride this one out.*

P: *It would be a shame if I added my story to the mix, wouldn't it?*

S: *Lose me from this show and it will close altogether, mush. Your last hurrah in the West End snatched from your arthritic grasp.*

P: *I hate the bastard press. Almost as much as I hate you.*

S: *Thanks for that.*

P: *In my experience paying them off always works. Skeletons come out the closet to scare us but then they go away again. Get your management to back-pay the child maintenance and the story should disappear. As for the landlord . . . you paid your debt to society. We have a show to get on. Don't let them derail us.*

S: *Thanks. None of it is what it seems. It's all been twisted.*

P: *Now I'm not the only one who knows you're a nasty piece of work.*

Text exchange between Hermia and Miriam

H: *According to the newspapers the star of our show is a violent, woman-hating psychopath.*

M: *Just reading it now. This is a disaster!*

H: You know, when I first met Simon, I was aware of a brownish tinge to his aura.

M: What does that signify?

H: It's not good. Guilt and some inner, spiritual struggles going on.

M: Well, yes. Illegitimate babies are one thing, but all that horrid violence!

H: I was rather wary of him. Instinctively, as a woman. But the next time I tuned in his aura had wisps of orange and purple. More mischievous and thoughtful. He was evolving, I decided.

H: Well, I'm glad to hear it. But it's not going to help our ticket sales I wouldn't have thought.

M: The story is spreading like wildfire. The Mirror, *the* Sun, *all the tabloids are gleefully reporting the story. 'Is Gaunt a Goner?' I expect the paps are camped outside his house. Laura will love that.*

H: That's another thing. Fancy changing your name to Gaunt!

M: Especially when you're fat.

H: Do you think they'll sack him?

M: I doubt that. Too late for the Palladium — we're about to open. But surely his casting for the TV version will be scrapped. Who knows? Maybe he just needs to do a benefit for single mothers, and all will be forgiven.

H: Jeez, the UK is a fickle place!

Simon Gaunt press statement, Monday, 28 August 2017
Following recent interest in my past I'd like to state the following:

1.   Many years ago, I was found guilty of a crime I didn't commit. I freely admit I was in the pub when the scrap happened, but I was in no way involved. The police arrested me along with everyone else. I just wanted the whole thing dealt with as quickly as possible and my solicitor at the time advised me not to contest the charges.

2.   Until last week I had no knowledge that my daughter Phoebe existed. I now look forward to meeting her and welcoming her as a member of my family.

3.   I appreciate that there is a continuing press interest. My wife Laura and I will be available for interviews and photo calls arranged via my publicist, Amanda Proud of Proud PR.

Note: Simon Gaunt is to star in *Leopard Spots* at the London Palladium opening tomorrow.

Ken Thomas's blog, Monday, 28 August 2017
So Simon Gaunt spent six months in a young offenders' unit? I wonder if there were any sordid encounters in the showers? My DMs are open.

Ken Thomas's Twitter, Monday, 28 August 2017
Seems there is a technical issue with my blog so will be tweeting for a while. Must mind my Ps and Qs!

Chapter 27

Jayne's diary, 10 a.m., Tuesday, 29 August 2017, London
Found myself with Gordon in wardrobe. Very red around the eyes. I was going to leave him to it but to walk in and then straight out again would have felt rather unfriendly. I started eating my sandwich (M&S tuna and cucumber. Posh!) and offered him my crisps. He turned his head away and said he doubted they were vegan-friendly. I looked at the packet and said, yes, they were, so he took a tiny one and nibbled it like a rabbit.

'Are you all right, then?' I asked. Had to say something.

'Not really,' he said. 'I'm trying to dress Peter and he's doing all he can to get me sacked!' He threw the crisp in the bin and crossed his arms, fuming. Trying to undress him more like, I thought. I'm not sure how much I'm supposed to know about what happened between them, so I had to tread carefully.

'That's not nice,' I said. 'What's his problem with you?'

'I don't know,' said Gordon.

'You must have some idea,' I said, looking him directly in the eye.

His chin trembled. 'I played with fire and I got burned,' he said and dissolved into tears. I put my hand on his shoulder. I didn't do a full-on hug in case I breathed tuna fumes all over him.

'Oh no!' I said, acting surprised. 'Like that is it?'

'Edinburgh last year,' he said, reaching into his jacket pocket for a tissue.

'Can't you just move on?'

'No! I tried – got a new man, but we split up. It's no good. I can't get Peter out of my mind!'

He looked at me pleadingly. He was gabbling now, words tumbling out, tears streaming down his face, mascara running everywhere. 'I'm a complete mess about it. I can't sleep, eat, nothing . . . I just want to be with him. But he hates me!'

'I'm sure he doesn't, Gordon. But it's probably very awkward for him. He's married. What did you think was going to happen?'

Gordon leant towards me, and I could see a hug was now my only option.

Just then Taffy came in. She stopped in the doorway and rolled her eyes.

'Oh dear,' she said. 'Like that again, is he?'

The sound of her voice caused Gordon to pause. He sat up again and looked at Taffy.

'I'm such a mess,' he said, shaking his head.

'Listen to me, boy,' said Taffy, moving closer to stand over him. Her tone was kind, but she was wagging her finger.

'This has GOT to stop. I put my reputation on the line to get you this job. You leave your personal troubles at the stage door, do you hear me?'

'Peter wants me sacked!' wailed Gordon.

'Well, I'm not surprised. Do your job, smile and nod and go home afterwards and no one will be able to sack you. Carry on like a hysterical schoolgirl much longer and we'll all be glad to see the back of you. I'm sorry you're suffering heartache but it's your own doing and not appropriate here in the workplace.'

165

As she spoke Gordon wiped his eyes and looked down at the carpet.

'Enough!' said Taffy decisively. 'Pull yourself together for God's sake. This play, this theatre, they are more important than you. Do you hear me?'

'Yes,' said Gordon meekly. 'I'm sorry Auntie Taff.'

Taffy's eyes flicked to me for a moment.

So Gordon is Taffy's nephew? That explains a thing or two.

Handwritten letter left in Peter's dressing room

Dear Peter,

Well, here I am. It seems as if fate wants us to be re-united whether we like it or not. When I got the call from Taffy I nearly wet myself. I know Edinburgh was a long time ago now and things got a bit messy. I'm sorry if I caused you any difficulties. But it will be different this time. I have learnt the art of discretion. I promise. I want you to know that my feelings for you haven't changed. I hope you feel the same. We can make this work. Age is just a number.

I can't wait for us to be together again.

Yours always,

Gordon xxx

Jayne's diary, 1 p.m., Tuesday, 29 August 2017, London

So, it's been announced that Simon will star in the TV adaptation of *Leopard Spots*. Maybe they've announced it now because he's on the front of all the papers and all publicity is good publicity, but I nearly fell over with surprise, especially as none of the others get a look in. They will be fuming.

And guess what? Peter's part is going to be played by Trevor! It seems a bit cruel. I mean, Peter is bound to be upset, to put it mildly. And right before the big opening night at the

Palladium! I'm sure some would say it is Trevor's play and he can do as he pleases, but he hasn't acted for years. They used to be friends. All a bit cutthroat. No one saw this coming. Perhaps this is what he planned all along? Then Simon has this to say in the press release:

'It is very difficult to imagine filming a version of the play without the inimitable Peter Milano by my side, but Trevor helped Peter to create the part and I'm sure will do a marvellous job.' I fully expect Peter to spontaneously combust when he reads that.

Can't help but notice that Laura turned up hand-in-hand with Simon smiling and kissing. What luck that the press was there to capture the happy scene.

Kitty Litter WhatsApp Group Chat

P: *I've a good mind to walk out of this theatre and leave you all in the shit.*

M: *Don't do that, Peter, we need you here tonight.*

H: *The timing of this is crazy. Have they no heart?*

P: *I honestly don't know if I can go on. My blood pressure is through the roof.*

H: *Harness your root chakra at the base of your spine, Peter. Do some deep breathing and count slowly from ten down to one.*

H: *Or Spud might have something herbal to calm you down.*

P: *Jesus Christ, I've never been so angry in my whole life!*

S: *Hey guys. I honestly don't know what to say. Showbiz is ruthless, we all know that. Like the hungry leopard. I didn't know they'd release it today.*

M: *Maybe to distract from the other story about you? Good news to cancel out the bad.*

P: *Oh, so it's good news now, is it?*

M: *You know I didn't mean that.*

H: *It might be helpful to all just be present in the moment. Here*

167

for each other. Let's just concentrate on tonight and exhale all this negative energy.

    M: *Yes, remember how talented we all are!*

    P: *I feel like punching someone.*

    S: *Don't Peter. Not with your brittle bones.*

    H: *Breathe, Peter, breathe!*

Fun facts: root chakra

One way to harness your root chakra's power is to ground yourself, a practice that is used to build a sense of security and stability in your mind, body, and spirit. Grounding techniques can help you focus on the present moment, and pull you away from distressing thoughts, unwanted flashbacks, and negative emotions.

Julian on what's to come

Sometimes, when something awful is about to occur, we are forewarned, as if the universe is trying to caution us, telling us to beware. That night in London there were sudden, explosive thunderstorms. Rain lashed down on the London Palladium, as if nature was trying to wash away the evil that was about to hatch there and fork lightning lit up the darkest Soho alleyways. Flash flooding brought the traffic on Regent Street to a stand-still. Jayne stirred in her basement bed-room and Robin placed a comforting arm around her.

Text exchange between Miriam and Hermia

    M: *What are we going to do about him?*

    H: *Don't worry. Be happy. Remember that song?*

Ken Thomas on Twitter

What to wear to tonight's Palladium opening of *Leopard Droppings*? A bin liner would seem appropriate but the great and the good will be there, so I'm thinking more smart-but-casual.

Trevor's opening night speech to cast and crew

'I guess we're not in Kansas anymore, folks! No, we most certainly are not. I know that today's announcement about the TV version of this wonderful play will not be great news for some of you. But listen – put it out of your minds. Forget all that, if you can, and concentrate on tonight. I beg you. Live in this moment.

What can I say, what words can I find to convey the pride and excitement that is welling inside me?

I sometimes wonder if it's all just a dream. I will wake up and have to face a cruel reality? But no, it is not a dream. We are really here.

And I want to thank you. Each and every one of you.

There was a time, in the not-so-distant past, when I was lying fallow, in the doldrums. My best work was considered behind me. I was a washed-up has-been. This was not my fault. My confidence had been destroyed. I seemed to have lost everything. All gone. And believe me when I say there were those who rejoiced in my downfall, who took pleasure in my humiliation and whose feet ground me further into the dust.

But somewhere deep inside me there was a glimmer, still. A secret knowledge that if I could claw my way out of the pit into which I had fallen, re-ignite the spark, then I could prosper again. Revenge, that is what tonight feels like. Revenge! See? The spark took light and now the fire is raging. Anything is possible.

There is nothing I need to say to you tonight about the play. My work as a writer and director is done. Complete. You know it, all of you. *Leopard Spots* is fighting fit and raring to go. In fact, the leopard is a racehorse in peak condition. Muscles rippling, loins twitching in anticipation. I, as the jockey perched

169

on top of this throughbred, just must hoist myself onto the stirrups and enjoy the ride. The prize is within reach.

I am not one for first-night gifts, but tonight I have made an exception. When you return to your rooms you will find something from me. It is a gift-wrapped ceramic leopard. Something I hope you will all treasure as a memento of this unforgettable night.'

Ken Thomas on Twitter
For some reason I seem to be persona non grata for *Leopard Droppings*. No trace of my name on the comps list, apparently. But fear not. I have connections. I'm going as someone's plus one, so unless there are WANTED posters with my eek on in the foyer, I'll be there.

Act Three
Chapter 28

Julian on opening night

It had been a fairly standard West End press night: red carpet outside the entrance of the Palladium, a heavy braided rope strung between brass poles holding the press at bay, posh cars drawing up, lightbulbs flashing.

VIPs walked along the carpet and were obliged to stop at the top of the stairs and smile for the photographers. (Ordinary members of the public were made to queue to one side and not get in the way before entering through a far less decorative door.)

Once inside you were pounced on by the publicists who ushered you to a corner where you stood under bright lights in front of a huge *Leopard Spots* poster. An eager, fresh-faced youth from marketing and social media (dressed in a leopard-print shirt which he looked very pleased with) thrust a microphone in your face and asked: 'Are you excited?' and 'What are you most looking forward to?' as he filmed you on his smartphone.

After this, another, more lowly, member of the team gently placed a hand on your back and guided you to the Val Parnell room where you were given prosecco and a free programme. I skipped the canapes as they looked as if they might have been regurgitated.

The room was buzzing and over-crowded and I was quickly air-kissing vaguely familiar celebs I didn't remember ever meeting before. Trevor Millicent gave me a bear hug; Lesley Joseph told me how much she loved last year's panto; Ulrika waved; Biggins hooted and someone from *Big Brother* spilled his drink down Alesha Dixon's dress. A pouting Laura Porter, pupils dilated like saucers, told me what a fan of mine her husband was and Katheryn, Peter's wife, offered a rather manly handshake.

I lost Ken in the melee but assumed I'd find him again once we took our seats. I've never been good at these showbiz occasions, where everyone is dressed up, a bit tense, some networking, others settling old scores, everyone hot and bothered and trying to look like they're enjoying themselves. It was a relief when the bell rang, and we all filed into the auditorium.

Inevitably, there was more waving and greeting once seated. Was that Anneka Rice? No, it was Richard Madeley.

Ken finally appeared, glowing and sweaty, saying he'd had a run-in in the loos with 'That dreadful political pundit man from the *Mail*' and his evening was in tatters, and did I have a tissue I could give him?

Finally, the lights went down, the incessant chatter stopped, the curtain went up and I breathed a sigh of relief.

The light on stage slowly grew brighter through a mist – warm yellow and orange then pink and white, as if it was the dawn of a new day, to reveal a very impressive set. A dilapidated colonial-style terrace, all faded glamour and chipped, peeling balustrades; 1940s rattan loungers scattered with cushions facing towards us on one side and a well-stocked, rather messy bar area on the other. Dusty, mismatched Turkish rugs and runners on the floor. Various louvred shutters and a door to the side.

Around everything grew vines and creepers with big, billowing banana plants and spiky tropical floras; shrubs seemed to

172

be invading at every opportunity. Hibiscus and passion flowers even grew out of the set and above the proscenium arch.

There was an audible gasp from the audience and a small, appreciative smattering of applause. The stage was empty, and we tuned in to the soundscape: exotic birds, crickets, distant monkeys chattering, the hum of insects which grew with the light then almost seemed to change to a purr or a growl. Was this the leopard of the title?

From stage right, Simon Gaunt finally appeared as Marwood Weston dressed in pale-denim dungarees rolled up to the knees and a straw hat. More applause. He was holding a battered wicker basket and secateurs, trimming the flourishing greenery, tutting and shrugging at the impossible task.

'What's the point?' he mumbled to himself. Then, spotting a new shoot on the other side of the terrace he slowly approached it, like a cat stalking a moth, then snipped it triumphantly.

'Gotcha!' he said holding up the offending tendril then tossing it into his basket. It was very funny, gentle visual comedy: a poor, defeated gardener taking delight in a small victory while clearly losing the larger battle.

Then he stops and listens. We hear a car engine, wheezing and coughing – clearly an old banger on its last legs. Simon hurriedly puts down his basket and disappears through the door at the side of the bar.

A man's voice calls 'Hello? Anyone home?' before Peter Milano enters through the garden downstage left. There is no spontaneous applause until he stands there expectantly, and we dutifully comply. He gives a slight nod as if to say: 'I should think so too.'

Ken turned to me and whispered: 'The clap he so richly deserves.'

A second later, Miriam Haughton follows him on. Her character is flustered and cross and she doesn't wait for any

173

recognition, just ploughs on, berating her husband for the disastrous 'holiday' she is enduring. Very good bickering scene. They work well together, Miriam delivering her spiky, vicious dialogue with perfect timing and Peter doing a good, world-weary, emasculated turn as a man torn between love and boredom.

They eventually go up the steps to the terrace and Peter as George impatiently rings the bell asking if there is any service: 'In this godforsaken place!' Simon re-enters, now dressed in an egg-shell blue linen suit, white shirt and yellow tie. That's my Jayne's deft quick-change, I thought to myself.

Simon, clearly now in the role of hotel manager, was hilariously pompous towards George as he listened to how these unexpected visitors needed somewhere to stay as their car had broken down and the chauffeur had to drive to the nearest one-horse town to try and get it fixed.

'Perhaps you need some grease on your input shaft?' he says suggestively, looking at Miriam as Geraldine, who takes a fan out of her capacious handbag and cools herself demurely. George demands drinks.

'It is a little early, but I'll see if the barman is available,' says Simon, bowing condescendingly before disappearing through the door.

The character of George reminds Geraldine about their honeymoon and the memory leads to a long, rather passionate snog before Simon re-enters only fifteen seconds later, dressed now as a waiter in a waistcoat and bow tie. The quickest of changes gets a roar of laughter and applause. This belongs to Jayne, by rights, if only the audience knew!

It was about now that Ken nudged me and said he needed to go to the bathroom urgently. I tutted and moved my legs to one side so he could get past. He had no doubt pigged out on the canapes and was now regretting it, I thought.

Another excellent scene ensued, a brilliant portrait of middle-class functioning alcoholics descending from romantic toasts to venomous, undignified bitching over two martinis. Peter swayed and slurred, Miriam's hair became dishevelled, and her blouse undone as she slowly homed in on Simon, her drunken desire increasingly uninhibited.

Hermia Saunders then glides onstage as Miss Simpson, the only other resident guest. She is a vision of camp in a pink satin kimono and turban, festooned in emeralds. Her arm is in plaster but supported by an expensive-looking floral sling. She disapproves of Geraldine and makes it clear that Marwood is her property.

Geraldine responds by asking about the spa facilities and Marwood, with a wink to the audience, says he will fetch the masseur. Another quick change and he's back in a white, short-sleeved tunic, holding a tray of massage oils. Geraldine, hiccupping, follows him off stage, with a triumphant backward glance towards Miss Simpson.

So far, Leopard Spots has been funny and clever – the audience have been completely thrilled by it.

Chapter 29

Julian on the shock moment onstage

This is when it happened. As I recall, Peter and Hermia's characters were left alone on stage. There was a deliberately awkward pause as they both realised that Geraldine and Marwood were going to the spa and, no doubt, going at it like rutting stags on the massage table at that very moment.

'Nice weather for it,' said Hermia, which got a laugh. She moved down stage towards the audience as she spoke, and Peter then staggered up stage and slouched into a creaking rattan chair. He then said his line: 'What is it about vodka? Turns her into a bitch on heat.'

It happened so quickly. Just a flash, like a stone shattering a car windscreen.

Something dropped suddenly from above. Heavy. Dark. The force threw Peter from his chair to the ground, and we heard an anguished groan. He lay there twitching. He half rose up again for a second. His face a mask of horror and surprise, a streak of dark blood, glistening under the lights, pushed its way down his face like lava. His mouth was open, his eyes staring upwards to the gods. Then he fell back again. But somehow the likeness seemed to linger in the air, briefly, like a ghost.

Those of us watching didn't know for a second or two if this was all a part of the play or not. We froze.

Hermia turned, took a step up stage, her hand clutched her throat. Then she screamed and turned helplessly to face the audience, her eyes wide with shock.

'Please! Somebody help!' Then she let out another scream, a full, throaty wail of utter terror, it seemed to me. This proved contagious and soon there was a wave of hysteria in the auditorium.

Simon ran on and put his arms around Hermia, and she collapsed, sobbing in his arms. People began to get up and call for an ambulance. Others began to cry, wailing with distress at what they were seeing. Trevor pushed his way out of his row of seats in front of me and ran towards the pass door to the left of the stage, followed by Peter's ashen wife, Katheryn.

In the chaos I thought I saw Ken too, scurrying along behind. The house lights came on, just as Miriam rushed on to the stage towards Peter, followed by a man I recognised as Spud, but then, very quickly, the curtain fell.

Everyone was now up on their feet, many now crying and comforting each other, some bewildered and pale with shock. Quite a few people clearly wanted to get out of there and were pushing their way towards the exits, but others were just stood, not knowing what to do, blocking the aisles.

Then the curtain suddenly went up again, as quickly as it had descended, and we all stopped and faced the stage. Trevor stood front and centre, his hands spread out in a calming gesture, palms down. He did a couple of up and down waves, indicating that we should be quiet and listen to him.

Behind him we could see Peter still lying where he had fallen, but now he was surrounded by quite a crowd, some kneeling, others crouching down – Miriam; Hermia; Spud; Simon; Katheryn; a pale, thin boy dressed in black; a grey-haired woman who, from what Jayne had told me, must be the wardrobe

177

mistress Taffy. And, unbelievably, my date for the night, Ken Thomas . . .

'Ladies and gentlemen,' boomed Trevor. 'I'm sorry to say there has been . . . a most terrible accident. The emergency services are on their way but the whole of Soho is gridlocked and they may be a while. Is there a doctor present who could attend to Peter, please?'

A woman near the front raised her hands and said: 'I'm a doctor!'

'Please, come through the side door,' said Trevor, pointing to his left. He then, ever the director, felt the need to say something conclusive.

'Thank you, everyone. I'm so sorry . . .' But even he couldn't think of anything appropriate. His chin wobbled slightly and he turned to the wings and in a shaky voice said 'Curtain down!'

And down it came, as he turned back towards his actors. The last thing I saw was Peter's lifeless legs. The rest of him was obscured by those trying to help. I don't know if it was the jungle setting or not, but I suddenly had the inappropriate vision of a pride of hungry lions in a feeding frenzy.

Police officer report

My name is PC Geoffrey Bacon. I was on duty with my colleague WPC Sharon Saddleback when we got an emergency call to attend an incident at the Palladium on Tuesday, 29 August 2017. We arrived at the scene at approximately 8.23 p.m. A man we now know to be Peter Milano was lying on his back on the stage and a doctor from the audience was attending to him.

We immediately cleared the stage and called for paramedics who arrived within six minutes. Mr Milano did not appear to be breathing and CPR was undertaken by paramedics. It was then Detective Inspector Serrano arrived and instructed us to move those present into the green room.

Fun facts: the Metropolitan Police Service
The official newspaper of the Metropolitan Police Service is called *The Job*. Published every two weeks, it is crafted for the benefit of police personnel and members of the public. There is no charge for the paper and it's available in every police station.

Jayne's diary, 1.15 a.m., Wednesday, 30 August 2017, London
I was getting Simon into his chef's costume when we heard the thud. It was such a deadly sound, it seemed to reverberate and we both immediately jolted upright, and listened, like meercats. Then there was Hermia's terrible cry for help and Simon went, sprinting onto the stage. People ran on from all directions, crowding around Peter.

The curtain went down then up again. Trevor appeared then a woman who I think was a doctor. I heard sirens and running feet plus all the noise from the audience, crying and carrying on. I didn't move as all this havoc happened around me. I was frozen. If the building had been on fire, I think I would have stood there still, clutching the chef's hat.

It was Taffy who came to me eventually.

'Come on love, we've been told to wait in the green room.' She had to pull me by the arm. Honestly, my legs were like jelly.

'What happened?' I asked.

'I don't know. There's a stage weight that fell down from the flies, apparently. Hit Peter. He didn't look in a good way.'

Simon was already in the green room when we arrived, sitting with his head in his hands. Spud was standing up, vaping furiously. Taffy sat me in a comfy chair and rubbed my shoulder and only then did I start to cry. Ken Thomas was also herded in, and sat silently, very red in the face and looking cross.

There was a policewoman there with us all. She wrote down our details and what our jobs were.

I asked if Peter was going to be OK, but she said she didn't know.

Simon got up and started making tea for everyone.

'What the fuck just happened?' he said.

Then Miriam came in, like a zombie, her eyes staring, white as a sheet, despite all the make-up. I got up and hugged her but she was rigid. Hardly breathing.

'You should sit down, miss,' said the policewoman.

The woman from the audience who was a doctor came in next, with Gordon, either side of Hermia, who was in a completely opposite physical state, hyperventilating and in a state of collapse. Her turban had been removed and her hair was a mess. She seemed barely conscious.

'Lie her down on that sofa,' said the doctor urgently.

'Try to take some deep breaths,' she said.

Gordon then flung himself at Taffy, weeping into her shoulder.

'I can't bear it!' he sobbed. 'Why Peter?'

'He'll be OK,' said Taffy, patting him on the back. 'Don't worry, love.'

Miriam sat in silence, a handkerchief pressed to her mouth as if she was going to be sick.

The doctor spent a few minutes with Hermia, took her pulse and wiped her brow with a wet towel before leaving.

'What about Katheryn?' I asked Taffy.

'She's with Peter. They're taking him out on a stretcher to the ambulance.'

Simon handed round the tea, although Hermia now had her

180

eyes shut, her broken arm in its sling resting on her chest, the other covering her face.

The only sound was Gordon's rasping sobs, which had subsided now, to a rhythmic, vocal grunt.

We all sat in silence for several minutes, the policewoman standing by the door as if on guard.

'How long do we stay here for?' Miriam asked.

'You will all be required to give a statement in due course, madam,' she said.

There was a gentle tap on the door and Trevor came in.

'Who are you?' asked the officer. A flicker of irritation crossed his face and Trevor gave a slow blink before saying: 'Trevor Millicent. Author and director. I need to say a few words to my company if that's all right?'

She nodded and held a pencil over her notebook, ready to take notes. I sensed Trevor liked this. Made him feel important. He then went around the room hugging everyone, which was a bit awks. Spud slid to the floor; Taffy rolled her eyes. Hermia stirred and managed to sit upright, her eyes still flickering, though, as if she wasn't all there. Trevor then stood in the middle of the room.

He gave a loud sigh, then said: 'This is not the evening we had planned.' He looked around at us all.

'I'm sorry to have to tell you this, but Peter has died.'

Gordon immediately wailed, Simon slapped the wall, Miriam covered her eyes and Hermia jerked her head from side to side as if refusing to accept what she had just been told. Spud ran his fingers through his hair and bowed his head. Ken looked blank.

'Oh, the poor man,' said Taffy, handing Gordon a paper tissue. I thought of poor Katheryn, their children, the sudden event that had just changed everything for so many people and tears ran down my cheeks.

Trevor continued: 'No one yet understands what happened,' he told us. 'A terrible accident. We must allow the police time to do their job. The theatre is under investigation. We must all wait here for now until we are told otherwise.

'As your director I say this. Sorry. Sorry to you all. Sorry you have witnessed such a terrible occurrence. There will be answers eventually. We are a family, and we will get through this together. Support each other. We have tonight lost one of our own, a much-loved colleague whom we have spent the last few months working closely with. I've known him for forty odd years. I never . . . This is terrible. I'm just . . . heartbroken.

'For once I don't know what to say to you. Cry. Pray. Do whatever it takes to get you through these dark and desperate hours. Right now, words are meaningless. As your director, as your friend I can only suggest one thing. A group hug?'

There was a sudden deadness in the air. I don't think any of us felt this was what we wanted to do right now.

'Come on,' he persisted. One by one we stood up and walked slowly towards Trevor who stood before us, arms outstretched, waiting, like that statue of Christ on top of some hill in Brazil.

Simon and Gordon were first, positioning themselves either side of Trevor, then Miriam shuffled awkwardly in front, her head turned to one side as if in distaste for such physical proximity. I stood beside her and could smell her Chanel N°5 perfume. Taffy helped Hermia to her feet, and she limply hung her one good arm around my waist. We all clustered inelegantly. It felt like a game of children's hide and seek.

But there was one person missing. 'Come on, Spud, my lad,' said Trevor sternly. Spud, like a moody teenager reluctantly joined us and stood behind Taffy, arms half-heartedly raised a bit and hardly touching any of us, but there were wafts of the sweet vape scent and that musty, dusty odour. We stood like that for half a minute or so, listening to each other breathe, to our hearts beat, perhaps.

It was the policewoman who brought the group hug to a merciful end, by clearing her throat.

'Ahem . . . We are ready to take you each through to another room separately to make your statements. Who'd like to be first?'

Fun facts: green rooms
Where actors meet before and after performances. Many actors also experience nervous anxiety before a performance, and one of the symptoms of nervousness is nausea. A person who feels nauseous is often said to look 'green', suggesting that is why the 'green room' is so called.

Kitty Litter WhatsApp Group Chat

H: *I can't sleep. Is anyone else awake?*

M: *I am. Staring at the ceiling. Sending hugs.*

H: *The whole crazy thing is going round and round in my mind on a loop.*

S: *Hi. It's had a weird effect on me. I've got an insatiable craving for Nutella.*

H: *Nutella is made with hazelnuts. Rich in phenolic compounds. Helps your heart stay healthy by reducing cholesterol and inflammation.*

S: *So, I shouldn't feel guilty?*

H: *Simply put, Simon, your heart is hurting. Your body is responding by demanding food that will restore it.*

S: *But it's 200 calories a spoonful. That's not so good, surely?*

H: *Just tune in to what your body wants.*

M: *I'm doing that right now and I'm hearing the word Diazepam.*

Jayne's diary, Wednesday, 30 August 2017, London

Was eventually given my phone back and allowed to leave at about midnight. There were press and photographers milling around but they took one look at me and lowered their cameras and notebooks. Probably thought I was the cleaner or something.

I stumbled out of the stage door and into Great Marlborough Street and within seconds Robin was at my side, his arms around me. It was only then I cried properly. Big, racking sobs. I suppose I'd been holding it all in trying to look after everyone else.

'Let's get you back to Camden,' said Robin. He hailed a taxi. Once seated I calmed down and started to breathe better. Opened both the windows. I leaned against Robin. Thank goodness for him.

Daily Express, Wednesday, 30 August 2017
By Ken Thomas.
Headline: Actor Peter Milano killed in Palladium horror

The theatre world was in shock last night following the on-stage death of actor Peter Milano during a performance of a new play at the Palladium in London.

Audience members screamed in horror when an object, thought to be a ten-pound iron stage weight fell from the flies above and struck the much-loved actor on the head during a press night performance of the new play, Leopard Spots.

Actress Hermia Saunders, who was on stage with him when the incident occurred, rushed to his aid, and cradled the blood-soaked Mr Milano in her arms. He appeared to mutter a few words and then fell silent.

Ms Saunders gave an anguished cry for help and several members of the cast and backstage crew ran on stage as the curtain fell. We saw no more, but the terrible image of what happened last night on the most famous stage in the world will be forever etched on the memories of everyone present.

The house lights came up and the director, Trevor Millicent, appeared front cloth to ask if there was a doctor in the house. A woman came forward and was ushered through a side door. Shortly after, we were told that the performance would not continue and were invited to leave. The audience, many of whom looked visibly shocked, some crying, filed out into the night. Peter Milano's death was announced by his agent on Twitter some hours later.

The tragedy ends the career of one of our most enduring stage and screen stars.

Peter Milano was born into a bohemian Brighton family in 1955. His father, Alfredo, was an Italian restaurateur and his artist mother (they never married) Marlene Evans.

His career began modestly enough in rep but his good looks soon caught the eye of the film and TV world and, by the early 1980s, he was a household name, first as a stage actor and then better known for his role as Eddie, an undercover cop in the long-running BBC series Night Manoeuvres.

He also spent some time in Hollywood, most notably in the film Don't Hurt Me *opposite Jayne Fonda with whom he allegedly had an affair. Sadly, the parts dried up and Peter returned to the UK where he married the heiress Lady Donna Ratcliffe in 1985. They divorced in 1990.*

He won a BAFTA nomination for playing the title role of a rugby player coming to terms with a Parkinson's diagnosis in Why Tim? *as well as numerous parts in various TV series during the 1990s such as* Bergerac, Midsomer Murders *and* Doctors.

Peter was a regular on the chatshow circuit where his many theatrical anecdotes and refusal to take himself seriously endeared him to audiences. More recently, his draw as a touring actor has allowed him to work mainly in theatre, ranging from popular farces to Shakespeare. He married again to property developer Katheryn Thorogood in 2007.

Leopard Spots, *the play Peter was performing in when he died, was an unexpected success. Somewhere between Joe Orton and Tennessee Williams in style, it started out at the Edinburgh Festival last August where, a hit with critics and audiences alike, it quickly built an enthusiastic following. It toured to packed houses this summer and was about to begin a triumphant run at the Palladium – which was suddenly vacant following a dismal production of* Cats.

Peter Milano was a highly esteemed actor admired by many. To die such a violent and public death while reaching for the very pinnacle of professional success is a tragedy worthy of the darkest drama. I have never known an evening in the theatre like it and I hope I never will again.

Jayne's diary, Wednesday, 30 August 2017, London

So, yes. Peter really had died on stage. Feels unreal. Terrible. His poor family.

Then there are the other things I remembered from last night. Robin. Was that all true? I got up and looked in the wardrobe. His clothes were gone. His rucksack too. All his things from the bathroom. That was true as well, then.

When we got back to the flat it was past midnight. Nathan was up, telling me it was all over the news, asking if I was all right. We all had some chamomile tea and talked about it for a while. Just impossible to comprehend. Robin kept saying he'd seen something. Things didn't add up, but he then went quiet. He wouldn't say any more about it.

About 2 a.m., Robin and I went to our room. I was tired but we had sex anyway. Quite tender and gentle this time. Then after, Robin got out of bed and got dressed. I asked him what he was doing, and he sat on the bed and sighed, looking upset.

'I've got to go,' he said.

'But it's the middle of the night. What do you mean, go?'

'I need to tell you something, then go. I'm sorry. I haven't been honest with you. I've lied. I didn't mean it to go on this long. I was going to tell you anyway.'

'What? Whatever are you on about?'

'Because of what happened tonight.'

'I really don't understand. You can't leave me here. Now. In your brother's flat!'

'Nathan knows. He's fine with it. You'll understand when I tell you.'

'For God's sake just tell me then.'

'I'm a surveillance operative. I work for the police, Jayne.'

'What do you mean?'

'The less I tell you the better. For your own good.'

'Robin, you're frightening me now.'

'I'm telling you the truth. My relationship with you – it just happened. I should have stopped it. But it all coincided.'

'What coincided? I thought you were an estate agent?'

'I'm not. I thought you must have guessed by now. I mean, come on, Jayne. An estate agent who never has any properties to sell?'

'You're blaming me for not knowing what you said was a lie? Am I stupid for trusting you now? That's just twisted. And nasty. Why couldn't you tell me what you are?'

'Because . . . Jayne, I'm undercover. We are investigating someone . . . someone you work with.'

'Who?'

'Obviously I can't tell you.'

'Spud. You kept saying I shouldn't trust him.'

'I – I can't talk about specifics. It's too dangerous.'

There was a long pause while I digested this.

'So I am – was – just a means to an end for you?'

'No. Not at all. Maybe to start with. It all just . . . it shouldn't have happened, should it?'

'No. Apparently not.'

'Look, I'm sorry. Really sorry. I never meant to hurt you. Or myself, for that matter.'

I could see Robin was crying. So was I.

'Because of what happened last night it's going to be a whole different investigation. I can't stay. It compromises both of us. Maybe one day . . . you and I . . .'

He shrugged.

'I'm not going to use the L word,' I said, trying not to sound desperate. 'But if I had to choose between you and Greggs, I'd have chosen you.'

I tried to look into Robin's eyes then, but through my tears he was all blurred.

Then he got up, quickly packed his things, and left.

He left me with so many unanswered questions.

Who was Robin really?

Who was he investigating?

Was that it? Would I ever see Robin again?

Nothing made sense.

I guess I cried myself to sleep.

Jayne's diary, Wednesday, 30 August 2017, London
When I woke up, I wasn't sure if it was all true or not. I'd slept really deeply. I'd had lots of dreams. I was on my own. Did Peter die last night? I opened my laptop and read the news.

Chapter 30

Police statement – delivered on the steps of the Palladium's stage door on Great Marlborough Street
'Good afternoon. I am Detective Inspector Anthony Serrano and I have an update for you on the incident at the London Palladium yesterday evening.

Our officers were called to the scene around 8 p.m. after the actor Peter Milano was struck on the head by a ten-pound stage weight that fell from the flies above him. Despite the best efforts of the paramedics, he was pronounced dead at the scene.

The autopsy on Peter Milano is to take place later this afternoon and we will update you as soon as we have any further news.

We realise that what has happened has aroused considerable media interest so I'd just like to add that at this stage it would appear to have been a tragic accident and we are not predicting any arrests.

Our thoughts are with Peter Milano's family, friends and colleagues at this difficult time.

Thank you.'

Fun facts: death in the theatre
1673: Molière, the French actor and playwright, who suffered

from pulmonary tuberculosis, died after being seized by a violent coughing fit while playing the title role in his play *Le Malade Imaginaire* (*The Imaginary Invalid*). The superstition that green brings bad luck to actors is said to originate from the colour of the clothing he was wearing at the time of his death.

Jayne's diary, Wednesday, 30 August 2017, London

Followed Rowanne's advice and had a long, comforting bath. It seems there are now two horrible events in my life, both beyond my control and neither of my making. Work and personal life have both imploded within a few hours of each other. You think everything is under control, bobbing along nicely and then bang! All change.

My mind is whirring and I'm having to reassure myself that it isn't my fault. Any of this. Thought about running away back to New Invention. But Taffy says the police might want to interview us again. We're still being paid so I have to stick around.

Jayne's diary, Thursday, 31 August 2017, London

Nathan has been very sweet. He'd gone to work when I got up this morning but left me a note saying he hoped I was OK and gave me his number in case I needed to talk. I do need to talk, but not to him, and I don't know what to say anyway. I suppose he knew all along about Robin so I'm not sure I can trust him either. He left me a thing called a croissant for breakfast, but I don't like the look of it; all stodgy and curled around itself like some sort of rodent.

I went to Greggs and had a vegan sausage roll instead. Well, it might have been two. I thought a break-up was supposed to take away your hunger and leave you all thin and pale but I'm ravenous. I can feel the eczema building up for an outbreak too. Cheeks and elbows this time, so I'm going to look like a pork scratching soon. Great.

I remember a Lily Savage line: 'I'm sick of fellas. Think I'll become a lesbian. At least you get to wear flat shoes.' Sort of lol.

Fun facts: a hot bath
In addition to reducing pain, soaking in warm water may also improve brain function according to recent reports. This may be because water immersion seems to increase a brain chemical called brain-derived neurotrophic factor and, at the same time, also reduces the stress hormone, cortisol. Relaxing in a warm bath also relaxes your blood vessels, because the heat causes them to dilate, making it easier for blood to flow through. This temporary decrease in blood pressure is similar to the effects of exercise and may have similar cardiovascular benefits.

Kitty Litter WhatsApp Group Chat
H: *Checking in. How's everyone coping?*

M: *It's very much the morning-after-the-night before. Poor Peter. When I woke up, I thought it had all been a terrible dream. But then I saw the news and this awful nightmare is true.*

S: *Did you hear the police report? A stage weight FFS. How the hell can that happen?*

M: *It had probably been up there for years, then some sort of vibration from the scene change dislodged it.*

S: *Could have been any one of us. Like when Hermia fell through the trap door in Brum. Peter was in the wrong place at the wrong time.*

H: *We are all in deep shock. This is going to affect us for a long time. Be careful. Our minds are in a very distracted state.*

M: *True. I nearly got run over crossing the road when I got out of the taxi last night.*

H: *Just sit quietly and sip chamomile tea.*

M: *I keep feeling cold, as if I'm sitting in a draught or something.*

H: *This is one way our bodies react. Keep warm. Comfort yourself. Stay hydrated.*

S: *God, it must be even worse for you, Hermia. I mean, you were right there when it happened.*

H: *So awful. I keep hearing that terrible gurgling moan he made in the first few seconds. He was still alive after the weight fell, you know.*

S: *I looked into his eyes. The expression was just, sort of . . . astonishment.*

M: *It is strange how time seemed to slow down. When I ran on it was as if I was watching myself in slow motion.*

H: *Shock again, Miriam. A dissociative, paranormal experience.*

S: *The fact that he was still alive then is really upsetting. Maybe if we'd done something differently, we could have saved him?*

M: *It was only seconds before . . . all that blood. It's such a blur.*

S: *I feel so gutted.*

M: *I had some Rescue Remedy in my dressing room. I wonder if that might have helped him?*

H: *I felt the moment when his spirit left his body. Like a butterfly. There was nothing any of us could have done.*

Evening Standard, Thursday, 31 August 2017, London
By Trevor Millicent.
Headline: Director pays tribute to Peter Milano

I have known and adored Peter Milano for over 40 years. He was a kindred spirit. We could not have been closer; we were like brothers.

We met at RADA when we were very young men learning our craft. Within weeks we were sharing a cramped flat in Finchley. He was devastatingly handsome and there was a steady stream of girlfriends all of whom he treated with courtesy and respect.

It was obvious to everyone that he was a major acting talent. Because we were so close, we were both delighted when we started our careers together at the Royal Shakespeare Company.

Competing for the same roles we never once fell out. We delighted in each other's success, and we supported each other always throughout our varied careers. Most of all I admired his raw talent. I watched in awe from the wings each night as his virile, enigmatic Count Paris strode the boards. He was simply magnificent.

Over time, work took us in different directions, but we never lost touch. We were there for each other during the trials and triumphs of life.

Now he has gone, and I am devastated. It is like losing a limb. He had never been more brilliant than he was in Leopard Spots. *All his accumulated experience and ever-blossoming talent was on display. He needed virtually no direction from me. I just handed him the script and he did the rest, instinctively, dazzlingly. He shone.*

Trevor Millicent: notes for archive
ES piece attached. How I managed to dredge up these compliments I've no idea. I was dry heaving as I typed. But needs must. One sometimes has to spread the BS quite thick for the sake of appearances. I'm not the only one doing it either: Ken Thomas wrote such a florid load of tosh about Milano in the *Express* yesterday I had to check he wasn't eulogising about Laurence Olivier. He must have been typing with one hand and wiping away the tears of laughter with the other.

Daily Express, **Friday, 1 September 2017**
By Ken Thomas.
Headline: Milano Death: how could it happen?

Doubts were cast yesterday on the circumstances of actor Peter

Milano's death. The star died when a stage weight fell on him during a press night performance of Leopard Spots *at the London Palladium on Tuesday 29 August, witnessed by a packed house of over 2,400 people.*

A theatre insider told the Express *that when he heard how Milano died, he was immediately baffled: 'There's no way a stage weight should ever be up in the flies. They are used to hold scenery in place in the wings. There are always weights knocking around but why and how would anyone carry one right up there? It is unheard of.'*

It is thought that Peter Milano died from his injuries almost immediately. Mrs Margaret Wilmslow, who saw it happen from her third-row seat in the stalls said: 'It was terrible, traumatising. Something fell down and there was the most awful thud. For a moment, we weren't sure what was happening, or if it was all part of the play. But then I saw the look of horror on the actress's face – the blood splattered on the stage, the look of shock on his face and I just knew. No one is that good at acting. It was an expression of complete terror.

'Peter Milano, who I've loved for years (he's the reason we bought tickets in the first place), slumped forwards and groaned. She – the actress – ran over, put her arm around him – the other was in a sling – held him by the shoulder and looked up then over to the side. There were screams. She called for help. By then people were starting to cry out in distress. Someone wearing headphones and dressed in black then came on fairly quickly and the curtain came down.

'How can such a thing happen in a play? And at the Palladium of all places? It will be a long time before I feel able to go to the theatre again. I haven't slept and I keep getting flashbacks. I shall expect a full refund, but you can't get through to anyone at the box office. I know someone has died, but I'm a pensioner. I saved up for a night out.'

Our insider, who wishes to remain anonymous said: 'Serious questions need answers, and soon, about what happened at the Palladium, otherwise what occurred that night takes on a more worrying aspect.'

A spokesperson for the Palladium said: 'All protocols are strictly adhered to by our highly trained technical staff, and we strongly refute any suggestion that anyone in our employment acted without adherence to the rules.'

The police have declined to comment and said their team of investigators were conducting their enquiries and a statement would be released in due course.

Fun facts: stage weights

A stage weight is a heavy object used in a theatre to provide stability to a brace supporting objects such as scenery or to stabilise lighting stands. They are made of cast iron with a malleable iron carrying handle. They usually weigh around ten pounds.

Jayne's diary, Friday, 1 September 2017, London

Peter's death all over the news. Strange to think he's gone. They've been showing clips of him in his heyday. So handsome and quite a star back then. The police are still investigating and say it's 'Too early to draw any conclusions.' Trevor was on daytime TV saying what a brilliant actor he was, so talented and 'instinctive'. Didn't get that impression from all the notes he gave him every day.

Met Taffy for tea in Soho. We walked past the Palladium. All the signage still up. Peter's photo. Policemen on guard at the front and at the stage door. Quite a lot of flowers left by the wall of fame. We stopped to read the messages. One huge bunch of pink lilies. The card said: 'To darling Peter, my one true love, GORDON XXXXX'.

195

'Ah, bless him,' said Taffy. 'He's in a terrible state. Taken it very badly, he has. Inconsolable, poor love.'

Fun facts: leopards

The largest threat to leopards is human activity. Urban expansion results in habitat loss and a decrease in food sources. Leopards are also hunted by poachers for their valuable fur and whiskers. Because leopards prey on livestock, ranchers will frequently poison the large cats in an attempt to protect their animals.

Instagram post from Laura

Hi guys. I know a lot of you have been worrying about me after what happened at the Palladium, and I wanted to let you all know I'm doing OK. I was in the third row, got a proper eyeful. It wasn't a nice thing to see, not on top of crab croquettes with a wasabi ceasar at Sticks'n'Sushi. That nearly came back up, I can tell you.

It's all been very hard for Si. That play has been his life for the last year and no one seems to know if it's gonna be scrapped or whatever. But it's nice to have him home in the evenings for a change. We've been snuggled up on the sofa, bingeing on Netflix to take his mind off things.

We've decided to go ahead with our party on Sunday. Just a small marquee in the garden. It's our fifth wedding anniversary after all and the caterers have been booked, hair, make-up, bouncy castle, *Hello* are covering it. Nine pages, they say. It's not fair on all those people to cancel. Life has to go on. We're going to raise a glass to Peter after we've renewed our vows. Will post on here to show you all. Wait till you see my dress. Stella McCartney! Whoop!

Kitty Litter Whatsapp Group Chat

M: *Simon, I think Laura's Instagram post is a bit insensitive.*

S: *Why is that?*

M: *The tone of it for a start. 'Life has to go on'? Not for Peter it doesn't!*

H: *I agree with Miriam. She should take it down.*

S: *I'm sorry you both feel that way, but we can't wallow in misery like you. We've got kids. Anyway, Laura does her own thing. I can't tell her to do anything.*

M: *Do you really think it is appropriate to have a party a few days after your co-star died?*

S: *Co-star is a bit strong. Fellow actor, maybe.*

M: *Look, I know there wasn't much love lost between you and Peter. We all had our issues. He was a difficult man. But there is such a thing as decorum.*

S: *And respect! Everyone can see Laura's using this awful tragedy to promote herself and raise her profile.*

S: *Fuck you. Don't insult my wife.*

M: *Please think about it, Simon.*

H: *It's a wrong move, I'm telling you.*

S: *I guess neither of you will be coming, then? Oh, silly me. You weren't invited in the first place.*

Text exchange between Katheryn and Simon

K: *Peter told me all about the money you scammed from him. His account is now frozen following his death but see below my bank details. Please transfer the £50K to me within 24 hours. Barclays Bank: account number XXXXXXX sort code XXXXXX*

S: *Kathryn, I don't know anything about this.*

K: *I have Peter's bank statements. He followed your instructions and placed the money into an account you directed him to.*

S: *What? I'm baffled, Katheryn! It is honestly nothing to do with me.*

K: *If I have to get police involved I will. I want that money back.*

S: *I am sorry for your loss.*

Daily Express, Saturday, 2 September 2017
By Ken Thomas.
Headline: Milano family threaten to sue theatre

The family of Peter Milano are contacting lawyers and intend to sue the London Palladium if the actor's death is proved to be due to negligence. Milano died at the theatre on Tuesday, 29 August when a heavy weight struck him on the head during a performance of Leopard Spots. *The Palladium have denied any responsibility and police investigations are still on-going.*

Milano's wife, Katheryn, released a statement yesterday saying: 'I am still reeling, trying to come to terms with the loss of Peter. The death of my husband is not something I will ever recover from. I simply don't understand how such a thing could happen. He Facetimed me that day, at teatime, as he always did.

'His last words to me were: "I love you. See you tonight." A couple of hours later I got a call with the terrible news. My world collapsed. Peter was my life. My everything.

'I need some answers. He was at work, doing what he loved. What was the health and safety like at that theatre? Things can't just fall out of the sky like that and kill an innocent man. My lawyers are contacting the theatre management. Someone has to answer for what happened. Peter didn't deserve this. He had so much to live for.'

Fun facts: lion death
On 3 January 1872, a one-armed lion tamer Thomas Macarte, known as Massarti the lion tamer, entered the lions' cage for a performance with a travelling menagerie in Bolton market.

Attacked by the lions, he attempted to fight them off with his sword and a pistol loaded with blanks but they overcame him. Although other members of the show eventually forced the animals back into an inner cage, they dragged Macarte in with them.

Police statement from DI Serrano
The autopsy report on Peter Milano has now been completed. The head injury caused by the stage weight that fell from the flies was a serious one. However, in addition to the head trauma, a three-inch stab wound passed between his ribs and into his lung. While the head trauma may have proved fatal eventually, it is this injury that is the primary cause of death.

Due to this new development, this is now a murder enquiry and the London Palladium is a crime scene.

Chapter 31

Kitty Litter WhatsApp Group Chat

S: *Have you seen the news? They're calling it murder.*

M: *I don't understand. How can it be?*

H: *It's just one terrible shock after another. I've had to go back to bed.*

M: *They are saying there was a knife wound.*

H: *Yes, the autopsy examination. But how?*

S: *Who would stab the poor man?*

H: *It's ridiculous, isn't it?*

M: *So, the stage weight that fell — that wasn't an accident?*

H: *Is that what they think?*

M: *Well, looks like it.*

H: *Was he stabbed before or after the stage weight?*

M: *After, obviously. He was speaking to you before, wasn't he?*

S: *The police statement doesn't say much. I guess we have to wait and see.*

H: *I can't comprehend any of this.*

S: *Peter is dead. Hit over the head by a stage weight then knifed in the back as he lay there.*

M: *Stabbed in those minutes before the ambulance arrived?*

S: *Hang on. We were all there on stage. That means we are all in the frame.*

H: *Us and the others.*

M: *Who else was there? Taffy, Trevor, Spud?*

H: *And Gordon.*

Simon Gaunt police statement

I met Peter at the read-through for *Leopard Spots*. Mid 2016. He was friendly, he liked a laugh and a beer and we were mates. Used to take him up the East End for pie and mash with my missus, Laura. She thought he was a real gent.

I was in the left wing, a few yards away from the stage. Jayne, my PA was getting me changed. I had just taken some paracetamol as I had a banging hangover.

When Hermia screamed, I legged it on stage. I thought something had happened to her. You hear a bird in trouble you wade in, don't you? I saw Peter on the floor by the chair. By that time others were rushing on. Hermia was clinging to me like a koala. Well, a koala with one arm.

Then Trevor arrived and took charge.

I know Miriam and he clashed quite a bit – some argy-bargy going on there – but I'm going to miss him. He was very patient and helped me a lot with the old acting lark.

I don't think things were too happy at home. Katheryn kept him on a tight leash, and I got the impression there were money troubles. He liked to gamble. But as far as I'm concerned, he was a diamond.

Harry Grimshaw police statement

My name is Harry Grimshaw. Or Spud. I'm a stage tech. Set changes. Props. Maintenance. Whatever.

I just do my job and I'm not really mates with any of this lot. Some of the actors speak to me. When they're bored. Or want something.

Peter asked me if I could get him some spliff last week. Said he couldn't sleep. I told him he could probably buy some if he hung around Leicester Square.

When it happened, I was under the stage where there's a storage area checking the canisters for the smoke machine. They're locked in a fireproof case. I heard the noise. Two noises. One was the weight landing, I guess, the other was Peter hitting the ground. At the time I just thought he's knocked something over or tripped. Then I heard a shout, footsteps. I locked the case and went up the stairs to stage right.

Peter was on the ground, Trevor, Hermia, Simon, Gordon and Miriam were trying to help him. I ran straight on to see what I could do. The curtain was just coming down. I could only see Peter's legs. People were crowding round him. Someone shouted to call an ambulance, so I went into the corridor and called 999. I thought he'd had a heart attack.

To be honest actors are all a bit up themselves. Always squabbling or shagging. I just leave them to it. Peter and Trevor hated each other's guts, I know that much.

Hermia Saunders police statement

I'm from America and I genuinely believe I was born to play the role of Miss Simpson. I was guided to the UK by higher forces. The magic that happened onstage every night between Peter Milano and me was something very special: when two flawed halves become a perfect whole. I had an intense admiration for him, and we both felt a psychic connection. His death has devastated me.

It is very painful to discuss what happened. We were both in the zone, you see. Not acting, 'being'. When the weight fell my soul shattered. I only have flashes, shards of recall. As Miss Simpson, I remember screaming and falling into someone's arms, nothing more. But as Hermia Saunders – nothing whatsoever. A blank. Dissociative amnesia.

Peter was highly respected within the company – he was the silverback of our troop of actors – but lately I have felt a dark, malicious presence in our midst. I have used my intuitive skills to home in on where this emanates from. And I see the letter G.

Miriam Haughton police statement

I was thrilled to be cast in *Leopard Spots* with Peter Milano. He'd always been very underrated as a comedy actor I thought, although I'd never worked with him before. We got on splendidly. He was a delight although I think he found touring a bit of a strain at his age. The more I got to know him the more I realised he was a complex character. Maybe that's true of all of us? Always professional, but he had a lot of insecurities.

I had finished my cocktail scene and it had gone very well. I was behind a screen, stage right, in the quick-change area. My dresser, Gordon, was getting me out of my costume and into a towelling robe. I was just drinking some Evian water. It was obvious something awful had happened. Gordon looked round the screen and said something like: 'It's Peter. He's been hit.' Gordon ran out there at once. Then I followed, half-dressed. Peter was on the floor; he was breathing but his eyes looked blank. He was clammy. Simon was holding up Hermia. By then people were rushing to help, calling for an ambulance.

Peter had a few run-ins with Simon over the last few weeks. He was jealous of Simon's top billing, and I believe they came to blows on one occasion. All a bit undignified, poor man.

Gordon Griffiths police statement

I met Peter when I was employed as a dresser for the Edinburgh run. Fair to say we liked each other. A lot. I bowed out of the tour for reasons to do with my mental health but when I was told Peter wanted me by his side for the Palladium, I knew I had to do it. Some things are just meant to be. You can't fight love.

I was dressing that old trout Miriam Haughton in the wings when . . . when Peter was hurt. I ran on stage. I just had to. Surprised myself. I faint at the sight of blood normally. I can't even cut my own fingernails. Such a nelly, I am. But I knew he wanted me to hold him. Hermia Saunders was hysterical. She had hold of him and wouldn't let go.

I pushed her out the way. And that awful man with the poison pen, Ken Thomas. What was he doing there anyway? I wanted my face to be the last face he saw. I've been compared to a young Keira Knightley, you know.

Peter, or 'Daddy' as I called him, was simply too good for this world. He was everything to me and I hope he knew that.

I know he was married. He was the original reluctant homosexual, which I think is a book by Christopher Isherwood, or was it David Walliams?

Peter radiated star quality, even as his life ebbed away. What a pro.

Trevor Millicent police statement

Peter and I go back together to RADA in the 1970s. More of a reliable workhorse than a thoroughbred, but I cast him in my play *Leopard Spots* without hesitation. He had the perfect quality of faded good looks and insecurity that the role required.

By the time I got to the stage, having pushed my way down the row – row D I think I was in – and through the pass door, there were a lot of people trying to help. Chaos. As the director of *Leopard Spots*, I felt I should take charge. I called for the curtain to be raised and informed the audience that the performance had been halted due to circumstances beyond our control and to ask if there was a doctor in the house.

A woman came forward and then I asked everyone to stand

back. We laid Peter on his back, and she began trying to find a pulse. I could see it was hopeless almost at once, but I didn't let on.

Such a tragedy. Everyone was enjoying the play so very much. Er, and for Peter Milano, too, of course. Such a sad loss.

Miriam complained about Peter daily, to me. Because she loathed him it was agony for her playing his wife. The groping, his tongue in her mouth. But George and Geraldine weren't supposed to be happy with each other. 'Use the hate, don't let it go to waste,' I told her. But maybe it got out of control.

Jayne Oxley police statement
I'm Simon Gaunt's dresser, or personal assistant. I got to know Peter quite well on the tour. He was a sensitive man trying to live up to his image. He could be difficult, and he fell out with some of the actors from time to time but that happens. On his own he was quiet and reflective. Sad, even.

I was with Simon in the wings, getting him into his chef uniform. Whatever fell was very heavy. I felt the thud through the floorboards. We stopped immediately and turned in the direction of the stage. Simon went out there when Hermia cried out. I couldn't go. I was stuck to the spot. They were all over him.

Then someone found a doctor in the audience.

Of course, there were arguments among the cast, but I can't believe that anyone would harm Peter deliberately. Not like that, surely?

Ken Thomas police statement
I was in the audience. I'm a theatre critic. When it happened, I was just on my way back to my seat after an urgent visit to the loo. I saw Trevor Millicent sprinting towards the pass door, so I followed him. I've known Peter for many years. My instinct as a journalist made me come backstage. Always on the lookout

205

for a story and here was one happening before my very eyes. I needed to see what was going on to report it.

But I really do object to being kettled here like this. Can I please go about my business now? I know nothing else that can be of interest to you. Am I free to go?

Julian on the investigation

Don't worry, dear reader, if you are as confused as DI Serrano was by all this. He was so busy scribbling down their statements he didn't have time to assess who was telling the truth and who was acting. A slippery bunch, theatricals. They lie for a living. They get awards for it, even. So busy was Serrano, scribbling in his notebook, there are vital signs of possible guilt that he would have missed: the flicker of the eyes, the change in skin tone, the moist palms. They were all suspects, but he didn't know them well enough to spot the clues they carelessly dropped in their haste to implicate each other.

Only one among them had the knowledge, tenacity, and intelligence to follow the trails and uncover the truth. Jayne didn't know it yet, but this was to be her mission.

Chapter 32

Ken Thomas's blog, Saturday, 2 September 2017

Can an evening in the theatre where the principal actor dies be considered a triumph? No. Which is most unfortunate because the West End premiere of *Leopard Spots* was on course for great success that night: everything aligned, as it occasionally does, making it a sparkling evening, memorable for all the right reasons. The actors hit their spots, the dialogue was lively, and the atmosphere was pleasantly electric. The audience, many famous names among them, were enjoying themselves immeasurably: rocking with laughter when appropriate, hushed with anticipation as the skilful plot unfolded.

Until.

Until pleasure turned to horror, beauty to ugliness, good to evil. All in a nanosecond.

I have witnessed death before. A lover in the 1990s, staring bewildered at the hospital ceiling, not understanding how love could lead to this. My poor, ancient father, struggling to breathe, gave me a pitiful look and then released himself from this life. I once held a young girl in my arms after she was run over by a 176 bus on Camberwell High Street and wept as she choked on her own blood then became still and glassy-eyed seconds before the ambulance arrived.

But I've never seen a death like Peter Milano's. Mid-sentence. An actor, acting, holding the audience in the palm of his hand for the climax of the play, the pinnacle of his career, the greatest performance of his life . . . and then, as if struck by a meteor, dead before our eyes, his blood glistening under the stage lights.

As a theatre critic, I have known Peter and his work for many years, of course. He has been around for as long as I have. I haven't always been kind about him, but I like to think I have always been honest. The relationship between a critic and those he criticises is, by its very nature, a fractious one. He didn't like me. I'm not in the business of liking anyone particularly.

But who did this terrible thing? And why?

Jayne's diary, Saturday, 2 September 2017, London
Nathan left for work early. I just lay in bed listening to the sound of the Camden traffic. I'm trying not to think too much as I don't think it's healthy. Not if they are negative thoughts, anyway. I feel as if Peter's murder was a cannonball fired into my life and I'm left surrounded by the wreckage. Job? Gone. Love life? Gone. Prospects? Nil. The only thing thriving is my eczema. That's blooming. Lol.

Wondered what my mother's advice would be and decided she'd say: 'Fresh air and exercise!' so I got up, showered, had some Weetabix and went for a walk along the Regent's Canal.

Was like being back in the Midlands. Saw pretty, painted long-boats in Maida Vale, then I went past the zoo and saw giraffes and some noisy hog things, then I ended up in King's Cross and had an ice cream sitting on the grass. You could get a proper dinner in the café back home for what it cost me.

Every time I had sad thoughts about Robin, I distracted myself with tongue twisters that I make up, like: 'Peter Piper placed a perfect portion of pineapple on his pretty partner Petra's palate.' I have to say it perfectly three times, really quickly.

Then I feel better. But if it stops working, I make up a new, more difficult one.

'Did, dib, dob said delightful Dolly Diamond deciding to dilate the dimples on her darling derriere despite Derek's dominant demand to desist doing distasteful displays of divinity during December.' I got a few funny looks from office workers eating their sandwiches.

As I was walking home again Taffy called. In a right state.

'It's Gordon, love. He's been called into the police station for an interview.'

'No! For what reason?'

'I dunno. But I'm worried. God knows what he said in his statement. You know what he's like. He's a bit all over the shop at the best of times.'

'Oh gawd. He might have spilled the beans about him and Peter.'

'Definitely. He'd have enjoyed the attention, wouldn't he? Loves the limelight does Gordon.'

'He'll probably start crying.'

'Oh, for sure. He ought to have some legal advice or a decent solicitor, but he doesn't understand. Off he's gone, skipping into the police station like Judy Garland down the yellow brick road.'

DI Serrano interviews Gordon Griffiths, 2 September, 2017

DI: Could you tell us when you first met Peter Milano?

G: At the Edinburgh Festival a few days before the play opened. I was employed as a dresser.

DI: And what do you remember about that meeting?

G: As soon as our eyes met I just knew there was going to be something between us, like when Cher meets Nicholas Parsons in *Moonstruck*.

DI: Do you mean Nicolas Cage?

G: Was he in it too? Anyway, it was really obvious. I practically left a snail's trail across the floor I was so turned on. I like older men. Not usually as old as him, but that's my type.

DI: So when did the relationship begin?

G: During the second week of the run.

DI: What happened?

G: Er, well, I'd been giving him looks, if you know what I mean. Flirting with him. Then I noticed it being reciprocated. One day he said the flies on his trousers needed repairing. 'See, here,' he said and took my hand and more or less shoved it inside. Obviously, I had a good feel. Who wouldn't? Like a draught excluder it was! Next evening, he invited me for a drink at his hotel, the Scandic Crown.

DI: Did you go up to his room with him?

G: Yes. Obviously. We didn't have it off in the bar!

DI: So sex occurred that evening?

G: Well, to be specific it was in the early hours of the next morning. He had to take Viagra and it took a while to kick in. We watched a film while we waited.

DI: And how was it?

G: The sex or the film?

DI: Was the sex consensual?

G: What does that mean?

DI: Did you participate willingly?

G: I was gagging, to be honest. I'd had six Bacardis by then. I'd have had it off with a table leg.

Kitty Litter WhatsApp Group Chat

S: *Hey. Everyone OK? Anyone got any news?*

H: *The papers are still full of it.*

M: *I called into the Palladium today. There are things left in my dressing room that I need. I have a lot of expensive cosmetics. But they wouldn't let me past the stage door.*

S: *Jayne had laid out nibbles in my room for all my mates. Cheesy balls, hummus. They'll be humming by now.*

H: *According to the papers the cops are still searching for the murder weapon.*

M: *The knife?*

H: *I guess so.*

S: *Heard from anyone else? How's everyone doing?*

M: *Jayne is still in London. Poor girl doesn't know what to do with herself.*

H: *Have either of you heard from Spud?*

S: *Not a peep.*

M: *Nothing.*

H: *I'm in dire need of the herbal remedies he was getting for me. It's rather annoying. I wish he'd answer my messages.*

S: *Probably done a runner.*

DI Serrano interviews Gordon Griffiths continued, 2 September 2017

DI: After you had sex with Peter that night at the Scandic Crown what happened?

G: Well, it took me a while to catch my breath.

DI: Did you stay the night?

G: No. That's where it got a bit unpleasant. I closed my eyes, post-coitally – you know that warm glow you feel after you've had a good rogering? I was just nodding off when Peter said I should leave, if you please! His whole tone changed. He said it shouldn't have happened, was all a mistake and would I please go and never mention it again.

DI: How did you respond to the situation?

G: I was livid. Treating me like a common prostitute, I wasn't having it! I said I was staying put and then he said if I didn't get out he'd call the police. I started to cry but he was like a block of ice. I might have shouted a bit. Threw a few things around the room. That's the Bacardi, too. I'm all right with vodka but Bacardi brings out the devil in me. I took some photos of him naked on the bed with my phone, which made him furious. He chased me, trying to get my phone. That's where the forty-year age gap came in handy. I grabbed my clothes and the used condom and left.

DI: What were you intending to do with the photos and the used condom?

G: Dunno. A keepsake? I wasn't thinking straight if you'll pardon the expression.

Chapter 33

Jayne's diary, Friday, 8 September 2017, London

Went to St Paul's Church in Covent Garden this afternoon as there was a mass, vigil thing, whatever you call it, in memory of Peter. I wore my black stage clothes. Eczema has now spread to my forehead and cheeks. I look like I've been attacked by a cheese grater. Got some hypo-allergenic foundation from Boots and smeared that over. Looked too pale so I had a go with some bronzer. Now my face resembles an unwashed casserole dish with all the crusty bits left on. Sigh. But I guess no one is going to be looking at me anyway, so it doesn't really matter.

St Paul's is the actors' church, apparently. Photographers outside. Lots of people hugging and looking sad. His family, I guess, at the front of the church. I sat near the back but Hermia, despite her sunglasses, saw me and gesticulated, so I had to go and join everyone from the play in the second pew. As I shuffled past some people, I caught a glimpse of Spud in the very back row. We had a second of eye contact then he bowed his head and turned towards the door, scowling as usual.

Miriam was wearing a black veil which Taffy told me she'd asked her to make the day before. She was crying. I saw her blow her nose through the veil, which seemed a bit odd. Hermia was in a burnt-orange chenille poncho thing, which hid her sling rather well. She had a sad, serene expression and Simon was in a black suit and tie, which is the smartest I've ever seen him. Laura rather stuck out in a primrose yellow bodycon dress with a huge Louis Vuitton tote bag that was twice the width of her. Taffy was occupied with Gordon who seemed to be gagging, maybe because he was stuffing a black hanky in his mouth, mascara running down his cheeks.

There was a bit of classical music then the vicar told us how the church was a place of comfort and refuge for everyone, whoever we were. Just as the buttresses and pillars of St Paul's supported the roof under which we sheltered, so must we, in our hour of grief, soothe and console one another.

He then introduced Peter's widow, Katheryn, who, bless her, managed to do a Bible reading. I never understand these, but apparently our father's house has many rooms and there's a place waiting for us. It was nice but I was just pleased she made it through. Bit of a kerfuffle from Gordon at this point. Sounded like a puppy being strangled, but Taffy managed to calm him down.

Then the vicar, with a wry smile, told us we were about to hear Peter's favourite song. I couldn't believe it when Jane McDonald then came on wearing a red trouser suit and sang 'Blame It On The Bossa Nova'. It was quite the star turn. She was brilliant and even though we were in a church, and it was a solemn occasion, someone started clapping. I turned to see who it was, and it was the same, rather bloated man I'd seen on stage after Peter was knocked down.

'Ken Thomas,' said Taffy with a disapproving sniff. 'Journalist.'

But then others joined in the applause. It was a moment of light relief, frankly, before Trevor spoke. At length. On and on he went about Peter, their time together at RADA, the 1980s, the ebb and flow of relationships, the triumph of *Leopard Spots*, how it was snatched from his grasp.

I heard my stomach starting to growl, so I surreptitiously reached into my Tesco carrier bag where I found half a Greggs cheese-and-onion bake from earlier. By pulling bits off and slipping them into my mouth I managed to stop the tummy noises. Lol. I wasn't really listening to the rest of Trevor's speech but I remember it finished with some Shakespeare:

'Like as the waves make towards the pebbled shore,
So do our minutes hasten to their end.'

Beautiful. That set Miriam off and Hermia gave her a tissue which got caught up in her veil.

The vicar then wound things up with talk about the fragility of life and the lasting legacy of an actor's work. I got the feeling he'd said these words before, somehow.

Then it was the inevitable 'Amazing Grace', before we all filed out into the sunshine, relieved it was all over. There was more kissing and hugging and Gordon lit a cigarette which he smoked furiously.

We headed to the wake which was at the Bow Street Tavern. I saw Robin by the church gates, trying not to be noticed. He was the last person I expected to see, and my jaw dropped open. But I didn't react. Just closed my mouth and walked past him. I wanted to go and speak to him, ask what the hell was going on, but I resisted.

I was rather pleased with myself. He was dressed in a dark suit, trying to blend in with all the mourners, I suppose. He averted his eyes, so hopefully he didn't see how bad my skin was. Taffy, bless her, saw him too, guessed what was going on and squeezed my arm.

'Keep your dignity, love,' she said.

215

At the pub, Trevor made yet another speech about how wonderful Peter was and what a loss and so on. The run was to be cancelled but he hoped to revive it next year, hopefully. Blah, blah. No mention of the fact that Peter has been murdered, very possibly by someone in that very room!

Simon then said everyone should get drunk, that's what Peter would have liked. No one needed much persuading, even if it was only four in the afternoon. I just had a pineapple juice and a ham-and-cheese toastie. I joined a sort of queue to speak to Katheryn and I told her what a lovely man Peter was. She thanked me, then I went to back to the corner where all us *Leopard* people were. Laura was actually drinking Malibu straight from the bottle.

Miriam asked me how I was, wasn't it terrible, and all that. Her veil had been pushed back over head by now, looking not unlike a hairnet, had she but realised. Then she looked over her shoulder, to make sure no one was watching and took my hand and pressed some notes into it.

'I want you to have this, Jayne,' she said. I was shocked. I knew it was money. Not sure how much. Quite a wad.

'It's not your fault you're now out of work,' she said, whispering at me. 'You're a sweet girl, a lovely girl. If you need any more let me know. I don't want you to worry. About anything. Promise me?' I could tell the alcohol was taking effect.

'I don't need this,' I said to her. 'I'm still getting paid.'

'Take it,' answered Miriam firmly, pushing my hand away. Short of causing a scene I couldn't think of anything to do but reluctantly accept the money.

'How's your mum doing?' I said, to break the intensity.

'Not great, I'm afraid. She gets lonely and I know I should go and visit, but with all this going on I just haven't been able to.' Miriam looked as if she was going to cry. 'I telephone every day, but I'm not sure she knows it's me half the time.'

216

I thought I'd donate the money to the Camden food bank. Then I had another idea: I could buy a train ticket to Redhill and go and visit Alice. Take her some flowers, maybe. She might not remember me, but a visit of any kind would break the day up for her a bit. I was about to suggest this to Miriam when we were interrupted by Hermia.

'A hard day for us all, but we got through it,' she said, patting Miriam on the knee. 'But guess what? My agent says work is going to be difficult for me now. I shall forever be known as the woman who was on stage with Peter Milano when he was . . . killed.'

Raised voices then boomed across the bar and everyone fell silent, and heads turned. It was a confrontation between Katheryn, who was shouting in her rather deep voice at Ken Thomas. They'd been talking for a while, but things had suddenly flared up.

'So, what are you even doing here?'

'I've known Peter for decades!'

'You've just come to gloat, haven't you? Going to write some more horrible things about him on your stupid blog?'

'How dare you! I have over five thousand subscribers. People of quality. Unlike the scrawny crowd of D-listers gathered in this shithole.'

'Get out! You're not wanted here!'

'I know more about your husband than you do, Mrs Milano.'

'Oh, fuck off you sad, vicious old fool. No one wants to know.'

'Oh, don't they? Well, how about I do leave? Yes. I shall go home right this instant and start writing something new. Something you and everyone else will be very eager to read, I assure you. The TRUTH about Peter Milano!'

As he staggered towards the exit he kept going. 'Yes, folks! Coming soon! The whole, unexpurgated TRUTH about your dear friend Peter fucking Milano!'

Shortly afterwards Julian Clary weaved his way elegantly through the crowd to me and suggested we share a taxi back to Camden.

'I think it's time to ejaculate ourselves from the premises,' he said, jerking his head in the direction of Gordon, who was busy being sick into Jane McDonald's handbag.

Ken Thomas's blog, Friday, 8 September 2017
Several of my readers (not to mention the man himself) have asked me over the years what my beef with Milano was all about. It seemed to them to be irrational and obsessive. Over the top. But it was not, and I have decided to tell you why. Then you will understand.

So, I have decided to tell everything. The truth regarding Peter. It cannot harm him now and I feel you, dear reader, deserve to hear it from me.

This I will begin in my next blog. We must all gird our loins. It won't be easy for any of us.

Fun facts: St Paul's Church, Covent Garden
Designed by Inigo Jones in 1631. The first known victim of the 1665-1666 outbreak of the Plague in England, Margaret Ponteous, was buried in the churchyard on 12 April 1665.

ADVERTISEMENT

219

Chapter 34

Jayne's diary, Saturday, 9 September 2017, London
Taffy called me in the middle of the night.

'Jayne, it's me. Listen. The police have just been here. Half a dozen of them. They arrested Gordon on suspicion of murder. Took him away in handcuffs, took all his things, his laptop, phone, diary, clothes, everything. How can they possibly think he did this?'

I did my best to calm her down.

'It's a mistake, Taffy. They'll realise soon enough. I suppose they got wind of his affair, his anger at being a jilted lover.'

'They've put two and two together and made five.'

'Poor Gordon.'

'He was in a terrible state, he was. White as a sheet. Bewildered. That's before the police arrived. I'd given him a Valium to calm him down, he's that upset. Still saying he loves Peter and can't live without him. In a terrible state. I'd just got him to sleep on the sofa when they came barging in.'

'They must have found his letters to Peter. I've seen them. "Peter, You're the One that I want. I want you even more than John Travolta wanted Olivia de Havilland." He does come across as a bit deranged.'

'He's highly strung.'

'He doesn't do himself any favours, Taffy. "Roses are nice, violets are fine, you be the six and I'll be the nine."'

'He's young and broken-hearted, in the grip of a childish infatuation. But he's not a murderer!'

'I don't think for a minute he had anything to do with what happened, Taffy. It might look suspicious now, but they will realise they've made a mistake. The police must have proof, surely?'

'I'm supposed to be looking after him, Jayne! Now he's in a prison cell.' I made myself a cup of Wulfie's tea and sat down to think.

Kitty Litter WhatsApp Group Chat

S: *Gordon nicked? Un-fucking-believable!*

M: *Terrible, isn't it? But who knows what the police have found out.*

S: *I don't think Gordon could hurt a fly – even if he wanted to.*

M: *I don't know about anything anymore.*

H: *He has bad energy. I've been aware of it since the moment he arrived.*

S: *He's a bit weird, I grant you. But so is Michael McIntyre and he hasn't been arrested.*

M: *Gordon is impetuous and unpredictable. I saw the way he looked at Peter.*

S: *Just a kid, though!*

H: *You heard of the babyfaced killers in Central Park? Two kids, only 15. Stabbed a complete stranger 30 times and threw him in the lake.*

Jayne's diary, 6 p.m., Saturday, 9 September 2017, London
So, Gordon has been charged with Peter's murder. This doesn't sit right with me. Not at all. He's a strange lad, but not capable of murder.

Called Julian several times for a chat. He says exercise is good for clearing the head, so we've been on long walks with his little rescue dog, Gigi. Very cute, although Julian says she's a feral devil dog and the only command she understands is: 'Get thee behind me, Beelzebub.'

However much we try to talk about other things we keep coming back to what happened to Peter.

Julian said that as I know all the people involved in this better than the police I could probably do their job for them.

I am a dresser, too, I reminded him. We see everything and remember everything. They've got it so wrong about Gordon. I just wish I could call Robin and tell him they're making a mistake.

'I expect they'll realise that after the interview,' said Julian, trying to reassure me.

'I'm not so sure. Gordon will be frantic, but Taffy thinks he will also enjoy being "important". He lives for the drama. God knows what he'll say to implicate himself. You hear about these false confessions all the time! Shall I call Robin?'

'Even if Robin would speak to you, there's no point in saying you're sure it wasn't Gordon without any evidence. I went out with a policeman once, for about twenty minutes, and although I enjoyed taking down his particulars, I couldn't just say "See you Thursday", he needed written confirmation. About everything. I dumped him in the end for a florist, as I recall. There's a lot to be said for a man who arrives for a date with a red-hot poker in full, magnificent bloom.'

I expect Julian is right. I need to think. Rack my brains and come up with some proof. There must be something I can do but I don't know where to start.

Julian on Jayne's newfound role

The dog walks with Jayne have become a daily thing. I'm delighted to have her company and there is, let's face it, a lot to digest.

She doesn't mind doing the necessary with the poo bags either, after Gigi has made herself comfortable, which is a boon, what with my back twinges. (I might be a renowned homosexual but I can't do bending at the moment. The shame of it. I don't suppose Craig Revel Horwood has this trouble.)

It is a part of my masterplan that Jayne becomes the amateur sleuth in this story. Of modest stock, her steely determination and devotion to justice will propel her in the readers' eyes to a rank above any dubious police officer. We can trust our Jayne to get to the truth and not rest until Peter's murderer is uncovered.

Following my pep talk, she is now homing in on the facts, chewing them over, slowly and methodically like a pensioner with a digestive biscuit.

If Peter was stabbed then there was only a small window of opportunity for this to have happened, she says. Between the time that the stage weight fell and the police arrived. What can she remember? What about the previous weeks? Was there some clue she has overlooked, perhaps?

Frustrated as she is, there's a definite sparkle in her eyes when she's thinking this all through. How wonderful to be that clever and determined. I spend most of the day wondering where I put my glasses.

Then, when we sat down on a park bench for our mid-walk rest, Jayne produced a Tupperware box containing four home-made macaroons.

'Delicious!' I told her. 'Still warm from the oven, too!'

'Well,' said Jayne. 'I'm not buying shop cakes anymore, not after what happened in Plymouth with the cupcake.'

Then she became lost in thought for a while. Clearly there was something rather significant about the cupcake.

'OMG!' she said, but quietly to herself, and began scribbling in her notebook.

'Well?' I asked. Jayne took a bite of macaroon.

'The cupcake. It wasn't curdled butter cream. It was poisoned.'

'Excuse me?'

'What happened at the Palladium wasn't the first attempt to murder Peter.' She stood up and brushed the crumbs off her lap. 'They tried before! It can't have been Gordon. He ate the cupcake intended for Peter and ended up in hospital, seriously ill.'

At this point I intervened.

'We don't speak with our mouths full in Regent's Park, Jayne,' I cautioned her. 'You're not in the Midlands now.'

Jayne's diary, Sunday, 10 September 2017, London
The police obviously don't know the half of what's been going on. I keep thinking things over in my mind. The more I think about it the more I realise that the one who knows more than anyone else is me – not that I understand it. Yet. I keep waking up in the night and scribbling things in my notebook. I'm doing a lot of speculating, but I feel like I'm on to something at last.

So. Presumably we can discount the doctor who came forward from the audience. That leaves those that were crowding over Peter after the stage weight fell. That is when it must have happened.

Standing in the wings I had a clear view.

Peter was lying almost centre stage, the bloodied stage-weight to his left side.

Hermia stood a little downstage, facing the audience, screaming.

Simon was first on. He rushed to Hermia, who pulled herself away towards Peter.

By then Gordon was kneeling next to Peter, stroking his forehead, about to kiss him.

Miriam then appeared and kneeled the other side.

Hermia pulled Peter up onto her lap with Simon's help.

Spud came on, leaning over Peter next to Miriam.

Trevor came on stage via the pass door, took Peter's arm.

Ken was hopping around everywhere – there wasn't much space left until Trevor moved down stage and asked for the curtain to be raised. A few seconds after his announcement, the doctor from the audience came and asked for some space around Peter.

Trevor told them to get back.

One of these people stabbed Peter – possibly even tried to poison him. It must be possible to work out who it was.

Jayne's diary, Monday, 11 September 2017, London
I had a restless night and got cross with Robin who I badly wanted to speak to. By the time I heard Nathan making his smoothie in the kitchen I was seething. I marched in and told him I HAD to speak to Robin. I don't normally get shouty, but I figured that if I wanted to get results it might be my only option. I've seen those 'Good cop/bad cop' interviews on TV where one of them suddenly turns nasty. Sometimes bears fruit, so here goes. I took a deep breath and began bellowing. I might even have thumped the kitchen counter a few times with my fist.

'Listen, Nathan. I don't care if Robin's an undercover secret service or whatever he calls himself. I don't care if it's unethical. So he was sleeping with me when he was supposedly investigating whatever the great crime of the century was that was going on in the company before Peter's death!' I was surprised how deep my voice sounded. Like Peggy Mount.

'OK! Calm down, Jayne.'

'I won't calm down. I think the police investigating Peter's murder are getting it wrong. Supposing I've got information that could help?'

'You need to let them do their job, Jayne. I'm not being rude, but you're just a dresser. Maybe you've watched too many episodes of *CSI*?'

'Oh, really? But what if I'm right and they're wrong? Is it not worth a few moments of Robin's time to at least hear what I have to say?'

'All right,' said Nathan, holding his hands up in surrender. 'I'll try calling Robin. Just . . . make a cup of tea and sit yourself down.'

I did neither, but stayed where I was, glaring, while Nathan went into his bedroom. I heard him talking urgently on the phone in a pleading voice. A minute later he came back.

'Robin is really sorry, but no. He can't. Not while things are at this critical stage. He said to give you his love.'

I was furious. 'He thinks I'm just a silly girl who needs to be cast aside while he deals with more important matters, does he?' I sat down on the sofa in a huff.

Nathan sighed and sat down next to me. 'I can't say much. But Robin's work deals with major crime syndicates. This is not just about Peter's death. I think, in his own way, Robin is protecting you.'

The mention of protection made me think of the condoms in the bedside drawer. 'Well, should you speak to him again, please tell him that I don't need that sort of protection. I am perfectly capable of looking after myself.'

I got up to leave, but then realised none of this was poor Nathan's fault. He'd been kind enough to let me stay in his spare room and here I was shouting at him and making demands.

'Nathan, thank you for speaking to Robin. I'm sorry for

shouting at you. If you want me to leave . . .'

'It's all right, Jayne. It is a stressy situation. I understand.'

We exchanged grim smiles and I went into my room to think things over and work out what I should do next.

I was going to show Robin that he underestimates me. I would prove him wrong. The dresser is always brushed aside, undervalued and overlooked. But without us the show wouldn't happen. And maybe without me this murder won't be solved either.

I got out my trusty notebook and read through my scribbled notes. I needed to gather more information, to sift through what I knew and see if there was any more information I might have overlooked.

I had to start somewhere so I decided to contact Miriam. Out of everyone in the company she was the friendliest. I'd talk to her and see what might come up. I sent a text.

'Hi Miriam. Are you free to meet up for a coffee? If you don't fancy Greggs I could push the boat out and meet you at Starbucks?'

I waited a long time for a response, but she didn't reply. Maybe she was driving and couldn't look at her phone. Driving down to visit her mother in the care home, maybe? In the absence of any plan B, I decided to boldly go to Summer Breeze myself and intercept Miriam there.

Fun facts: how to spot an undercover cop
Keep an eye out for brand-new hoodies or other casual active-wear. Undercover cops frequently deck themselves out with hooded sweatshirts, warm-up jackets, and other sports-themed apparel to blend in with the crowd. While none of these items are suspicious on their own, they can look out of place when paired with other, less casual accessories.

Chapter 35

Fun facts: the cost of care homes
Fees will vary depending on the area you're in and the home you choose. On average, it costs around £800 a week for a place in a care home and £1,078 a week for a place in a nursing home. However, these are average figures – individual care homes may charge more or less.

Jayne's diary, Monday, 11 September 2017, London
When I arrived at Summer Breeze, I was in a bit of a tizzy, wondering what I was doing there. Nerves, I suppose. I'd had the whole journey to question the wisdom of what I was doing. So, I waited under a sycamore tree in the car park to gather my thoughts. I had to do this, I told myself. I was determined to speak to Miriam about Gordon's predicament.

Then, as I gazed at the glass entrance doors, trying to pluck up the courage to enter them, I saw a man dart out and head towards a battered old vintage car. He stood there, fiddling with his keys and rolling up the sleeves of his floral shirt. With a smile of satisfaction, he got into his car and roared off. It was that journalist Ken Thomas. What business did he have here?

I took out my notebook and listed the times he'd been seen before: at the Bath first-night party being thrown out by the security; on stage at the Palladium where Peter was murdered; at the wake, shouting at Katheryn, and now here, at Miriam's mother's care home. Curious.

I waited until I was sure he was gone for good then walked across the car park to the entrance, doing my best to look calm and relaxed.

There was a friendly nurse at the desk, wearing a name badge. Constance.

'Hi, Constance,' I said. 'I was wondering if Miriam Haughton was here, visiting her mother?'

'Not yet, but she is expected,' she smiled. Constance sounded Polish and wore a thin navy-blue cardigan over her nurse's uniform.

'Maybe I could wait? I've come to see Alice.'

'Ah, how nice!' smiled Constance, getting up and leading me down a corridor. 'You've been before, haven't you? I remember. She is popular today.'

'Oh, I hope she isn't too tired?' I said.

'I doubt it. She's having good day. Sleep most of the morning,' she told me with a chuckle. She seemed to be sucking on a boiled sweet.

'See these pictures?' She stopped at some cheaply framed drawings that lined the corridor. 'They are for sale, if you are liking them?' There were some cheerful flowers, some childish scribbles and some abstract art.

'Very nice,' I said.

'Our residents paint very well, yes?'

'They do,' I agreed.

'This one is Alice's,' said Constance, pointing to a staring face, gender non-specific, painted in dark colours.

'This was a few weeks ago when she was not so happy.'

'Do you know why?'

'It happens. I can't remember. Someone came, I think, that

229

upset her no end. Her daughter. Yes. She was distressed about it for some days. But you know, with the dementia, this happens. Then they forget, fortunately!'

'Ah, bless her,' I said.

'You want to buy one?' Constance asked hopefully.

'Maybe on my way out later,' I said diplomatically.

'OK,' she said with a shrug. 'All proceeds go towards our Halloween party. We are hoping to get enough for a Bruno Tonioli tribute act.'

'Is that expensive?' I asked doubtfully.

'Not so much. Thirty pounds,' said Constance. 'But he come in a see-through shirt, waves his arms around then does the splits.'

'Excellent,' I said.

We walked a little further along the corridor and then she stopped and opened a door.

'Alice. Another visitor for you,' she said, raising her voice as people do for the elderly. She gestured for me to go in.

Alice was sat in her chair by the window, eating a choc ice with a folded piece of paper on her lap. She smiled at me, but I don't think she remembered me.

'Hello Alice,' I said. 'I'm Jayne. I met you before with Miriam. You told me to come and see you again one day, so here I am.'

I gave her some delphiniums I bought from the station.

'They're lovely, thank you,' said Alice. 'Sit down, my dear.' I sat next to her, and she smiled at me blankly. 'What's on television tonight, do you know?'

'Oh, er, not really. What do you enjoy watching?'

'It's all rubbish, isn't it?'

'My father likes *The Chase*.'

'Never seen that. What's on tonight?'

'We need to look in the paper and find out for you.'

'Have you been on holiday?'

'No. I work in the theatre with Miriam.'

'My daughter works in the theatre, you know.'

'Yes, I work with her.'

'She's an actress.'

'I'm her dresser.'

'I was an actress. A proper one. What's on television tonight? Is there anything good on?'

'Miriam told me you were an actress. You were very talented.'

'Oh. Was I? Yes, I must have been. Very busy I was, once. I had an excellent review. Ken wrote it. He left me a copy. Poor Ken. Would you like to read it? It's years old. Wherever did I put it?'

Alice looked around the room, then with a tut to herself, picked up the folded piece of paper from her lap and handed it to me. I read it while she polished off the rest of her choc ice.

Daily Mail, Wednesday, 9 June 1982
By Ken Thomas.
Headline: *A Midsummer Night's Dream*, Wyndham's Theatre

Shakespeare's perennial masterpiece shines brightly in Tom Stoppard's production at the Wyndham's. The youthful, talented company of actors perfectly inhabit the world of sprites and mere mortals. It looks beautiful, too – Hugh Durrant's characteristically extravagant set shimmers with dewy summer colours and his costumes, restrained for the humans, let rip with fantastical shapes and colours for the spirits. Puck sprouts vine shoots and nasturtium leaves with red and yellow blooms that bob and bounce provocatively as he leaps about the stage.

But the stars of this play are Oberon and Titania and we are in very safe hands here. A smouldering Peter Milano is simply

231

magnificent as the King of the Fairies while Alice Haughton deliv-
ers a mesmerising Titania.

The physical attraction between Milano and Haughton is tan-
gible (and if rumours are to be believed requires little acting).
Bare-chested and exuding animal charisma, Milano's Oberon
makes rash wantons of us all, while Haughton brings such rare
presence and beauty to Titania we believe his jealousy without
question. They are the Richard Burton and Elizabeth Taylor of our
time. It is a rare, life-affirming thing to see two actors so in tune,
so in their prime, so brimming with talent and animal magnetism.
Catch them while you can.

It would be a tragedy for the future of the West End stage if, as
is rumoured, this pair were to be lured away to Hollywood.

So, Alice knew Peter! And Ken Thomas knew both of them!

'Wow,' I said, trying to digest this new information but sound
as calm as possible at the same time. 'That's a glowing write-up.'

'What's on television tonight?' repeated Alice.

I needed to know more about her time acting with Peter and
how she knew Ken, but I wasn't sure how to proceed.

'Why do you say "poor Ken?"' I asked gently.

Alice turned her head slowly in my direction and gazed at me
blankly with sad, watery eyes.

'Ken has always kept in touch. When everyone else abandoned ship he was there. From time to time, anyway. I guess we
have a strange kind of bond, you know.'

I didn't know but said encouragingly: 'Yes, I'm sure'.

Alice was talking, but not particularly talking to me. I
thought if I said too much, I might interrupt her flow. I listened
to her rambling, hoping I might be able to make sense of the
odd snippet.

'I enjoyed those days,' she said. 'All the fuss and attention. It
all came . . . naturally. All those lines I used to remember!'

232

Miriam had shown me photos of a much-younger Alice and now I could see the remnants of her beauty still there deep in her eyes and in the way the light settled on her cheeks. Inner beauty, maybe.

'There were always photographers jumping out at me. Everywhere. Do you like that woman who reads the news and nods her head all the time? I don't. She shouldn't do it. Irritating. Is she on tonight?'

'What was it like acting with Peter Milano?' I asked casually.

'Fiona Bruce! That's the one. Nod, nod, nod. Why can't she just read the news and keep her head still? I've got the foot lady coming later. Always asks me what colour I'd like my nails. I say green and then she paints them pink!'

I heard the stamp of a court shoe on lino and turned to the doorway.

'Jayne? What are you doing here?' It was Miriam and she looked furious.

I stood up to greet her, but Miriam grabbed my wrist and pulled me into the corridor outside Alice's room.

'Well?'

'I was waiting for you. I sent you a text and didn't hear back. I need to talk to you.'

'Why are you bothering my poor mother?'

'We were just chatting. When I came here with you, she told me to call again and—'

'She is a vulnerable old lady. Stay away from her.'

'It was you I came to see, Miriam. You didn't answer my text and I knew you'd be coming here, so . . .'

'I've got better things to do than reply to texts from a stupid, whining dresser. What is it you want? More money?'

'No! Miriam I thought we were friends. We need to help Gordon, go to the police and tell them they've made a terrible mistake.'

233

'Oh shut up! I'm not going anywhere with you! Gordon is a mad, vindictive little queer boy and he can rot in prison for all I care.'

'He's innocent, Miriam. He didn't murder Peter.'

'Well, the police think otherwise, don't they? And I know whose judgement I have more faith in.'

'And I know I'm right. Listen to me, please!'

'I've listened to enough of your drivel. I've had weeks of it. Leave it to the police and remember your place: I hate to be brutal but you're a common, provincial little nobody who thinks too much. The police have their man. Get over it. Log on to Tinder again and find another estate agent to fill your empty days.'

Miriam flicked her hands at me as if I was an annoying fly.

I found myself back under the sycamore tree in the Summer Breeze car park. I was reeling from Miriam's cruel words. I could feel my skin prickling, which was always the start of a new outbreak. I considered leaving a note on the windscreen of her Alfa Romeo which was parked just a few yards away. No. She had made her position very clear and I would be getting no help from Miriam. At least I knew what she really thought of me now.

I left the car park and began the walk to Redhill station.

Did I really think too much, as Miriam said? Now I had plenty more to think about.

I knew that Peter and Alice starred together in a hit production of *A Midsummer Night's Dream* in 1982.

Ken Thomas was also mixed up in all this.

My next move should be to go and see him . . .

Chapter 36

Jayne's diary, Tuesday, 12 September 2017, London
Found one of Robin's socks under the bed. Made me stop and wonder what on earth I was doing here, in his brother's flat. It's just a bit bizarre. Nathan just says things like 'You'll understand one day.' Well, maybe I will and maybe I won't.

I slept with the sock under my pillow. Then this morning I thought that was sentimental and silly of me, so I put it in the laundry basket.

Went for my daily dog walk with Julian. Thank goodness for him. He was agog about my trip to see Alice.

'How rude of Miriam!' he exclaimed when I told him what she said. 'I mean, you might be a bit rough around the edges and you wouldn't get into Ascot with anything you have in your wardrobe, but she's hardly blue-blooded herself!'

He then, very kindly, slipped me a piece of paper with Ken's address on it.

Julian on Ken
Well, yes, I did give Jayne Ken's address. She'd have found it on her own, one way or another, but I wanted to hurry this story along. This year's panto script won't write itself. And let's face

235

it, none of us want a scene where Jayne trawls through the electoral register before calling out 'Eureka!'

I also texted Ken to say my friend was on her way over to talk to him about Peter so could he please be kind. This saves me writing another load of minty dialogue from Ken. I think we've all got the general idea as far as that's concerned.

I'm not being funny but we're on the home straight now according to my editor, and she should know. She's got a grab-a-granny Kenyan Safari holiday booked, so completion date is coming through in red capitals at the bottom of her emails.

She's got it into her head that she'll be having a rampant affair with the park ranger – sultry looks across the campfire and tent flaps left invitingly open, that sort of thing. In my experience, these literary types have overactive imaginations, but she's got her bikini wax booked so what do I know?

I hope she packs lubricant and antibiotics though, that's all I'm saying.

Jayne's diary, Tuesday, 12 September 2017, London
Hampstead is all very twee and genteel, although the block where Ken lives looks suspiciously like ex-council. First floor. He buzzed me in and was waiting at the door, wearing a rather forced smile. His face was all shiny and moisturised and the flat had a self-conscious look about it, as if he'd had a quick tidy up before I arrived.

Small kitchen/diner/lounge. Whiff of last night's pizza coming from the bin and plenty of bottles on the counter: booze mainly, but a few dusty olive oil and balsamic vinegar bottles too. There was a lumpy armchair and a green two-seater sofa facing the TV and a little desk in the corner with his computer on it. He followed my gaze to it.

'Where the magic happens,' he said with a simper.

236

'Amazing!' I said. 'Lovely flat. Thank you so much for letting me come.'

'No problem at all,' he said, waving away my thanks. 'Any friend of Julian's is welcome here.'

'I'll try not to take up too much of your time. I brought you this as a thank you.' I gave him the bottle of Whither Hills sauvignon blanc that Julian plucked from his wine cooler as I left.

'It'll help to loosen his tongue,' he said with a knowing wink. Ken's eyes lit up.

'My dear, thank you so much! I was going to offer you tea but it would be rude not to open this, don't you think?' he said, reaching into a cupboard for two wine glasses.

As he poured the drinks and placed some crisps in a bowl on the coffee table he began talking.

'You want to know about Peter Milano, I gather?'

'I read a lovely review you wrote of *A Midsummer Night's Dream* in 1982. Beautifully written, very complimentary.'

'Yes,' agreed Ken. 'I was resident theatre critic for the *Mail* for several years. The public hung on my every word. Until I was sacked. Alice Haughton was quite extraordinary. Ethereal. Mesmerising.'

He took several gulps of wine and re-filled his glass. I'd only had a sip of mine. His eyes were rather bloodshot.

'And Peter? He was good too?'

'Not as good as Alice, but good enough,' he said grudgingly.

'You said in your blog the other day that you were going to tell the truth about Peter. Do you mind if I ask what that is?'

Ken inhaled loudly. 'Bold, aren't you?'

'I'm interested in the truth,' I said, holding his gaze.

'Be careful what you wish for,' he said menacingly, reaching for the bottle again.

I decided to wait. I sensed he wanted to tell me more but was hesitating, percolating. He got up and paced the room a few

237

times, as if wrestling with his own demons before, finally, the words came gushing out in a fierce torrent.

'That poor girl Alice . . . So sweet. Naïve. She was in love with Peter. But he destroyed her. Ruined her! Peter stole her career. Her whole future. Trashed it, wilfully. Now he is dead I can reveal all. I am writing a major piece about this for a national tabloid. Negotiations are almost complete. The truth about Peter Milano.'

'Can you give me a sneak preview?'

'Yes!' he cried.

Ken staggered over to his desk and opened a drawer where he rummaged around frantically.

He found what he was looking for and thrust it at me triumphantly.

'Here. Read this. It is an article I wrote about Alice in 1983. It was never printed. They stopped me from telling the truth then, but they won't this time.' He slumped into his armchair, conveniently close to the now almost empty bottle of wine which he finished hungrily as I read.

Unpublished article by Ken Thomas, Thursday, 13 October 1983
Headline: Down the rabbit hole with Alice Haughton

Alice Haughton's face is instantly recognisable these days. She is one of the mainstays of London's glittering West End where she has starred in a handful of consecutive hits for the last few years, and she has walked off with armfuls of awards and five-star reviews. Her bird-like beauty has graced scores of magazines and newspaper articles while theatre lovers wait with bated breath for her next role.

Inevitably, her private life has also been the subject of much speculation in the less savoury publications and it is a measure

238

of her star quality that she could look fabulous even when photo-
graphed late at night leaving Sheekey's or Annabel's on the arm of
handsome co-star Peter Milano, of whom more later.

But things change. Six months ago, she abruptly stopped work
to have a baby. A happy occasion, one would hope, although the
reality may be somewhat different.

I had supposed she lived in a splendid penthouse somewhere
like Mayfair but as I discovered, it is wrong to assume anything.
Instead, I was summoned to a modest flat in a, shall we say, gritty
part of South London to meet the star.

Not too concerning in itself but then I was greeted by a wan,
unsmiling Ms Haughton. Wearing slippers. Her newborn daughter
was asleep in a crib in the cramped, cluttered lounge. Strangely, no
agent or publicist was present. But things were to get stranger still.

We sat down with two mugs of weak tea, and I began by asking
her how she was enjoying motherhood.

'Bit of a shock,' she said, gazing over to the baby. 'She's very
angelic, don't you think?'

To be honest I couldn't see much apart from a crown of dark
hair and a bundle of white blankets.

'Might I ask about the father?' I say gently.

'Peter Milano is her father. Obviously. He's the only man I have
ever slept with. But Peter doesn't acknowledge that she is his
daughter. Must be the milkman. He's gone off to America, hasn't
he?'

Is she getting some support from her family? It seems not. The
Haughtons are strict Catholics and her unmarried status on top
of her scandalous choice of career means she has no contact. The
situation is very sad and a horribly sudden change of circumstan-
ces. But this is 1983 – surely, she can return to work when she is
ready? She huffs at this suggestion.

'Really?' is all she says. 'Showbusiness feels like a distant, un-
happy memory, to be honest. I never much liked it, anyway.'

239

I leave Alice Haughton feeling very sad. She may have lost so much in her life, but she has gained, too. A beautiful baby. And, of course, she still has her talent and her beauty. No one can take that away.

'Oh my,' I said, handing the yellowing page back to Ken. 'Why was it never published?'

He turned his eyes to me and his complexion flushed pink. 'Because there are times when the truth is inconvenient.'

'But poor Alice!'

'You think I didn't fight to get it out there? But there were higher forces at work. Peter always denied he was the baby's father, accused Alice of sleeping around. His agent got him an audition in Hollywood, and he was off. Family life was not good for his image.'

'I guess not.'

'But there were photos of Alice buying cut-price baby food at Deptford market while the father of her child was rolling around half-naked on a beach with Jane Fonda in a terrible film!'

'How could he be so heartless?'

'Peter never had a heart. He was a rogue.'

We sat in silence for a moment. I felt a wave of gratitude towards Ken for sharing this information with me. I was shocked and grateful. It was, after all, going to be Ken's big, lucrative, newsworthy scoop to finally reveal what he knew after all these decades of silence.

'Ken, thank you for—'

My words were cut short as the front window of the lounge seemed to suddenly explode and I was thrown to the floor.

Shards of glass flew towards us, shattering the overhead light. Ken somehow ended up whimpering behind the sofa. I was frozen.

It finished as suddenly as it started. We both slowly peered around us. The broken ceiling light swung mockingly backwards and forwards and there, on the table, was a large masonry brick, dust rising from it as if it had just been catapulted into Ken's Hampstead flat from outer space.

'Are you OK, Ken?' I asked.

He didn't answer but pointed at the rock. I saw now that a piece of paper was roughly taped to it.

'What is it?' whispered Ken.

'Do you want me to look?' I asked. He nodded; eyes wide with fear.

It took a moment to detach the message but I uncrumpled it and spread it on the table. Written in big, crooked capital letters were some words which I read out to Ken:

'STAY QUIET OR ELSE!'

'Go home. Quickly. And stay there,' said Ken.

'You can't stay here, Ken,' I said.

'Too right I can't!' said Ken, grabbing his keys and jacket. 'I shall go and stay with my friend Damien. He lives in Ealing, but it's no time to be picky. You had better forget everything I have told you, for your own good.'

A few minutes later, I was on the Tube back to Camden. I could see a small piece of glistening glass caught on my trainer. Poor Ken had been quite shaken up and couldn't wait to leave his own home. But despite what he'd told me I knew I couldn't forget what I'd learned that evening. I had to plough on. Even if I hadn't got the faintest idea where it was all leading.

241

Chapter 37

Jayne's diary, Tuesday, 12 September 2017, London
When I got off the Tube, I called Julian, but he couldn't really talk as he was working, presenting the LGBT+ Bus Shelter of the Year Awards. He said he'd get sacked if I told anyone, but the top prize was going to High Wycombe.

'You wouldn't believe it, Jayne. They've not only got a rainbow-painted awning but hanging baskets and heated seating! It's dreamy. A well-deserved win. Must dash.'

Now I was back in the safety of Nathan's flat, where I was introduced to his boyfriend, Darius. Darius clearly goes to the gym a lot and wears a vest. They kindly invited me to join them for dinner. I didn't tell them about what had happened, it was just good to be safely home, doing something normal. I realised I was starving, too.

We had roast chicken with potatoes, carrots, and spinach and then a Greek dessert that Darius had made called something like balaclava, but not that. They were really nice and friendly but when they drew the curtains and put on a DVD of *Brokeback Mountain*, I decided I'd better give them some space, so I thanked them and said I was going for a lie down.

'You don't need to go, Jayne,' said Nathan. 'We're not planning on re-creating the scene in the tent, you know.'

'I've never seen the film, but I don't mind what you do!' I laughed. 'I'm tired, though. If I fall asleep on the sofa my snoring might disturb your viewing pleasure. Thanks for the lovely dinner.'

Fun facts: Greek dessert
Baklava, a rich pastry of layered filo dough, nuts, and honey, is a classic Greek dessert with roots tracing back to the Byzantine Empire. Its history reflects the influence of various cultures on Greek cuisine.

Jayne's diary, Tuesday, 12 September 2017, London
Truth is, I wasn't tired at all, but I needed to get my thoughts in order. I now knew that Alice and Peter allegedly had a child together that Peter never acknowledged.

Ken knew and is now being threatened.

But who is the crazy person throwing bricks through windows? And what has the past got to do with the present? The murder?

I needed to keep going and investigate more. I just didn't know what or who to believe.

The trouble with theatricals is they thrive on gossip, rumour and exaggeration. They can't help it. They live for the drama and as we all know, Chinese whispers can distort the facts in no time.

I remember once being told by a certain actress she'd heard that the leading male actor in the company was a foundling, who'd been abandoned when he was eight weeks old wrapped in a copy of the *Staffordshire Gazette* in the public toilets in Battersea Park, poor boy.

I made a few discreet enquiries and got to the truth, which was a tad more mundane: he'd once adopted a two-month-old Staffie pup from Battersea Dogs' Home. In the telling and re-telling it had somehow morphed into an episode of *Long Lost Family*.

I needed facts. I googled Peter Milano, and hidden away in a section about his ill-fated foray into Hollywood I found a review of the one film he'd made there.

Time Out, Wednesday 5 September, 1984
By Lindsay Point.
Headline: *Don't Hurt Me* is a tough turkey to swallow

Sometimes a film is so bad it's good. It might, in ten or twenty years' time, gain a cult following in independent cinemas frequented by dope-smoking mature students. Not in this case. Don't Hurt Me *is so bad it is surely destined to be forgotten quicker than a husband's business trip 'massage' with extras. In fact, as soon as I've filed this review, I'm going to deny I ever saw it.*

Quite what possessed Jane Fonda and Peter Milano (who? Well, exactly) to join forces for this turkey beats me. It's basically a story about a divorcee who meets a gigolo. And then . . . oh, I just can't. The beach scenes look nice, I'll give them that. Jane in a sarong. Whoever-he-is in a pastel linen suit. Mute the dialogue and you might have a Bon Jovi music video. On the other hand, you might not.

Take my tip: Don't Hurt Yourself by watching this shitshow. Stay home and self-harm instead. It will be less painful.

Text exchange between Taffy and Jayne

T: *You OK, love?*

J: *Not bad. A lot going through my mind, trying to make sense of it all.*

T: *Good luck with that, love.*

J: *Did you know about this film that Peter was in with Jane Fonda?*

T: *God, yes. Everyone was banned from talking about it but it's how he met his first wife.*

J: *Who was that?*

T: *Well, he flopped in Hollywood then came back home with his tail between his legs. No one wanted to know, and it was all doom and gloom until Lady Donna – who was the only fan of the film and a fitness fanatic – singled him out. She LOVED that film. And she wanted to make Peter a star, you see.*

J: *He'd have loved that.*

T: *Wouldn't he though? Anyway, I was calling to see if you've heard the latest?*

J: *What's that?*

T: *Brace yourself. Apparently, there are rumours that* Leopard Spots *might continue its run one day. But with Trevor taking over Peter's role!*

J: *What?!?*

T: *I know, love. Bit tasteless, isn't it? I mean, the Palladium is still a cordoned-off crime scene.*

J: *I'm speechless.*

T: *Who knows if it's true or not. I need to go and spread my whiskers now. Ta-ra, love.*

Jayne's diary, Thursday, 14 September 2017, London

The police have finally finished their search of the Palladium. Taffy and I have been sent to pack everything up backstage, while the crew dismantle the set and lights onstage.

It was different from a normal pack-up day where everyone is bustling about trying to get the job done as quickly as possible so we can move on to the next venue. The rumours about the run continuing with Trevor in it didn't seem to be true. This all felt very final. Plus, it was sad going back to where Peter died, re-visiting the scene.

In their fruitless search for the murder weapon, the police

245

had turned everything upside down so it all looked messy. Lots of grey dust from the fingerprinting. There was an atmosphere of death, somehow.

'Giving me the shivers in here,' said Taffy.

'Me too,' I said. For a while we just stood in the corridor not sure where to start. Then Taffy rolled up her sleeves and put on her determined look.

'Right then. We've got a job on our hands here, Jayne. I'll start sorting the costumes into the trundle wardrobes and props into the wheelie skips. You clear the dressing rooms.'

On the night of the murder everyone had left their personal belongings behind. Now I was given a box for each dressing room and told to put their stuff in so it could be returned to them. It was difficult going into Peter's room. Still a whiff of his aftershave in the air, but it all looked forlorn, abandoned. I felt myself about to cry so I had a big sniff and pulled myself together.

The police had been poking around and dusting for finger-prints. There were flowers, which were dead, so I threw them away, keeping the messages. I put all his personal bits and pieces into the box to be given to Katheryn. Make-up. Hairbrush. Scented candle. First-night cards from friends and family were pinned on the cork board next to his mirror, so I took them down and put them in the box too. Then in the bottom drawer, tucked under the lining, I found a card which the police had obviously missed.

[Teddy bear image.]
I know this is all you dream of. Now is your time to shine.
Sending you on your way with love,
Gordon. Xxx

I decided Katheryn probably didn't want this and put it in my pocket.

Hermia's room was quite a job to sort out. Make-up, brushes, bottles of cosmetics, primer, moisturiser and cleanser, incense burner, dirty cotton wool pads all strewn over the dressing table. A half empty bottle of whisky. These I put into plastic bags and packed in the box. An ashtray overflowing with cigarette butts and roaches overturned on the floor, which I emptied and washed in the sink. Clothes, underwear, a sling had been flung onto the armchair, so I folded and packed these too.

Simon's room was the worst, though. All the food I'd laid out for his friends was still there, stale, mouldy and dotted with mouse droppings. Flies everywhere. I tipped the lot into a bin liner. He didn't use much make-up, just anti-shine cream and powder. In his ensuite there was a small mirror with smear marks on — I guess from his pre-show 'livener' of 'Charlie' as he called it.

Finally, Miriam's room, which was very spick and span. Everything just so, her expensive make-up organised and laid out on a small decorative towel with brushes to the left, foundation, lipstick, eyeshadow and blusher to the right. I transferred everything into the box. Her good luck cards weren't on display, but piled neatly in a drawer. Being nosey, I looked through them all. I'd done this with everyone else too. Heartbreaking, really. All that goodwill, all those hopes, wishes and congratulations, dashed and destroyed in a second, to be replaced by sudden, unforeseen tragedy and sadness.

Then, at the bottom of the pile was a folded sheet of A4 paper. It looked like it might be a bill or a bank statement. I unfolded it and read. It was a computer print-out from a DNA Testing company.

Saturday, 21 July 2017

The results of the analysis are shown in the following table.

Based on our analysis it is proven that Sample A is the biological father of Sample B.

For a second I didn't quite understand what I was reading. I thought it was some kind of blood test that was none of my business. But then I read it again and realised the significance of the information. DNA . . . Proven . . . Biological father . . .

Suddenly my heart was thumping in my chest and my mouth went dry. Holding the paper in my hand, I paced up and down. This information proved that Miriam was Peter's daughter.

My mind flashed back to mid-July in Brighton when Miriam wanted Peter's hairbrush so desperately . . . this must have been when she wanted to order the test. A strand of hair to send off . . .

I read the analysis for a third time and then fixed my eyes on the date. About a week after the hairbrush business. We had been in Birmingham. That was why Miriam had been in such turmoil, disgusted by the kissing scene with Peter. Well, no wonder. It was also only a few days before Hermia fell through the trapdoor. Just a coincidence?

My breathing became faster and shallower, and I covered my mouth with my hand as I had the thought: what if that wasn't an accident but an earlier attempt on Peter's life?

I took my hand away from my mouth and formed a fist with it and gently thumped myself on the forehead. Think! Maybe . . . Could Miriam have been so horrified by the news that Peter was her father, the man responsible for her mother's ruined life, that she was the one who wanted him dead?

Suddenly I knew what I needed to do. Go to Birmingham. Back to the theatre and see what I could find out there. There is clearly more to this story than the police are willing to see.

Fun facts: DNA
DNA is found in every living organism, including bacteria, plants, animals, and humans. The structure of DNA is similar in all organisms, with only minor variations.

Trevor Millicent: notes for archive
Out of the ashes rises a phoenix. I feel the first stirrings of a new masterpiece. A play within a play. The starring actor is murdered, but by whom?

Chapter 38

Jayne's diary, Friday, 15 September 2017, Birmingham
By the time I arrived in Birmingham and took the short walk along Dudley Street to the Alexandra Theatre, I had formulated my plan. I had to somehow blag my way in and get under the stage to see what I could find where Hermia's trapdoor fall happened. So long as Jake was working the stage door today, I thought I had a good chance. And there he was, sat just inside in the little cubby hole.

'Jayne! There's a surprise!' he exclaimed. Like all stage-door workers he loved gossip. He would have been glued to the news about all that happened at the Palladium and as I had been at the eye of the storm, there was lots I could tell him, and I intended to use this to my advantage.

'Oh, Jake,' I said, opting for a wan smile. 'It's good to see you.'

'Let me make you a cup of tea, girl,' he said, giving me a hug across the counter. 'It must have been terrible for you,' he said, patting me gently on the back. 'Tell Uncle Jake all about it. I remember that weirdo Gordon hanging around here. If only I'd known what he intended to do. But they've got him now.'

It wasn't necessary for me to express my doubts about Gordon's involvement in Peter's murder. In fact, if that's what

Jake believed, it could be to my advantage. If he thought I was snooping he might not give me access to under the stage.

'It's been awful, Jake,' I said, with a crack in my voice.

'Did you see it happen? Was there a lot of blood?'

Sympathetic as he was, Jake clearly wanted the gory details. Never mind my PTSD.

'I was just a few feet away,' I told him. 'I saw everything.' Jake gasped, clearly thrilled.

'Tell me everything,' he said. It was a wonder he didn't open a bag of popcorn. I relived it all for him including, possibly embellishing, the salacious aspects that I thought he'd enjoy, right up until the moment the police said we could finally go home.

Jake drank it all in, clutching an invisible string of pearls around his throat, wide-eyed with the horror of it all.

'Oh, Jayne!' he said, exhaling loudly. 'You poor thing. But you're home now, where you belong. Going to your dad's for a good rest, I hope?'

Now was the time to put my plan into action and hope it worked.

'I've got to go back to London. Still things to sort out.'

'Why are you here then, girl?'

'Well, I'm hoping you can help me, Jake.'

'Of course!'

'You remember the night Hermia had her accident?'

He nodded. 'How's she doing? Still plastered up?'

'She is,' I confirmed.

'Expect she has trouble rolling her spliffs with her right arm out of action, eh?' He pursed his lips and nodded knowingly.

'She's still pretty traumatised by everything, I'd say.'

'I bet she is.'

'I'm here because she's lost an earring. Great sentimental value. Ruby. A present from her husband. She thinks it must

251

have fallen out when she fell through the trapdoor here that night.'

'All those weeks ago and she's only just realised?' Jake looked doubtful.

'Well, she is quite dizzy, as you know.'

'Ain't that the truth!'

'She thought she'd lost it at home. Turned the place upside down. Now she's convinced it's here. Under the stage. I've been sent to look for it.'

'You want to go down there, girl?' he looked horrified. 'It's filthy. Manky. Mice and rats and gawd knows!'

'It would be worth it if I could find the earring, though. Hermia would be so happy. Just a quick look around.'

I realised Jake was worried that I'd expect him to come with me and chivalry wasn't one of his qualities.

'I know you can't leave the stage door. I'll just nip down. I've got a torch on my phone.'

'I'd come with you but I'm expecting a delivery of hand sanitisers. We've got *Annie* opening next week and you know how germ-ridden children are,' he grimaced.

Jake directed me to a small door at the back of the stage. 'When you get down there turn right and you'll be under the stage. Go straight ahead. Trapdoor is about fifteen feet away. Go carefully, won't you?'

'Thanks, Jake. I'll take good care.'

'If you're not back by midnight I'll send a search party.'

I took a deep breath, switched on my torch and descended the narrow concrete stairs. I was nervous about what I might discover. It was pitch dark with just a few cracks of light coming through the stage floorboards above me. I could just about stand up, but I felt the soft stroke of cobwebs in my hair.

The air was dry and dusty. I swept the torch beam slowly from left to right and moved cautiously forward, listening to the sound of my own breathing. I found the trap door mechanism. A few feet to the right was the equally ancient operating mechanism, a large wrench with a handle and some spoked, inter-connecting wheels, like a giant version of inside a clock.

Here and under the trapdoor were footprints and scuff marks, no doubt from the night Hermia fell through. There was a large metal bolt fixing it shut. It was intact, I noticed. For the trapdoor to open someone must have opened that bolt.

There wasn't much else to see. I swung the torch around a few more times. Some boxes in the far corner, a mound of forgotten old theatre drapes. Nothing. Then something weird glinted in the torchlight.

What was that? A small, flat object. It looked out of place there, when everything else was had an undisturbed, graveyard feel to it. I moved towards it and poked it with my foot. Plastic. I picked it up for a closer look. There was a strong, unpleasant scent. I didn't want to but I forced myself to sniff it. Fish! I held it at a distance and shone the light on it. Sardine-flavoured vape.

Spud! Spud had been here.

There was a sudden loud creak behind me and a fan of light which jolted me back to the present.

'Find anything, girl?' called Jake.

Suddenly I wanted to get out of there.

'Nothing,' I called back. 'Coming back up now.'

Back at the stage door, Jake made more teas and although my mind was racing with other thoughts I had to listen politely as he told me about his night out at the Nightingale and then about his plans to decorate his lounge.

'What do you think? Jasmine White or the grey of Elephant's Breath?'

'Oh, er, yes, that sounds lovely,' I said, my expression glazed. I excused myself and went to the loo to think in peace.

253

Spud was involved somehow. Maybe he knows some secrets. Was Spud the murderer?

Or maybe he was in cahoots with Miriam – I had noticed weeks ago that there had been some strange behaviour between them. Robin had always been suspicious about Spud. He needed to know about my discovery. It was AWKS but I had to make contact. I knew he wouldn't answer his phone and I didn't fancy the indignity of being ignored, so I decided to send a message. To emphasise the urgency, I used capital letters. In bold.

Text message from Jayne to Robin
J: I AM AT THE ALEXANDRA THEATRE. SUB-STAGE THERE IS EVIDENCE ABOUT SPUD THAT YOU NEED TO KNOW ABOUT. SEND SOMEONE ASAP

Robin might not be speaking to me for whatever reason, but he read my message, that much was clear. I saw the double tick.

Five minutes later, as Jake and I were finishing our tea, I heard police sirens and they were headed our way. Suddenly police burst through the door with sniffer dogs demanding to be shown sub-stage.

'What?' said Jake, his jaw dropping.

'I called them,' I said. 'I can't explain why, but I had to.'

Jake lifted the counter and took the police and the dog handlers through, glaring at me as he went.

'What's going on?' he asked.

'Sorry, Jake,' I said. 'But it is important.'

When he came back, we stood in silence, Jake looking pale and worried as another police officer stood guard next to us.

A few minutes later, I heard a dog's excited barking from below us followed by running footsteps and a bustle of activity from the men in uniform.

'We've found something,' I overheard. Then Jake and I were

told to leave immediately as crime scene tape was unfurled across the stage door.

'I'm going back to London,' I told poor, bewildered Jake.

'Oh,' he said. 'I see. I didn't expect to find myself in the midst of a drama when I woke up this morning. But you never know what the day ahead holds, do you?'

'Just think,' I told him, 'You'll have something to talk about at dinner parties, won't you?'

'Ah, yes,' he said, his eyes sparkling. 'I will! And you see that crime scene tape? That's just the shade of orange I want for my dining room.'

As I sat on the train back to Euston, I felt pleased with myself. I had thought to look where Robin and his police friends hadn't. And now, given the flurry of sudden activity, something important had been discovered. My money was on the murder weapon. The knife. I'd led the police to its whereabouts.

But how had it got from the London Palladium to the Brum Alexandra? The answer seemed to lie with Spud, who was now in it up to his neck.

I couldn't help feeling impressed with my own sleuthing abilities. I might be a humble dresser, but my powers of deduction were superior to those of secret policeman Robin, it seems. Lol.

I have left several messages for Ken, but he hasn't responded. I hope he hasn't encountered any more bricks.

Voice message from Taffy to Jayne

'Hello my lovely. Just been to see Gordon at Brixton prison. He's doing all right. Better than I thought. I expected him to be destroyed. He's got a good solicitor and they're doing their best to get him out on bail but doesn't sound too hopeful.

He looks shell-shocked, poor lamb. They've got his letters to Peter and these incriminating photos though, see, and the police see him as some kind of stalking blackmailer. Load of

255

old tosh. They've got no evidence. How could they have? It's all just circumstantial, see.

Anyway, he's a fickle lad, always has been. He's now got the hots for Detective Inspector Serrano. Says he's been giving him the glad eye. Playing footsie under the table during negotiations. It's all in his imagination. But at least it's taking his mind off things.

He's sharing a cell with a man in his forties. Shoplifter. He's looking out for Gordon, which is nice. They seem to be getting on OK. Keep your chin up, I said to him. Bye love.'

BBC BREAKING NEWS: second arrest over Palladium mystery

Birmingham Gazette, **Saturday, 16 September 2017**
By news desk.
Headline: Police close Alexandra Theatre

Mystery surrounds the sudden closure of the Alexandra Theatre in Birmingham yesterday. Officers and dog handlers swooped on the theatre, evacuating the building and sealing all entrances. Performances of The King and I *starring Matthew Kelly have been suspended.*

A police spokesperson said that they were investigating a 'significant discovery'.

A major haul of class A and B drugs is rumoured to have been found, but this has not been confirmed by police who are remaining tight-lipped.

Theatre manager Zoya Bajwa said: 'We hope this unforeseen matter can be dealt with swiftly so we can get back to business. We apologise to our customers who were looking forward to seeing this wonderful production. We are cooperating with the police, but they have given us no indication of what it is all about.'

Matthew Kelly, who has shaved his head to play the role of the King of Siam, said 'Such a shame, isn't it? Is it a drugs bust? I hope they haven't found my stash of senna pods. I've had to console myself with a very large glass of merlot. Cheers m'dears! Does anyone know if we'll still get paid?'

Stage door man Jake McIntosh, who was on duty at the time of the raid, said he was shocked by the sudden events. 'One minute I was having a cup of tea with a friend and the next minute we were turfed out onto the street! All I can tell you is that they were very interested in something they'd found sub-stage. Maybe that's where Lord Lucan has been hiding all these years?'

There is some speculation that the drama is somehow connected to the ill-fated play Leopard Spots *which played to full houses at the Alexandra just a month before the on-stage death of Peter Milano at the London Palladium on 29 August.*

Meanwhile, a second person has been arrested by police investigating Milano's murder.

A man, believed to be in his thirties, was taken into police custody late last night. No further details are available at this time.

BBC breaking news: Second person arrested in Milano murder

The person arrested by police yesterday in connection with the murder of Peter Milano has been named as Harry 'Spud' Grimshaw, a theatre technician.

The police statement reads: 'Harry Grimshaw is currently under arrest and is being questioned. This is a fast-moving situation, and we will update you as soon as we have any more information.'

A police spokesperson would not confirm whether a raid at the Alexandra Theatre was related to their investigation.

Meanwhile, it has also been reported that Peter Milano's body has been referred for a second autopsy.

Jayne's diary, Saturday, 16 September 2017, London
Taffy called me, all breathless.

'You'll never believe this, but Spud has been arrested. I didn't see that coming, did you?'

I didn't let on, but yes, I did see it coming. In fact, my poke around the dusty sub-stage at the Alexandria set this whole investigation on a completely different course. I made it happen! I got quite a buzz out of it, actually. Plus, the fact no one, apart from Robin, knew it was me. I expect this is how arsonists feel when they set fire to a building and then stand and watch all the fire engines arriving.

I'm more powerful than I thought. Powerful, but confused, too. I thought they'd found the murder weapon at the Alex. No one was saying anything about that. Seemed to be about drugs.

'Is that why Peter's body is now being sent for a second pathology report?'

'Exactly. They're looking for drugs in his system, see.'

'Do you think Spud is the murderer?' I asked Taffy.

'God knows, love. It's the drugs, isn't it though? But maybe Peter found out about them and that's why he got bumped off. I don't know. That kind of thing happens all the time. Drug dealers. They're like the fucking mafia.'

Kitty Litter WhatsApp Group Chat

H: *Well, I've just had my belongings from the dressing room uncoremoniously delivered to my home in a taxi.*

M: *Me too.*

S: *Yeah, same.*

M: *Charming way to find out that we are no longer gainfully employed. Looks like the play can't run with Trevor in the role. It would have been a bit off, anyway.*

S: *Trevor is fuming. He wanted to carry on, says it's health and safety gone mad.*

M: *Tasteless of him. You know Spud has been taken in for questioning?*

H: *I sense no malevolence in Spud. Just a poor, damaged soul. Gordon, on the other hand . . .*

S: *Where am I going to get my coke from now?*

M: *Really, Simon!*

S: *Laura says you can buy it from the nail bar in Chingford. Apparently if you ask for a Magic Dip Full Set in Lucky Lavender you get three grams of Colombian wrapped in a tampon as you leave. Happy days.*

M: *I don't want to hear this.*

S: *Soz.*

H: *Do you think any of us will ever work again after all this?*

S: *Well, a little bird tells me Trevor's creative juices have been flowing thick and fast.*

M: *Meaning what exactly?*

S: *Well, just between us, he wants us to all get together and workshop an idea he's got for a new play.*

H: *About what?*

S: *About a murder. One of us did it but no one knows who.*

M: *Rather ghoulish.*

H: *Cathartic, though, maybe?*

Police interview with Harry Grimshaw AKA Spud conducted by Detective Robin Kowalski and DI Serrano. Grimshaw's solicitor Jemima Odebayo is also present.
Robin: The time is 2.35 p.m. on Saturday, 16 September, Detective Robin Kowalski interview with Spud Grimshaw. Also present is Mr Grimshaw's lawyer, Jemima Odebayo.

Robin: Good afternoon, Spud. You remain under caution.

S: And you remain a bit of a knobhead.

R: I'd like to talk to you about your relationship with Peter Milano.

S: Would you?

R: In your initial statement you told us that he approached you asking if you could sell him some spliff as he was having trouble sleeping. Is that correct?

S: Yes, and I told him to hang around Leicester Square and the dealers would find him.

R: You know about the movements of drug dealers, do you?

S: I don't know about their movements, but I know where they sell drugs. Anyone who has walked around London knows, they're hardly discreet.

R: Why did Peter ask you, do you think?

S: I don't know. But whatever the reason I was unable to help him with his enquiries.

R: The thing is, Spud, since our last interview we have made an interesting discovery. Under the stage of the Alexandra Theatre in Birmingham we have found a large quantity of class A and class B drugs.

S: Lucky you. I suggest you have a party down the nick and all get smashed.

R: Don't try and be clever.

S: So, you found a stash three hundred miles away from here. What's that got to do with me?

R: You tell me. You were working there eight weeks ago. You had access to that space. Secret. Safe. Dry. Perfect. Your job as a techie gave you the ideal cover.

S: Oh, come on, officer. You'll have to do better than that. I never went down there. There have been other shows, before and after us. Why don't you go and finger them with your highly imaginative theories?

R: If you never went down there how do we explain the presence of a vape with your DNA on it?

S: (pause) Er, you put it there, maybe?

260

R: I'll tell you what I believe, Spud. You had some grudge against Peter Milano. The incident when Hermia Saunders fell through the trapdoor at Birmingham was a mistake. That was your first attempt to kill him, but it went horribly wrong. At the Palladium, you decided to finish the job. The stage weight that struck Peter on the head had your fingerprints all over it.

S: I'm a stage technician. I move weights around every day. It's part of my job. Is that all you've got?

R: We found the drugs, we found the vape, we have your mitts on the stage weight. It's not looking good, is it, Spud?

S: Circumstantial bollocks. Trying to fit me up. You need to do better. The clock is ticking, you can only hold me for twenty-four hours, isn't that right?

R: Detective Olive Tamworth has just entered the room.

Note handed to Robin from Detective Olive Tamworth
Extra info on the weapon from the pathologist. The fatal wound indicates the weapon used. It was a six-inch serrated knife, similar to a Spyderco Harpy CO 8S serrated pocket knife. Commonly used by stage technicians.

R: I have been handed some new information from Detective Tamworth, just given to us from the pathologist report regarding the knife used to stab Peter Milano. Do you own a Spyderco knife, Spud?

S: No comment.

R: Did you stab Peter Milano with a Spyderco knife on Tuesday, 29 August at the London Palladium?

S: I'd like to speak to my solicitor privately, please.

R: The time is 2.42 p.m. and this interview is paused at the request of Spud Grimshaw.

Fun facts: how to behave during a police interview

You must remain polite, calm, and aware of your rights. Avoid volunteering unnecessary information, speculating, lying, making self-incriminating statements, discussing the case with others, arguing, making jokes, and interrupting the officer.

Police interview with Harry Grimshaw continued

R: Resuming the interview with Harry Grimshaw on Saturday, 16 September at 3.55 p.m. So, Spud. I take it you have now spoken to your solicitor? Is there a statement you'd like to make regarding the knife?

S: I don't have a Spyderco knife.

R: Not now you don't. Because it's missing, isn't it?

S: I've never had a knife like that in my kit.

R: A stage technician without the correct tools?

S: Maybe I'm not very good at my job. Something you could relate to, I'm sure.

R: Depends which job we're talking about, doesn't it? I don't doubt you weren't very good as a stagehand. Because that was just your cover. You had other fish to fry, like transporting drugs from one part of the country to another. Hiding them in various convenient locations, didn't you?

S: Don't know what you're on about.

R: And a nice little business selling them on the side to the cast of *Leopard Spots*.

S: Not me, Guv.

DI: We have now received Peter Milano's toxicology report. Which shows the presence of alcohol, cocaine, and marijuana.

S: I'm shocked to hear it. Shocked, I tell you.

DI: You need to wise up, son. Stop being clever. Have you thought about how long you'll be banged up for?

S: I was hoping to be out by Friday. I've got tickets for the opera.

R: Here's what we've got, Spud. We've been following you for months. You're part of a drug gang. A syndicate. You'd sell it on the side to make a bit of extra cash. Your Tinder profile was a way to find new customers. But you're the mug who does the high-risk stuff, handling the gear, moving valuable stock from one city to the next, hidden in the truck with the set, sometimes storing it in the dark recesses of provincial theatres until such time as it is needed. Unfortunately, your vape addiction puts you in the frame at the Alex.

DI: Milano found out somehow. You had instructions to silence him. You tried to make it look like an accident.

R: But we've got your fingerprints on the stage weight.

DI: He wasn't quite dead though, so you made sure with the Spyderco knife you carry as part of your stage gear. Bish, bash, bosh. Job done.

S: No! Listen, OK. I'll admit the drugs stuff. I owe them money and it was the only way I could pay them off. They had me by the goolies. Yes, I admit I sold a bit of gear. Nothing much. Coke, spliff, pills. But not murder! I don't know anything about what happened to Peter. It's nothing to do with me. You've got to believe me!

DI: The evidence is clear, Spud.

R: We are going to take you to the front desk now where you will be formally charged with the murder of Peter Milano.

Fun facts: cocaine

The indigenous people of South America chewed the leaves of erythroxylum coca, a shrub of the coca plant. Natives of the current region of Colombia, Peru, and Bolivia used coca leaves for their nutritional value and as a stimulant and anaesthetic. The leaf also was an important part of social, tribal, medical, and religious rituals.

R: *Hey. Just to say well done. We charged Spud for Peter's murder.*

J: *Is this a thank you, then?*

R: *We wouldn't have got him without you.*

J: *Well, good. Glad I could help. And Gordon?*

R: *Gordon is being released.*

J: *Quite right too.*

R: *But he could do with laying off the love letters to DI Serrano or he'll find himself nicked for harassment.*

J: *Lol. Life is funny, isn't it?*

R: *Why?*

J: *Well. Tinder. I matched with two people. Little did I know that one was a killer and the other was a police officer.*

Jayne's diary, Tuesday, 19 September 2017, London

Went for a quick drink with Taffy and Gordon. Both cock-a-hoop, obviously.

'How was prison life?' I asked him.

'It stinks,' said Gordon. 'My Givenchy Pour Homme was confiscated; in case the alkies drank it. And the food was virtually un-eatable. I'd have given my right arm for a saveloy. All those men in tracksuits, though, that was quite a turn-on.'

'Talking of which,' I said, seizing my opportunity. 'You might want to cool it with Detective Serrano.'

'Oh, he's so lovely, though!' said a slightly tipsy Gordon. 'The world-weary eyes, the stubble, the handcuffs . . .'

'I don't think its reciprocated, love,' said Taffy gently.

'We'll see, won't we?' said Gordon. 'Faint heart never won the fat lady, after all.'

'Maybe just live a quiet life for a bit?' I said. 'You've been through a lot.'

'My mind is reeling,' agreed Gordon. 'I've got all these

different emotions going on. Heartbreak for Peter, lust for my Serrano and loathing for Spud. Tears, hot and cold flushes, all at the same time. I don't know if I'm coming or going or if I've already been. Let's order some more voddy, shall we?'

I left them to it. In fact, I had the perfect excuse: a message from Katheryn.

Voice message from Katheryn Milano to Jayne
'Jayne, it's Katheryn. I wonder if you might be able to help me? Peter's body has been released by the coroner so I'm able to go ahead with funeral arrangements. I want Peter to be buried in his wedding suit. "The happiest day of my life," he always said. It's what he would have wanted.

'The thing is it's going to be a snug fit. He was a slave to the sourdough . . . Might you be able to come over with your sewing kit and work some magic? I don't know who else to ask and I know you're a whizz with that sort of thing. Let me know, would you? I'll book an Uber if you can make it.'

Jayne's diary, Wednesday, 20 September 2017, Oxfordshire
I was driven to a village in Oxfordshire and deposited outside the large barn conversion where the Milanos lived. Lots of glass and that yellowy brick work and a pristine, recently mown front lawn. I had my portable sewing machine with me.

Katheryn was waiting for me in the porch and came to greet me, along with two small, yapping dachshunds with whirling tails.

'Thank you so much for coming,' said Katheryn, giving me a rather stiff hug. Come inside for some tea.'

Inside was all very spacious, bleached-oak floorboards and that modern sort of furniture in bright primary colours that you see in magazines but I never thought anyone actually owned. Everything just so. Lots of flowers on every surface. A

265

few photos on display – Peter and Katheryn's wedding, them on a yacht somewhere, Peter shaking hands with Cliff Richard. Or it might have been Ann Widdicombe.

I made a fuss of the dogs while Katheryn boiled the kettle. She opened a cupboard full of crockery and reached for cups and saucers then thought better of it and got out two mugs. Posh olive-green ones in a matte finish.

'What are the dog's names?' I asked.

'Molly and Diva. The short-haired one is Diva and the long blonde one is Molly. Or if you want to call them both at once you just shout 'Maldives!' That was Peter's little joke. We went there for our honeymoon.'

'How have you been?' I asked.

'Oof!' she exhaled and seemed to deflate and shrink. She sat on a stool, head bowed, waiting for the tea to brew.

'I don't know, Jayne.' She crossed her arms as if holding her emotions in. 'Life can just change so suddenly. From first night to funeral, just like that.'

'Does it help that Spud has been charged?'

'I don't know. I guess it is a relief. But fancy being killed by someone called Spud. Like something out of a 1940s thriller.'

She got up with a sigh and poured the tea.

'Are you hungry? I can make you a sandwich.'

'No, I'm fine thank you. I went to Greggs earlier.'

'Bless you for coming all this way. I didn't know what to do about the suit. Then I remembered Peter telling me what a genius you were, making Hermia that sling when her arm was broken, and I decided you'd be the one to reach out to.'

'No problem. I'm happy to help. I have Peter's latest measurements. The costumes were updated for the Palladium, so I'll know what adjustments to make.'

'Shall we go up, then?' She carried the two mugs of tea and led the way up a wide wooden staircase.

'We've got a humungous loft conversion here, which Peter rather pretentiously called "the Studio", but it's just all junk, really. I like all the showbiz stuff kept *well* out of the way. There's a table you can work on. I've hung the wedding suit next to it. You'll see. Avocado green linen, Jasper Conran. And really, there's no need to double-stitch, or whatever you call it. Just tack it into place. It's not as if he's going to go jogging in it, let's face it.'

We reached the top of the stairs and Katheryn waved me into a large space with slanting walls and several skylights and turned away.

'You won't mind if I leave you to it, will you? I've got to go and do battle with the caterers. Apparently, no wake is complete these days without mini-Yorkshire puddings filled with Aberdeen angus and a dollop of horseradish. I'm not paying £1 a piece for those. You can get forty sausage rolls for £2.50 at Iceland. I might be a grieving widow but I'm not being ripped off by those crooks. Yell if you need anything, won't you?' Katheryn clattered down the stairs.

I scanned the room. As loft spaces go it was certainly big and bright. It was bigger than most flats. Shelves were neatly filled with books, scripts and photo albums. Wider, lower shelves seemed to be occupied with understandably unwanted ornaments and ugly vases.

There were filing cabinets at one end next to a small designer desk, a few scattered chairs, some art works leaning against the doors of two built-in cupboards containing old costumes, including one labelled 'Oberon' which must have been what Peter wore for *A Midsummer Night's Dream* with Alice. Ironing board and steam iron, lamps, wooden bowls, a toolbox, general bric-a-brac.

I placed my sewing machine on the table and took off my cardigan. There was Peter's suit hanging forlornly on a hook.

I took out my tape measure, consulted my measurements chart and calculated that the trousers and the jacket would both need to be adjusted by three inches. I checked the seams. Plenty of spare fabric.

With scissors and an invisible marker pen I set to it, unpicking the original stitching. I'd done this sort of job many times before – actors eating too many post-show dinners – or in reverse, with secret bulimics melting away, their ensuite bathrooms reeking of air-freshener that everyone was too polite to mention.

Once finished I pressed the suit, gave it a quick steam and hung it back up to admire my handy work. Yes. It somehow looked much more alive now. A job well done. It felt good to do something, however small, for Peter. I felt I had done him proud. Of course, he would be wearing the suit inside the coffin, and no one would see, but that was not the point. He would look smart and that was because he had been dressed well. By me.

Katheryn's petulant voice wafted up the stairs: 'Cheesy balls? We are burying a much-loved star of stage and screen. It's not a *Love Island* reunion, darling!'

I decided to bide my time and wait until her call with the caterers was finished. I wandered about the loft, gazing at the bookshelves, occasionally taking out a script or a photo album to glance at.

On an upper shelf were some aged box files, dated 1985-1990; an era of Peter's life that I was curious about. I lifted it down and placed it on the table to see what I could find. It was a mishmash of newspaper clippings, articles, letters and legal papers.

I picked out a few.

Sunday Times, Sunday, 8 June 1986
By Tamara Seply-Court.
Headline: At home with Peter Milano and Lady Donna
Ratcliffe

To celebrate their first wedding anniversary, the actor Peter Milano and heiress Lady Donna Ratcliffe invited us to share a rare glimpse of their life outside the spotlight.

Surprisingly their wedding was not a society affair, as Lady Donna explained.

'Just a private wedding in a small-but-beautiful chapel in Paris with a reception afterwards for fifty guests in the Hôtel de Crillon in the Place de la Concorde,' she said.

The next day the happy couple drove away in a powder-blue convertible Bentley, heading south.

'We didn't want any fuss,' smiled Peter, gazing lovingly at his wife as the happy couple sat together in the sunny drawing room of their Knightsbridge mansion flat.

'It was perfect,' agreed Lady Donna, beaming with happiness. 'Just a few close friends and family.'

But since then, it has been back to work with a vengeance. Peter's portrayal of an international rugby player diagnosed with Parkinson's disease in Why Tim? *won universal praise and a BAFTA nomination.*

'There are lots of projects in the pipeline,' he says cryptically. 'Stage and screen . . . I can't tell you the details, but I'm very excited.'

This is quite a turnaround for an actor who two years ago saw his career derailed after a disastrous trip to Hollywood which produced just one ill-fated movie: Don't Hurt Me.

'I thought it was what I wanted at the time. To be a big movie star. But I loathed Los Angeles. It's full of broken dreams. I was terribly, terribly homesick.'

269

'Peter is too good for America!' said Lady Donna fiercely. 'We are lucky to have him back here where he is appreciated.'

'My wife is my biggest fan, as you can see,' blushed Peter.

'Showbusiness chews people up and spits them out sometimes. That isn't going to happen to Peter. His star is rising, up, up and away!' she laughs.

And were there any plans to start a family?

'Neither of us have any desire for children,' said Lady Donna firmly, shaking her head. 'I'm just not a very mumsy sort of person.'

'Definitely not,' agreed Peter. 'We are in complete agreement for once! I've never wanted children. All that mess and noise.'

'We might get a dog, though,' added Lady Donna.

'I'll get you a houseplant first, darling. Let's see how that goes, shall we?'

The Daily, Friday, 7 March 1986
Review of *Why Tim?* (a Ratcliffe TV production)

This beautiful film of a heartthrob athlete struck down in his prime will touch a million hearts. Based on a true story and sensitively portrayed by Peter Milano, we follow the tragic story of a man who has everything suddenly taken from him, but who finds a new sense of purpose in accepting his illness before going on to inspire and give hope to others.

Peter Milano gives the most subtle, nuanced performance of his career. The scenes of bewilderment where he slowly realises that his sporting career is over are truly heart-wrenching.

So much is conveyed without words in the hands of this master craftsman. He glares at his shiny, new wheelchair, forlorn hatred showing in every facial twitch, before climbing into it with a grim determination to overcome, to find something new to make his life meaningful. We understand. The camera loves him. This is television acting at its finest.

270

Letter from Eric Adams to Ken Thomas
16 November 1983

Dear Mr Thomas,

Please accept this correspondence as a formal notice to cease and desist ALL activity with regards to Peter Milano and Lady Donna Ratcliffe. The nefarious actions you continue to undertake again Peter Milano and Lady Donna Ratcliffe not only constitute interference with the aforementioned's business, but slander and misrepresentation. Therefore, this conduct is actionable under UK law.

While we certainly hope this is not necessary, we are prepared to pursue whatever avenues are necessary on our clients' behalf to ensure the protection of their reputation and that their business operations continue uninterrupted. We demand that you immediately cease any and all conduct aimed at disrupting or harming Peter Milano and Donna Ratcliffe.

Yours sincerely,

Eric Adams, solicitor

Fun facts: Lady Donna Ratcliffe
The fabulously wealthy Lady Donna Ratcliffe, only heiress to the media tycoon Rupert Ratcliffe, was used to having everything she wanted. She married Peter Milano and wanted him to be a huge star. Which he was not. His career was all but over when they met. No matter. She began a media onslaught of wildly complimentary articles and profiles, praising him and emphasising his talents, virile good looks and fine character.

She even set up a TV production company with the sole purpose of casting her husband in starring roles, which would then be given five-star reviews by the press outlets she controlled. Within two years Peter was back in the game, looking good and with a rosy future beckoning. Lady Donna got what she wanted. Always.

Jayne's diary, Wednesday, 20 September 2017, Oxfordshire
Katheryn seemed to have finished her angry phone calls, so I closed the box file and was lifting it back onto its shelf when an envelope fell out. It was addressed to Peter and postmarked Deptford.

Inside was a letter. Inside the letter was a photograph of two children. A little girl of maybe two and a younger child of about one year.

15 July 1985

Dear Peter,

I'm enclosing a snap of the girls in the hope that you might find it in your heart to help us. You haven't paid any maintenance and we are really desperate now.

I have literally nothing and the landlord has just put the rent up again. My family want nothing to do with me.

Please, Peter. Look at your children in this photo. How can you leave us destitute while you have so much?

Forgive me writing to you but I really don't know what else I can do.

I don't want you back, I am no threat to your new marriage or your career. I just need a little money for food.

I am begging you.

Alice

Jayne's diary, Wednesday, 20 September 2017, Oxfordshire
I slipped the photo into my pocket and quickly put the letter

back in the box and went downstairs. Katheryn was sitting in the kitchen with a notepad and pen.

'All done. Wasn't too tricky,' I said. 'I've pressed it and hung it up, ready for . . .'

'Thank you so much Jayne. I'm going to pay you for your trouble.' Katheryn reached for her purse.

'No, really, please don't think of doing that.'

'But I must, Jayne. It only seems fair.'

'No, I won't accept anything. I did it for Peter. I was very glad you asked me.' Katheryn put her purse down again.

'Did you sort out the catering?'

'Eventually. I had to fight my corner. It's an absolute racket, you know. They're getting sandwiches and mini pizzas. And I'm putting £200 behind the bar. After that people can pay for their own bloody booze.'

Poor Katheryn. She was talking ten to the dozen as a means of keeping her feelings at bay, I thought. I just listened, nodding occasionally.

'Then there's this place to worry about. Too big for me on my own. And too many memories. The market is quite buoyant now so I'm going to sell. Two million, I reckon, if I can find a Russian oligarch. They're buying country houses, you know, to keep their mistresses in. Shall I call you an Uber?'

Fun facts: Peter Milano
Peter's first wife, Lady Donna Ratcliffe, went on to marry an Italian noble, Alessandro Romagnoli, a descendent of Marquese Marianna Reggiani Romagnoli. They now live in a spacious villa in Via dei Coronari in Rome with a Bengal cat called Pietro.

Jayne's diary, Wednesday, 20 September 2017, Oxfordshire
As the Uber drove me home I thought about what I'd learned today.

The sad begging letter from Alice . . . so there were *two* children? Why couldn't Peter have helped them, just a little?

He had a beautiful house, where Peter should have enjoyed the autumn of his life. But why wasn't he happy? Why wasn't that enough?

Actors were such complicated people. And poor Katheryn, trying to be tough and in control, struggling to maintain her dignity, never mentioning the revelations about Peter's dalliance with Gordon or drugs. How humiliating for her.

Then there was the posh wedding to Lady Donna, conveniently positioned to revive Peter's image and career. Did Peter love her? Or was she just a means to an end?

I wondered if I'd ever understand it all. To borrow a phrase of Julian's I was feeling 'tired and emotional'.

Statement from Lady Donna Ratcliffe

I am sad to hear of the death of my former husband Peter. Despite our difficult divorce, I have always wished the best for him. I treasure the memories of our happy times together. May he now rest in peace.

Kitty Litter WhatsApp Group Chat

H: *All this media attention is driving me insane.*

S: *I can't go to the pub without being papped.*

M: *It feels as if our lives are falling apart at the seams, through no fault of ours. I'm going to call Equity and see what they plan to do about it.*

H: *Tell them that seeing my face in the papers is just adding to the trauma of what I've already been through.*

M: *We might be entitled to some compensation.*

S: *Career and marriage down the shitter. Just like that.*

H: *I've tried thinking positive thoughts but when I try and tune in to the future it's just a misty blank.*

S: *Like inside Peter Andre's brain.*

M: *Harsh.*

H: *If only Lorraine Kelly could be caught having an affair with Mick Jagger. That would take the heat off.*

M: *That's vulgar. I hear she's lovely.*

H: *What a shame.*

S: *We are soiled goods I'm afraid, ladies. No one will touch us with a barge pole.*

M: *We'll be lucky to get invited onto* Tipping Point *after this.*

H: *Don't say that, please. I'm having a bad enough day as it is.*

Press announcement
Lord Andrew Lloyd-Webber to unveil a memorial plaque to Peter Milano beneath the stage of the London Palladium this Friday, 22 September at 1 p.m.

Chapter 39

Text exchange between Jayne and Ken

J: *Hi Ken. Are you OK?*

K: *Well, I'm in Ealing.*

J: *I've never been there.*

K: *It's a shithole.*

J: *Ah. Sorry to hear that. There's something I need to know: who do you think chucked the brick through your window?*

K: *I don't know. I don't think it was an Amazon delivery.*

J: *Lol. You don't have any idea?*

K: *Not really. I'm not a very loved person.*

J: *But what is it they don't want you to leak? What information.*

K: *I can't tell you. And it would be dangerous to tell you. They might come after you.*

J: *Could you meet me somewhere and we could talk in private?*

K: *No. Absolutely not. I'm not breaking cover for you or anyone else.*

J: *I could come to you?*

K: *No. No. No. Try to understand that I am in hiding. Scared for my life.*

J: *All right, Ken. I'm sorry. Take care of yourself, OK?*

K: *I'm on eight Imodium a day. That's how scared I am.*

Jayne's diary, Thursday, 21 September 2017, London

All roads lead to her: Alice Haughton. So, I decided to go and see her again. And I wouldn't be hiding in the car park this time, I decided. I would be confident. A woman on a mission.

Furthermore, I wanted to make sure that Miriam was out of the way. I emailed her agent.

Dear Eugenie,

I understand you represent the actor, Miriam Haughton. We produce the award-winning ITV series Vera *and would like Miriam to come and read for a major role in a forthcoming episode, tomorrow afternoon at 2 p.m. if possible.*

We apologise for the late notice, but Brenda Blethyn has asked to meet Miriam personally and we hope this will be convenient.

The episode is to be filmed over ten days in August in the Gateshead area of Newcastle.

The address for tomorrow's meeting is:
Lavender Tower
Media City, Manchester M50 2EQ.

We do hope Miriam is able to make it. Please let us know at your earliest convenience,

Kind regards,
Ophelia Buttox (producer)

P.S. The part does require a Geordie accent!

Of course, it worked like a charm and Eugenie's breathless confirmation of the meeting arrived in my inbox within ten minutes. Good. Miriam would have a nice day out and Alice and I would not be interrupted.

Jayne's diary, Thursday, 21 September 2017

When I arrived at Summer Breeze residential home, Alice was in her room, sat in her usual chair, lost in thought when I entered. She remembered me almost at once.

'Helga, isn't it?' she said after a momentary blank stare.

'Jayne,' I corrected her. She nodded.

'How nice to see you. Anything worth watching on television tonight?'

'I doubt it. How have you been?'

'You're from the theatre, aren't you?'

'That's right.'

'Actress?'

'No. A dresser. But I know you were an actress once. I've been reading about *A Midsummer Night's Dream* that you did.'

Alice looked up sharply.

'Yes,' she nodded. Then after a moment's pause: *'What angel wakes me from my flowery bed?'*

'You remember the lines!'

'Most of them. I can't remember what I had for breakfast, but I remember Titania. And Oberon . . .'

I decided now was the time. I took out the photo of the two little girls I had found in Katheryn's attic.

'Do you remember this from a long time ago?' I passed Alice the photo. She stared at it for ages.

'Yes,' she said quietly. Her eyes filled with tears. I hated to upset her, but I knew I had to press on.

'Can you tell me about it?'

'My girls. My girls,' she said, trembling. She pointed to the younger child, stroking her face tenderly with her finger. 'That's my baby girl. And Miriam . . . inconsolable she was to lose her little sister. I thought she would never stop crying.'

'What happened to her?' I asked softly. Then Alice began to

talk, her voice quiet at first, but getting angrier and more upset as she went on.

'I couldn't keep her. Not both. There was no money, and I could not cope. I begged Peter for help, but he was off living the high life. They could have given me just a tiny amount to look after them. But Lady Donna wouldn't budge. Threatened they would get Miriam taken away as well.'

She paused and looked at me, the pain and heartbreak visible in her eyes.

'All these years I kept quiet,' she continued. 'Protecting Peter's image. His precious career. Ken tried to help. Sent a bit of money when he could. But they threatened him as well.'

Then a slow smile crept across her face.

'But he got what he deserved in the end.'

'Who did?'

'Peter. He got what was coming to him. I'm just happy I got to see it.'

I couldn't quite comprehend what she'd just said.

'You saw it? You were at the Palladium that night?'

Alice nodded.

'Yes. Not very good seats. Upper Circle. But I saw enough. My daughter invited me.' She handed me a *Leopard Spots* programme.

'She sent this with the ticket. How nice!'

I opened the programme and pointed to Miriam's photo. 'This one?'

Alice shook her head. 'No. The other one.'

A note fell out of the programme. I picked it up.

'Please come. It's going to be a night to remember.'

In that split second, I knew who Peter's killer was.

I suddenly had a lot more questions to ask, but just then the door opened, and the nurse, Constance, came hurriedly in and stood with her hands on her hips.

'I've just had an angry Miriam on the phone from Manchester. You're not supposed to be here, are you?'

I stood up. 'Sorry. Goodbye, Alice,' I said before I fled.

Popbitch, Thursday, 21 September 2017
We are pleased to report that a disgraced comedian's fame-hungry spouse is keeping herself occupied. She may be filing for divorce but between meetings with a celebrity lawyer, who's represented everyone from Prince Charles to Paul McCartney and Fiona Shackleton, she's also in negotiations with *I'm a Celebrity Get Me Out of Here!* Not to mention a cosy dinner at Nobu with a Premiership footballer . . . Busy, busy, busy!

Chapter 40

Julian on the latest reveal

A quick update on my editor: she's had enough of the shallow literary world and as soon as this book is done and dusted, she's going to dye her hair blue and start a new life as an environmental activist.

'I just want my grandchildren to have a future!' she says.

Well, not if they've inherited her dress sense.

As for the matter in hand, can I say how pleased I am with the way my Jayne has evolved. It is thrilling for me, as her friend, so see how she has grown in confidence. Her exploratory visit to Birmingham bore heavy fruit and she has not looked back since.

She has always been self-reliant and sharp, but now there is a new buoyancy, an assertiveness, that is thrilling to see. She has the bit between her teeth and is poised, ready for the final chase. Jayne knows she has the imperative forces of integrity behind her. Within her. She will not be thwarted in her pursuit of justice.

Ladies and gentlemen and non-binary gender variants, we are headed for a climax and no mistake. I haven't been this excited since I got locked in a horse box with Prince Harry. Talk about Red Rum.

Jayne's diary, Thursday, 21 September 2017

Once again, I felt cast aside by Robin. He accepted my tip-off in Birmingham and sent the sniffer dogs in to find Spud's drugs stash under the stage of the Alex, but apart from a brief text exchange there had been no other contact. No doubt he was taking all the credit for himself, and my involvement was to be brushed under the carpet.

What is painfully clear is that there are two things going on: my relationship with Robin and our feelings for each other, be they good or bad, are one thing. My determination to expose the real murderer is another. The two things aren't mixing well. Feelings and facts, it seems, are not compatible. I had to find a way through this and make sure that my head ruled my heart. For now, anyway.

But now I needed Robin's cooperation for the final sting and was receiving nothing but disdainful silence from him. Messages and texts were going un-answered and once again I felt like I was the annoying ex who wouldn't go away. Well sod that for a game of soldiers.

There was one thing I *could* do. I cornered Nathan in the flat. I knew he was in touch with his brother, and I also knew I had to be very firm about what I wanted or my plans would fail.

'Listen, Nathan. I need to see Robin. Today. It is urgent.'

Nathan sighed and offered me a sort of shrug. 'He's busy, Jayne. Your relationship issues—'

'This isn't about our relationship!' I snapped back. 'I know I am being cast as the desperate, spurned girlfriend in all this, but this is about Peter Milano's murder.'

'Leave that to the police.'

'I tried that, and they arrested poor Gordon. They got it wrong before and I'm sure they've got it wrong a second time.'

I surprised myself how calm and collected I was.

'If you won't contact Robin and bring him to me – today

– then I will go to the police. But I can assure you Robin will not come out of this well.'

I was channelling Helen Mirren in *Prime Suspect*. But it was the only way to deal with the situation. I knew I needed results this time.

Nathan sighed and called his brother.

'Ten tonight. He'll be here,' he said. Then he went out without so much as a goodbye. Poor Nathan. I felt sorry for him. It was his flat after all and here I was calling the shots. But ultimately it didn't matter what Nathan thought. He would understand one day. I needed to tell Robin what I had found out and I needed his help to do what was necessary. I paced up and down for a while then called Rowanne.

'You're absolutely doing the right thing', she said. 'Remember, one day this will all be over and we can go to Greggs and have a laugh like we used to. Love you!'

Robin arrived ten minutes late. Typical. He looked strained and rather cross. Like Nathan, I think he was expecting a tirade from a wronged girlfriend. But, it wasn't about that. It was, frankly, more important and this was no place for high emotions and girly tears.

There was an awkward silence when he walked into the flat.

'Why don't you sit down?' I said. I didn't choose to sit myself. I stood and read from my notebook. I now knew who had murdered Peter and I needed his help.

Then I told him what I had planned for the next day at the plaque unveiling, when all the relevant people would be present. Robin rubbed his eyes after I'd finished.

'I can't be a part of this, Jayne. If what you are saying is right, I need to inform my guvnor.'

'No, Robin. It has to be done the way I say, or it won't work.'

'I'll get the sack if you're wrong about this. I can't be a part of it, sorry.'

'Yes, you can, and you will. Because otherwise I'll tell your big, important guvnor that you were sleeping with me during the undercover operation.'

Robin looked at me in disbelief. 'You wouldn't do that to me, would you?'

'Watch me,' I said simply. 'Unless you do as I ask, I definitely would.'

He gave wry smile of defeat. 'OK. Miss Whiplash. I'd better do it then, I suppose.'

I had won. Robin agreed to play his part in my plan. I granted him a brisk hug of gratitude. But when the hug turned to a kiss, and I felt his hands wandering down my back I pulled away. This was no time for frisky nonsense.

Julian on Jayne's breakthrough

Jayne came round to my place that morning to get ready. She looked fine, I assured her. Perfectly appropriated clothes for an unveiling. I wanted to add a diamante brooch to her jacket lapel, but she wrinkled her nose at the idea. She did accept a little concealer and powder, though. She seemed a bit on edge.

'Everything OK?' I asked.

'Well . . .' she said. 'Hopefully. All the work I've been doing at the kitchen table has paid off. I now know who killed Peter.'

'It wasn't Gordon?'

'It wasn't.'

'Spud?'

She shook her head.

'Oh my. And what are you doing with this information?'

'Well,' she took a deep breath, held on to it for several seconds and then exhaled. 'I'm going to expose them.'

'At the unveiling?'

'Seems appropriate, don't you think?'

'Oh Jayne!' I squealed in a rather homosexual way. 'What

a marvel you are. I wish I could come but I've got to go and record a podcast with some frightful new comedian no one has ever heard of.'

I could see her eyes were sparkling. Jayne's inner brilliance was about to illuminate the mystery that she had been gnawing at for so long. I'm not a tactile person but I gave her a long, tight squeeze.

'Good luck. Go get 'em,' I whispered in her ear.

Ken Thomas on Twitter

At the Palladium awaiting arrival of a VIP to unveil Peter Milano's plaque which will be cheek by jowl next to Bruce Forsyth's. Would Brucie be thrilled? 'Nice to see you, to see you nice!'

Fun facts: Bruce Forsyth

Bruce Forsyth didn't find stardom until the age of 30, when he was chosen to host *Sunday Night at the London Palladium* on ITV. Before that, he was a jobbing performer on the variety circuit. 'I gave myself five years and I thought, if I don't do any good in five years, I don't want to end up being a frustrated performer [so] I'll get out of the business,' he said. 'And the five years were nearly up, and I got the job at the Palladium.'

Kitty Litter Whatsapp Group Chat

M: *Getting ready for the Palladium unveiling. Not sure if we are expected to wear black or not. Anyone know?*

H: *I think smart, but it isn't a funeral.*

M: *True.*

S: *Since Laura buggered off no one's making other people do any sodding laundry here. I'm in jeans and a creased old T-shirt.*

M: *Well, wear a blazer for the sake of decency.*

H: *It all seems so final, doesn't it?*

285

S: *Is it OK if I bring my new bird with me?*

M: *No Simon. Not appropriate.*

H: *Press would have a field day and the focus should be on our dear, departed colleague Peter.*

S: *Fair enough. She's got a bit of a hickey on her neck anyway.*

M: *Oh, please!*

S: *Soz.*

H: *Listen. I was doing some psychic healing last night and Peter came through.*

S: *As in 'followed through'?*

H: *No, Simon. You can be a sceptic if you choose, but I want to share with you both that Peter is now at peace. He is happy on the other side and wishes us all the best.*

S: *Did he mention who is going to win the World Cup next year?*

M: *Ignore him, Hermia. I find it very comforting that Peter has communicated with you. Very thoughtful of him.*

H: *He wants us all to be at peace.*

M: *I just need to put this awful business behind me. It's put me off theatre. I only want to do television work from now on. But not Vera.*

H: *What's wrong with Vera.*

M: *I've got my reasons.*

Trevor Millicent's draft speech for the unveiling of Peter Milano's plaque

Thank you all for coming. I know Peter would be delighted to have this lasting memorial here, at the most famous theatre in the world. The theatre, after all, was arguably the place of his most accomplished achievements.

In years to come I feel sure that Peter Milano's name will be spoken in the same breath as David Garrick, Sir Donald Wolfit and Sir Laurence Olivier's.

As the great playwright Arthur Miller put it, 'All the world's a stage, and all the men and women merely players. They have their exits and their entrances; And one man in his time plays many parts.' How true. And what a man Peter was. *(Note to self: check authorship of this quotation).*

I am therefore delighted to take this opportunity to announce some very exciting news. It is my intention to immortalise my dear friend Peter Milano in a new play tentatively titled *Un Amico di Dorothy*.

Exciting investment opportunities will be available soon and I hope to premiere the piece at the Soho Theatre next spring.

Jayne's diary, Friday, 22 September 2017
I knew this was it. I just didn't know how I was going to do it or if the words would come out. I had never been this nervous before. I kept thinking about my mother and her words: 'You can do anything. You are clever.'

At noon, as instructed, we gathered together underneath the stage of the Palladium. There, on the brickwork right below centre stage, next to Bruce's interred ashes and a brass name plate in memory of the agent called Billy Marsh, was a small, red square velvet curtain.

Jayne's diary, Friday, 22 September 2017
Everyone was there, murmuring quietly. Katheryn looking stoical, Miriam in a smart polka-dot dress with a white jacket; Hermia in something floaty, and her arm in what looked like a new silk patterned sling; Trevor, acting as if he was in charge, arranging people in a semi-circle; Simon, looking scruffy and hungover was chatting to Taffy, who had her arm around a pale and tearful Gordon.

Ken Thomas was there too, stood quietly at the back, but I think I was the only one who recognised him: still fearful for his safety, he had disguised himself with a flatcap and a big, bushy false moustache.

We all stood there, not sure how to behave, exchanging small talk in hushed voices. It was a bit like being at church.

'He'd have loved this,' said Simon.

'He would, bless him,' said Taffy, dabbing her eyes with a big, white hanky.

There was sudden loud whisper from Hermia.

'Pssst! Jayne? Would you mind, honey? My sling has come undone.' She waved her plastered arm in the air.

'Of course,' I said obligingly and went to help her, folding it over her arm and then reaching both ends behind her neck.

'Thank you. I knew it was a bit loose but it's difficult to do a knot with one hand. I could do with a dresser with me full-time!'

I suddenly stopped. My mind was whirring, my fingers were trembling but then I somehow continued and got the knot tightly tied. My heart was pounding so fast I turned away from Hermia in case my thoughts showed on my face.

There was the sound of footsteps hurrying down the concrete stairs towards us. It was Lord Andrew Lloyd Webber, who had agreed to do the unveiling. He stood by the side of the little curtain.

'Hello! Hello!' he said in his familiar, friendly voice, his big, sheep-like eyes gazing slowly around as he nodded an all-purpose greeting. I thought I saw Trevor do a kind of curtsey in Lord Andrew's direction.

'Thank you all so much for being here. This is very poignant, very sad. But the right thing to do. Peter Milano was one of our most treasured actors and I was genuinely thrilled when I heard he was joining us here at the Palladium. Fate, as we know, stepped in and . . . it's heartbreaking. To show, in some small way, our respect and affection for Peter, who was taken too soon, and in such an awful way, I hope this little plaque will be a nice, lasting memorial. He'll be here, with Bruce, for as long as this theatre stands.'

Sir Andrew smiled sadly then pulled the string to reveal a shiny brass plaque that said simply:

PETER MILANO
ACTOR
1955-2017
'You often meet your fate on the road you take to avoid it.'
- Goldie Hawn

There was a smattering of applause and a sigh from Hermia who hugged Miriam then proceeded, rather awkwardly, to hug everyone in the room.

'Er, I shall leave you all here for a moment of reflection,' said Sir Andrew. 'I have arranged for tea and refreshments for you all in the dress circle bar.' And then he slipped away, tripping up the stairs with more enthusiasm than he had descended them.

I looked towards Robin, and he gave me a nod. Now was the time. I was just clearing my voice to speak when Trevor's loud, confident voice echoed around the room.

'Before we all go our separate ways, I feel it would be appropriate for me to say a few words,' he began. There was an audible groan from the room.

'I know Peter would be delighted—'

I had to do it now.

'Excuse me,' I said. 'But *I* need to say something.'

Trevor glared indignantly.

'You? I rather doubt that you have any great wisdom to impart, Jayne. Why not run along to the dress circle and take the cling film off the sandwiches?'

Everyone was staring at me now. I took a deep breath.

'Thank you for that suggestion, Trevor. I know I'm just Jayne the dresser. A person of no great interest. No one takes any notice of me. But I take notice of you. And I speak the truth. Now is the time to share it.'

I looked at them all, one after the other.

'Peter was murdered. Not by Gordon and not by Spud. I knew that the police had got it wrong, so I've been doing my own investigation. Hard to work out who was responsible for his death because you all hated him. Every one of you. I had to do some digging. Now I know.'

'Is she drunk?' asked Trevor.

'No, I am not,' I said with a shrug. 'I'm a dresser. A dresser sees everything,' I continued, raising my voice a notch.

'I speak to everyone, I overhear things, I see things I'm not supposed to see. And, you may be surprised to hear, I have a brain. A clear mind, unfuddled by drink or drugs, ego, jealousy, rage or all the other regrettable demons that you all struggle with, it seems to me.'

'Rude!' said Miriam.

'Miss Marple is in da house!' muttered Simon.

'Stop this, Jayne,' hissed Miriam. 'You're making a fool of yourself. It is all sorted out now. The police said!'

'It was Spud,' said Hermia. 'Which is why he was arrested and why he has been charged.'

'Surely that's an end to the matter?' said Simon.

'Spud had a hand in Peter's death. We all know that,' I said, raising my voice a little more. 'But he had no idea of the deadly intent of the actions he helped with.'

Fun facts: the London Palladium

The London Palladium was hit by an unexploded German parachute mine on 11 May 1941. The bomb fell through the roof and became lodged over the stage. A Royal Navy bomb disposal team arrived; but when they touched the fuse-locking ring in order to remove the fuse, the bomb started ticking again. The area was rapidly evacuated, but the bomb didn't go off. Two of the bomb disposal team cautiously returned, extracted the fuse and removed other hazardous components, rendering the mine 'safe'. It was then lowered to the stage and disposed of.

Julian on Spud

Well, I'd better come clean about Spud. Now is as good a time as any. Many years before the events in this book took place I fell into bad company. A group of us would meet every Friday night. Stimulants were involved. Spud was the dealer and would arrive with his bag of goodies for us to purchase. He was always very quiet and businesslike. I got the impression we were just one stop on his rounds.

It was a sordid time in my life and one I deeply regret. After a few months of this nonsense, I extricated myself from this circle of friends and the reader will be pleased to know I have kept myself nice since then. I would just add, though, that the quality of the cocaine Spud sold us was most excellent. More of a health supplement, really.

Don't hate me. We all make mistakes – you should have seen the leggings my editor wore to our meeting last week. The words camel and toe spring to mind.

Jayne's diary, Friday, 22 September 2017

'Simon. You charmed him, like the rest of us, with your cheeky-chappie act. You hid from him your own dark secret. You needed money. Lots of it. To pay the debts you had run up with your ridiculous, nouveau-famous lifestyle and your glamorous wife's compulsive spending. In Peter, you saw a chance. You took him to the pub and talked him into a fictional get-rich-quick scheme and he was stupid enough to fall for it. When he threatened to expose you, you panicked. Peter's death must have suited you very well. How convenient.'

As I spoke, Simon began to sweat and his fists clenched. 'Oh, come off it, matey. We had a flutter on the horses, that's all!'

'Then we have you, Trevor. Brooding for years about your career, snuffed out by Peter for a laugh. How he stole your lime-light. *Leopard Spots* is your revenge, is it not? You wanted the starring role in the TV adaption of your smash-hit play. Peter was in the way. How opportune that Peter was dead and the starring role conveniently available.'

'Peter and I enjoyed a lifetime of mutual respect for one an-other. You wouldn't understand that!' barked Trevor furiously.

'Ken. You were silenced from telling the truth about Peter for decades, knowing that he had behaved appallingly and yet never faced the repercussions he deserved. You made it your mission to torment him as much as you could – who knows how far you were prepared to go in your quest for justice?'

Ken's voice was a bit muffled from behind his moustache. 'Utter tosh! My weapon of choice is the pen, dear girl. Much mightier than the sword, as you shall find out in my next blog.'

'Miriam now. What can you possibly have to gain from Peter's death? We all know you hated the kissing scene. Understanda-ble. But why so much, and so suddenly?

'A sordid truth had emerged. Peter was the father who had abandoned you as a child. Your mother Alice's distress bruised your heart. If you could tell Alice that Peter was dead, she might smile again.'

'This is too much,' said Hermia.

'No, Hermia. It is not enough, in fact. Because now we come to you. Hermia Saunders. Sweet, friendly, emotional psychic Hermia Saunders . . . that's the name you acquired during your stay in America. But your passport confirms that you are actually British. Born at Lewisham Hospital.'

'Rubbish!' Hermia was glaring at me now.

'Your real name is Nigella. Mother: Alice Haughton. Father: Peter Milano. Younger sister to Miriam. You'd been tormented by not knowing who your real family were for years. A twist of fate was going to allow you to uncover the secret – starring alongside Miriam in *Leopard Spots*. Finally, the two sisters were united, and you met Alice for the first time since you were adopted at the tender age of one.

'You drew Spud into your plan. But I don't believe Spud understood how deadly your plans really were. There was a mishap in Birmingham. It was Peter who should have fallen through the trapdoor, not you. But you turned this to your advantage. A better – more underhand – plan. You then tried to poison him with the cupcake I gave him in Plymouth. Spud had access to plenty of drugs, but that was foiled when Gordon ate it instead.'

Hermia rolled her eyes at me. 'A nice little story, but where on earth is your evidence?'

'Coming right up, as they say in America. Months ago, Spud and I matched together on Tinder. Nothing came of that—'

'You were too busy with your highly sexed estate agent, as I recall!' scoffed Miriam.

'Whatever,' I continued. 'But two days ago, "Spud" sent me a message on Tinder, asking me to visit him on remand. He is facing life in prison for a murder he didn't commit, and he wanted to tell me the truth.

'So, I went. Spud explained everything. Hermia said she wanted to teach Peter a lesson. Scare him, that's all. It was to be a prank. You wanted him to go up to the flies and balance the stage weight on top of the scenery wall, high above the stage. You told him exactly where to put it.

'Then during the scene change, as that wall flew up and

another came down to replace it, the weight would be dislodged and crash down onto the stage. Right next to Peter, she said, giving him the fright of his life and hopefully ruining his press night performance. Spud refused, knowing it could go fatally wrong.

'You then blackmailed him, threatening to go to the police about his drug selling, unless he did as you asked. You were having sex with him. He was mesmerised by you.

'You deliberately gave Spud the wrong measurements, placing the weight exactly above Peter, not a few feet away as he thought. But it didn't kill him as you'd hoped.

'As he lay in your arms, shielded from view by Peter, you swiftly put plan B into action. You produced a knife that you had stolen from Spike's kit and, during the mayhem, stabbed him in his back, puncturing his lung.

'The blood-curdling scream you let out was one of relief, not horror. A lifetime of pent-up anger and frustration finally redressed.

'Where is the knife now, *Nigella*?'

Hermia threw her head back in defiance. 'You tell me. Without the murder weapon this is all pure fiction!'

'I *will* tell you. When you asked me to re-tie your sling I couldn't for a moment. And that is because I was used to tying it for you on the *other side*. You've been wearing that for weeks. It isn't a real cast anymore, is it?'

I could see fear creeping into Hermia's eyes, and I sensed she was about to make a run for it. I grabbed her arm and pulled it out of the sling. With one tug the fake plaster cast snapped off and a bloodied knife fell to the floor with a metallic clunk.

Robin then came forward from the shadows where he had concealed himself and handcuffed a struggling, screaming Hermia.

Ken Thomas on Twitter

Stop press! Hermia Saunders has just been arrested at the London Palladium for the murder of Peter Milano!

Chapter 41

Ken Thomas's blog, Friday, 22 September 2017
I feel dutybound to now reveal to my followers the true story of what I know about Peter Milano's life and the secrets I have kept hidden for so long.

I first encountered Alice Haughton during an amateur production of *The Importance of Being Earnest* in a room above a pub in Wandsworth. Her Gwendolen was sublime and I marked her for future greatness even then.

Her star was in the ascent, and I was working as a theatre critic. Her youthful Titania in *A Midsummer Night's Dream* in 1982 had the West End in raptures. Everyone wanted to see the beautiful, talented actress who seemed to live and breathe her role. She was simply mesmerising.

It was during this production that Alice met Peter Milano, who shone in her reflected glory as a virile Oberon. Together they were the talk of the town, photographed together at parties and restaurants. The golden couple of their time. Romance was inevitable.

Alice was madly in love with Peter and assumed that they would marry and settle down together. But Peter was less enthralled. Keen to build his profile on the publicity surrounding him, he went to Hollywood and abandoned Alice, who by now was pregnant with Miriam. Sure that he'd hit the big time, Peter blocked all attempts at communication from Alice and made a stinker of a film with Jane Fonda.

When Hollywood spat him out, he came back to London and to a grateful Alice, sponging off her while he tried to pick up the pieces of his failing career. Soon Alice was pregnant with their second daughter, Hermia.

But before she was born Peter met the rich and powerful Lady Donna at a party. He saw his escape and grabbed it. Alice was cast aside. Penniless and striving to cope, she begged them to help her. They refused, Peter denying all knowledge of the children as Alice sunk deeper into debt and misery.

Unable to cope, she made the heartwrenching decision to have Hermia adopted, sure that she'd have a better life elsewhere. She never knew what became of her.

While Alice's life and career were ruined, Peter married the money and used Lady Donna's powerful contacts to supress any rumours or negative stories about him. Despite his mediocre talent, Peter's career flourished while poverty and psychosis slowly engulfed Alice.

Hermia Saunders police interview with DI Serrano, Friday, 22 September 2017

DI: Do you have any knowledge about the death of Peter Milano?

Hermia: I do, yes.

DI: Were you responsible for Peter's death?

Hermia: Peter was responsible.

DI: The knife was found hidden about your person.

H: I can't deny that.

DI: Why did you kill him?

H: Once I found out who he was and what he'd done it was the only decent thing to do.

DI: What did you find out?

H: That he was my father.

DI: How did you find out?

H: Drink and drugs! Don't you just love 'em?

DI: How did you find out that Peter was your father?

H: Miriam and I were on our second bottle of malbec. Actresses on tour. You know, bonding. Telling each other about our lives. I revealed that I was adopted. Told her about my awful, religious parents in America and what a hellish childhood I had. I showed Miriam the only thing I had from my past. A photo of myself as a baby. My birth mother had sent it with me. There was another child in the photo, but I never knew who it was. Miriam recognised herself! She remembered the cardigan she was wearing. Handknitted. Pink. White daisies around the collar. We were sisters.

DI: Then what did you do?

H: Opened another bottle and rolled a joint. The next day Miriam took me to meet our mother. Alice. There were a lot of tears and she confirmed that I had been adopted when I was a few months old. Then she dropped a bigger bomb. Peter Milano was our father.

DI: But Alice Haughton is resident in a dementia care home. How could you be sure?

H: Quite. She once told Miriam that Ian McKellen was her dad, conceived in the toilets of the Donmar Warehouse after a party. So, I told Miriam we needed a DNA test. We got some hair from his hairbrush and sent it off with our own samples. It came back positive for both of us.

DI: Is that when you hatched your plan for revenge?

H: Yes. Once I'd stopped hyperventilating. I am psychic. I knew in my heart that the universe had brought me to this place for a purpose.

DI: To kill your own father?

H: To right the wrong that this man had inflicted on three innocent lives. The man who had abandoned us and caused all this pain.

DI: And so, Miriam was a part of this? You planned it together?

H: No. My sister was not involved in what I did. I acted alone. It was my preordained task.

Miriam Haughton police statement

Together, Hermia and I discovered that we were sisters and that Peter was our father. I thought that her ideas about what to do with this information were just ramblings. She was in shock.

I swear on my mother's life I never for a moment thought she would do what she did. Finding all this out – it must have tipped her over the edge. From what she has told me, Hermia has had the most awful life. Unloved. Emotionally abused. Banished. To find out that there was another life she should, could have lived . . . with me! With our dear mother!

And she has struggled as an actress, fought and grafted . . . To think that Peter could have helped her made her furious. I can't believe this was a cold, calculated murder. She was surely deranged, not responsible for her actions. Imagine how the flood of distressing information overwhelmed her sense of reason!

The man who abandoned us and caused all this pain . . .Peter Milano.

Hermia Saunders police statement

My parents emigrated to America with me when I was a toddler. I was told I was adopted when I was twelve years old. I was already a rebel, getting into trouble and playing truant.

After that I just got worse. My Bible-bashing parents thought any bad behaviour was down to my illegitimate birth and my desire to become an actress was another manifestation of my dubious origins. I ran for the hills as soon as I could.

New York, Chicago, partying hard, trying every which way to make it as an actress. I changed my name and had some work done on my face – anything I thought might make me employable. I picked up a few parts in experimental plays, background work in TV, nothing special.

I always knew I was 'different'. I had visions from another time, flashbacks, out-of-body experiences. I knew I was born in England, so I dreamed that I was related to someone important. The royals, maybe? Or Dean Gaffney?

It was only when I was in San Francisco, working with a goofy bunch of oddball actors called The Spiritual Stargazers, that I delved into my psychic powers. I could tune in to people's souls, past and present. I knew what people were thinking about. It was pretty crazy. I could heal them. Then I did some work on myself. How about healing me?

I intuitively knew I needed to come 'home'. To the UK. I don't know why, but I felt that this is where my destiny as an actress lay. Then everything happened as if guided by an extrasensory force.

First audition I got was for *Leopard Spots*. I felt I was on my way. That *Leopard Spots* was such a runaway success took us all by surprise. It was then, during the tour, that everything changed and went into another gear.

I started getting weird psychic sparks, especially from Miriam. There was something there that interested me, so I got her drunk one night and that's when everything started to become clear. Sisters? It was me that suggested we both take a DNA test.

'We've got to be sure about this, Miriam,' I reasoned. It was true. We *were* sisters. Peter was our father. So *this* was what the universe had planned for me!

Then there was Spud, the sex and his super-strong skunk. I was losing my grip on things. I could feel the earth giving way beneath me but there wasn't anything I could do, nothing to hold on to.

This is when the darkest ideas started to grow in my mind, like poison mushrooms. I tried to regulate my thoughts but it wasn't possible. I told Miriam that Peter deserved to be punished and she agreed. To begin with I wanted to expose him. Then I wanted to harm him. Finally, I wanted him to pay with his life.

But even that wasn't enough. I needed it to be grand. Theatrical. Peter loved theatre, so he should die in one. Poetic justice.

That night I had terrible nightmares. Dreams in which I was pushing Peter off a cliff or running him over in my car. I woke up screaming.

After receiving the DNA proof, Miriam and I got drunk together again and talked over how we could punish Peter in the worst way possible. But the next day Miriam backtracked. Said she'd had too much wine. She hated Peter, but he was still our father and our mother had loved him passionately. We must leave it to fate to dole out just desserts. Karma would find him, not us.

I pretended to agree with her. Of course, it was all talk. We'd all done things in our lives that we regretted. Peter was a cad and a rat. Those were his issues to deal with himself. We must rise above it all. We gave each other a hug. We were sisters reunited, at last. Without Peter we wouldn't exist.

But I couldn't stop now, this was what everything had been leading up to. I would carry out the plan without her. Better that way. But I had to be clever about it. It must seem like an accident.

As my plan formulated in my mind it became apparent that I would need help. Spud. A bad boy. My dealer. The final part in the jigsaw. He was a member of the crew, but that was just a front. I knew enough about drug dealers from my time in America to recognise the type. He was certainly busy doling out drugs of all kinds to the cast. The dope he sold me wasn't the half of it. He was also infatuated with me and rather good in the sack. I offered him some cash. I just wanted to scare Peter, I said. The old letch needed putting in his place.

Our first attempt, in Birmingham, went horribly wrong. Peter changed the blocking on the night, Spud opened the trapdoor at the wrong time, and I fell into it and broke my arm. But we vowed to learn from our mistake. I then tried to poison him with Jayne's nasty little cupcake but the idiot boy Gordon ate it instead.

Finally, my secret, solo plan became more operatic. A public execution, I decided, was the only way to satisfy my emotional needs. I wanted him to die in full view of his audience. Nothing must go wrong this time.

The Palladium was perfect. The most famous theatre in the world. Press night – better still. Everyone would be attending. The witnesses would be of the highest calibre. But what about the details?

Hermia Saunders police statement continued
I spotted the opportunity. During the first act Peter was direct-ed to sit on a wicker chair set upstage at the end of a scene. There was a brief blackout during which a new piece of scenery would fly in. Every night I heard the clunk of the flat moving above me. If something heavy were balanced on the top of that flat, directly above Peter's chair, it would become dislodged in the change . . .

I told Spud the weight wasn't going fall anywhere near to Peter. I just wanted to ruin his scene, make him wet himself. I gave him the exact measurements from the wing to the point on top of the flat where he was to place the stage weight. See?

It was feet away! Then, during the scene, I would move Peter's chair . . . right under the spot.

The night it happened I had second thoughts. I decided to give Peter a chance to redeem himself. I went to his dressing room just after the half and confronted him.

'I am your daughter,' I told him, plainly. 'I am your daughter with Alice. The child that you never cared for that she had to have adopted.'

I don't know what I expected. A glimpse of remorse, of fatherly love? He screamed at me to get out.

'I didn't care then and I don't care now!' were his words. So his fate was sealed.

A sixth sense ten minutes before curtain up told me I needed a back-up plan in case the stage weight didn't do its job properly. I invited Spud to my dressing room for a quick knee-trembler and while I relieved him of his tension I also relieved him of the knife he carried on his waistband which I slipped into my sling.

This turned out to be a wise move as, once struck by the stage weight, Peter remained horribly alive.

In the ensuing melee as he lay spread across my lap, I deftly stabbed him in the back. The final hiss of air from his lungs was the moment I knew I had succeeded in my mission.

Fun facts: childhood trauma
Childhood trauma is an event experienced by a child that evokes fear and is commonly violent, dangerous, or life-threatening. Also sometimes referred to as adverse childhood experiences or ACEs, there are many different experiences that can lead to trauma. Unfortunately, it is all too common. An estimated 46 per cent of children experience trauma at some point in their young lives.

Jayne's diary, Sunday, 23 September 2017
There was no reason to stay in London any longer.

I phoned Taffy to tell her I was leaving. I felt a little tearful talking to her.

I suppose it was Taffy that taught me a dresser's real role is to watch and listen. Know everything that is going on.

'You should be a detective with that brain of yours,' she said. 'Much better paid than this lark.'

'Oh no,' I said. 'I don't think the police are very nice people. Besides, I'd miss the ironing too much.'

I left Nathan a note thanking him for letting me stay, with a box of Celebrations and a bunch of hydrangeas.

Jayne's diary, 7pm, Sunday, 23 September 2017
I was at Euston when I got a text from Robin.

'Don't go,' he said. 'I'm coming to find you. I'll be there in ten minutes.' My train was leaving in eight minutes.

'Too late,' I texted very slowly. 'I'm sorry, Robin.' Who knows if I did the right thing?

'I love you,' he replied.

'Controversial,' I said.

There weren't any seats on the train, so I stood in the space by the toilet. But at least it left on time. There was a tired-looking mother with two young children sharing the cramped space, so we began chatting and I shared my Greggs' sausage rolls with her. I'd bought two. I was on my way back to New Invention.

Julian on Jayne's success
I saw Jayne before she went home. She was tired I could see, but also flushed with success. There was now a confident sparkle in her eyes that was new and exciting.

'I want to go home and bake some macaroons,' she said. 'Feel normal again.'

'Sorry to see you go,' I said truthfully. 'I've got used to your company.'

'But what if things have changed forever?' she asked suddenly. 'I think all this drama might have altered me, you know.'

'Only in a good way I expect,' I assured her.

'It's funny,' she said, 'A murder, and no one could work it out but me!'

'That's because you're clever,' I said. 'It's no mystery to me.'

'I don't think of myself as clever,' she said with a shrug. 'I just observe things.'

This was the joy of Jayne. And a testament to the power of her quiet, steady, contemplative nature. While the rest of us dash around, trying to keep up with the expectations our lives demand of us, Jayne sits serenely in the background, centred, instinctively wise and untroubled by the trivia and nonsense of this earthly life.

'You're New Invention's gift to the world,' I told her.

Trevor Millicent: notes for archive
I despair of the state of British television. I thought a TV play about what happened at the Palladium (working title *The Passing*) was a wonderful idea and I was perfectly placed to write the screenplay. But no. It seems Channel 5 are already making the documentary. If they dare to ask me to contribute as a talking head, they will get a very un-broadcastable response indeed.

What's more, there are rumours that that tired old hasbeen Julian Clary is turning the whole thing into a camp cosy-crime novel, although I'd have thought he was too busy fingering Graham Norton to find the time. I'm livid.

Chapter 42

Eight months later

Daily Telegraph, Tuesday, 8 May 2018
By Ken Thomas.
Headline: 'The showbusiness trial of the century' begins at the Old Bailey.

The much-awaited trial of Hermia Saunders began yesterday morning. Many hundreds waited outside the law courts and the public gallery was crammed with people straining to catch a glimpse of the accused.

Ms Saunders finally took to the witness box after several days of jury selection. She looked pale and thin, dressed in a navy skirt suit and pale yellow blouse.

Asked how she answered to the charge that she murdered Peter Milano on the evening of Tuesday 29 August 2017, she answered: 'Not guilty'.

Fun facts: The Old Bailey

On the dome above the court stands the court's symbolic gilt bronze statue of Lady Justice by sculptor F. W. Pomeroy (made 1905–1906). She holds a sword in her right hand and the scales of justice in her left. The statue is popularly supposed to show blind Justice, but the figure is not blindfolded: the courthouse brochures explain that this is because Lady Justice was originally not blindfolded, and because her 'maidenly form' is supposed to guarantee her impartiality which renders the blindfold redundant.

The Telegraph website, Thursday, 10 May 2018
By Ken Thomas.
Sensational scenes at the Old Bailey today when the star witness for the prosecution, a dresser from Wolverhampton called Jayne Oxley claimed that the police investigation into who killed Peter Milano was inept and hasty.

Horrified by the arrest of her fellow dresser, Gordon Griffiths, she launched her own painstaking investigation to discover the real culprit. Without her amateur sleuthing, the innocent Griffiths would still be languishing behind bars.

Miss Oxley, speaking quietly but determinedly, was in the witness box all day, explaining how she looked at all the suspects, uncovered dark secrets and finally reached her conclusions. The jury looked on in astonishment as she explained the lengthy process she had undertaken and the final realisation of where the missing murder weapon had to be.

When she finally finished giving evidence there was a spontaneous round of applause from the public gallery, although the judge put a stop to it immediately.

'I share your admiration for the witness, but I must remind you that this is a solemn court of law and such outbursts cannot be tolerated.'

Old Bailey trial transcript, Thursday, 10 May 2018
Defence barrister: Miss Oxley, is it true you were in a relationship with a police officer at the time of the murder?

J: I didn't know he was a police officer. He told me he was an estate agent.

DB: I see. There is a reason for that, ladies and gentlemen of the jury. The man in question is a member of our brave Special Operations Undercover Force. He cannot be named due to the sensitive nature of his work. I have interviewed him and can vouch for his excellent character. And where did you meet him?

J: On a dating app called Tinder.

DB: Is that where you meet most of your gentlemen friends?

J: No! He's the first person I've met.

DB: Oh, come now Miss Oxley. A reasonably attractive woman like you, travelling around the country, young and carefree. I expect you have men in every town.

J: I'm not a slag, if that's what you're trying to imply.

DB: And where did you and this 'estate agent' go on your first date? To the pictures? A candlelit dinner?

J: No. To a pub.

DB: Your second date?

J: Er, for a walk.

DB: More specifically, you willingly accompanied him to an empty property where you instigated sex in the bathroom, I believe.

Prosecution barrister: Objection! How is this relevant?

Judge: Mr Parker-Knoll?

DB: The witness's testimony is central to the defence. I think we have a right to know what sort of woman we are dealing with. According to what she told this court yesterday, she is motivated by the highest moral principles. Whether that is true or not remains to be seen.

Judge: Very well. But please keep your questions relevant.

DB: As you wish, your honour. Your third date, Miss Oxley?

J: We had sex up against a lawn mower. I don't recommend it but maybe you should try it some time.

Judge: Miss Oxley, please. Confine yourself to answering the questions. There is no need to embellish matters.

J: Keep your wig on, Grandpa. He started it.

Judge: Can we wind this up, Mr Parker-Knoll?

DB: Quite, your honour. Miss Oxley, was your investigation into the murder of Peter Milano a revenge against your former partner, to humiliate him and by association, the police?

J: My aim was to find the person guilty of Peter's murder and to show it wasn't Gordon.

Newspaper headlines
Jayne vs The Judge!
Game, set and match to Miss Oxley
Milano case: defence slammed for sexist questioning of 'Miss Marple'

Jayne's diary, Monday, 14 May 2018
Today has been completely crazy! Apparently, I'm the 'star' witness of the whole trial. A car picked me up this morning and took me to a TV studio where I was interviewed by Susanna Reid, then I went on *Loose Women*.

They all said lovely things about me, how I caught the killer, outsmarted the cops and was 'The Dresser Detective'! But the most amazing thing was when I went into Greggs and someone recognised me. 'It's you!' they shouted Then everyone started clapping and patting me on the back. They wouldn't let me pay for my sausage roll.

Tomorrow, I'm going on *Woman's Hour* and *The One Show*. And I've had a weird email from someone called Zac Burger-something-or-other from Columbia Pictures who says he wants to turn my story into a movie. Julian says I should say yes but only if they cast Scarlett Johansson as me. Lol.

The sentencing of Hermia Saunders
By Justice Dame Amelia Thornton. Old Bailey Court.
Thursday, 17 May 2018. Transcript.

Hermia Saunders, you stand to be sentenced by this court for the crime of murder on the evening of Tuesday, 29 August 2017. An audacious and carefully planned assassination that dispatched a much-loved actor in full view of the general public at his place of work, the London Palladium.

Using bribery and blackmail you enticed Harry Grimshaw to help you with your murderous intentions. Your plea of not guilty due to insanity has been rejected by the jury.

Plans of the theatre rig and set design found in your possession clearly indicate the thought you had put into what was to happen. Your writing is on those papers and an arrow points to the exact place a ten-pound stage weight was to be placed.

Coerced by you, Grimshaw followed your exact instructions and placed the weight carefully, half on the beam and half resting on the top of a flat, a piece of scenery which hung above the stage ready to be used in due course in the theatrical drama in which you were employed.

In a scene during the performance of *Leopard Spots* that evening, in which you participated seemingly without a care in the world, Peter Milano sat, as he always did, on a chair.

Seconds before, you had moved that chair to a position directly below that weight. On cue, the fly man pulled the rope to fly in the piece of scenery and thus dislodged the stage weight which duly fell down to the stage, injuring him as you watched from just feet away.

In the mayhem that followed you produced a knife from the sling you were wearing and deftly stabbed Milano in the back, ensuring that if the blow to the head did not kill him, then this new injury surely would. You then hid the knife inside the plaster cast you had on your arm.

You then played the part of a shocked and distraught colleague, gave interviews extolling the victim's virtues and talents, attended his memorial. You even attempted to keep your close connection to the victim quiet by intimidating the journalist Ken Thomas, and threw a masonry brick through the window of his home with a threatening message attached.

You would have escaped justice were it not for the suspicions of Jayne Oxley, a dresser, who, thanks to her tenacious amateur detective work, uncovered the true story of your relationship with Milano, your grievance towards him and your repeated attempts – via the open trapdoor, a poisoned cupcake and this final successful plan – on his life. The court thanks Miss Oxley and commends her for bringing this case to a just conclusion.

Whatever his shortcomings as a father, Peter Milano did not deserve to die.

As far as the murder is concerned, I am required to pass a life sentence and to determine the minimum term you must serve before being considered for release.

Before sentencing, I must now record further circumstances which are relevant to understanding this case.

You were adopted as a baby and raised in America. To discover that Peter Milano was your father was a great shock to you. You held him responsible, not only for the misfortunes of your own life and the insecurity you endured in your career, but also that of your sister Miriam Haughton and your birth mother, Alice.

I accept that you had feelings of anger and despair. You blamed him for your mother's fractured life and your own consequent unhappiness. You acted in the heat of these revelations. I shall take that into account when deciding the minimum sentence.

However, the devious nature of your crime, the careful

planning over days and weeks, together with the enticement and manipulation of Harry Grimshaw lead me to believe this was not a crime of passion but a calm-and-calculated murder of revenge as you tried three times to kill him.

At the time, you were starring in a play in which you played a cold-hearted killer with blood on your hands night after night; you were also the murderer in real life – hiding in plain sight.

I take into account your previous good character. But in the circumstances of this case that carries little weight. Bearing all these matters in mind, the aggravating factors would increase the sentence to twenty years. The effect of your circumstances with regard to your depressive illness allows me to reduce that minimum term to a period of eighteen years.

Julian on the final bit

Well, there we are. That's about the size of it, as the scaffolder said to the chorus boy. I hope you've enjoyed my efforts and that you're not one of those annoying readers who goes around spotting loose ends or points of logic and then writes dreary letters to the poor author.

As far as I can see, it all makes perfect sense, but if there is a whoopsie here or there we must blame my editor. Mixing as she now is with those strange people who wear dungarees and live in tree houses, I hear she has started smoking dried seaweed.

Her mind is befuddled, her personal hygiene has gone out the window and she's started saying 'innit?' at the end of every sentence. Off you go now. I tire of this nonsense.

Aftershow snacks

Peter Milano

Peter's ashes were interred sub-stage at the London Palladium, alongside those of Bruce Forsyth and Des O'Connor. He did not get star billing, his plaque being smaller than the others and placed somewhat disdainfully to the left, away from his more-famous neighbours.

Katheryn Milano
Katheryn quickly found a buyer for the barn conversion and now lives in a riverside penthouse in Chiswick. She has become a keen wild swimmer and, so far, has only had three episodes of gastroenteritis.

Ken Thomas
Ken is now the crime correspondent for the *Evening Standard*. He regularly visits Alice at Summer Breeze and sometimes takes her out to the theatre. He has a new ginger kitten called Popper.

Miriam Haughton
Miriam continues to act and visit her mother as often as possible. She visits Hermia every week in prison and together they are writing a play about their relationship which they hope one day to take to the Edinburgh Fringe Festival.

Hermia Saunders
Hermia is currently serving her life sentence at Styal Women's Prison in Cheshire. She is adjusting well to prison life and works in the kitchens, although she is not allowed access to any knives. Her psychic readings are popular among the inmates, and she holds palm-reading workshops on the third Thursday of every month.

Simon Gaunt
Simon was declared bankrupt in 2021 and divorced from Laura soon after. They share custody of the children. He is planning a national tour next year the title of which is *Broke Bloke*.

Trevor Millicent
The TV version of *Leopard Spots* has not yet been greenlit by the commissioners at the Beeb. The development team at Tiger Aspect have re-imagined the play with musical numbers and it is now set in Whitstable.

Alice Haughton
Alice's health has greatly improved and she has taken up pétanque which she plays locally on Tuesdays and Thursdays. Katheryn, appalled by Peter's actions, donated a large part of his estate to cover all costs for Alice; she can now stay at Summer Breeze stress-free for the remainder of her days.

Harry 'Spud' Grimshaw
Spud is behind bars, serving a three-year sentence for his part in the drugs operation at the Alexandra Theatre in Birmingham. He is an active participant in the prison Bible group.

Robin Kowalski
Robin was dismissed from the police and is now working at Foxtons.

Taffy Evans
Taffy is back on the road, working as wardrobe mistress for a national tour of the musical *Hair* starring Les Dennis.

Gordon Griffiths
Now living at the New Beach caravan park in Dymchurch, Kent with the reformed shoplifter he met in Brixton prison. He still holds a candle for DI Serrano.

Jayne Oxley
Jayne is currently in Singapore, dressing for an international

arena tour of *The Lion King*. The show will move on to Daegu, Seoul, Busan, Taipei, Kaohsiung, Bangkok, Hong Kong and Auckland. She is very happy, although, as she told Rowanne, you can't get a decent sausage roll out there. There has been some light flirting with a sound assistant called Jonathan, but Jayne rather hopes it doesn't come to anything.

Julian Clary

Continues to flourish in his chosen career as a camp comic and renowned homosexual. His long-running tenure as the star of the London Palladium panto eventually came to an end in 2024 when he was replaced by Andi Peters. Future ticket sales were moderate. He now lives happily in Chipping Norton with a lesbian called Bertha. They have five dogs, numerous cats and two Indian Runner ducks called Jacques et Jill.

Acknowledgements

I'm not one to gush but praise be to my literary agent, Eugenie Furniss, for her faith in this book, to Sam Eades for her enthusiastic commissioning followed by cheery walks in the park to clarify my idea and to my editor, Sophie Wilson, for her firm but fair work with the scissors. I now understand what 'we'll put this bit aside until later' really means.

Credits

Julian Clary and Orion Fiction would like to thank everyone at Orion who worked on the publication of Curtain Call to Murder in the UK.

Editorial
Sam Eades
Sophie Wilson
Anshuman Yadav

Copy editor
Francesca Brown

Proofreader
Francine Brody

Audio
Paul Stark
Louise Richardson

Contracts
Dan Herron
Ellie Bowker
Oliver Chacón

Design
Charlotte Abrams-Simpson

Editorial Management
Charlie Panayiotou
Jane Hughes
Bartley Shaw
Lucy Bilton

Finance
Jasdip Nandra
Nick Gibson
Sue Baker

Marketing
Ellie Nightingale

Production
Ruth Sharvell

Publicity
Sarah Lundy
Sian Baldwin

Sales
Catherine Worsley
Esther Waters
Victoria Laws
Rachael Hum
Ellie Kyrke-Smith
Frances Doyle
Georgina Cutler

Operations
Jo Jacobs